REJECTED

A CONTEMPORARY STORY OF HAGAR

ELIZABETH SIMON

LIZARD BOOKS LLC

Book Cover by NeatDesign

First edition 2025

The Scriptures quoted are from the NET Bible® https://netbible.com copyright ©1996, 2019 used with permission from Biblical Studies Press, L.L.C. All rights reserved.

Publisher's Cataloging-in-Publication Data

Names: Simon, Elizabeth, author.

Title: Rejected : a contemporary story of Hagar / Elizabeth Simon.

Description: Port Charlotte, FL: Lizard Books LLC, 2025.

Identifiers: LCCN: 2025923642 | ISBN: 979-8-9927467-3-0 (hardcover) | 979-8-9927467-2-3 (paperback)

| 979-8-9927467-4-7 (ebook)

Subjects: LCSH Human trafficking--Fiction. | Surrogate motherhood--Fiction. | Hagar (Biblical

figure)—Fiction. | Nicaragua--Fiction. | Mexico--Fiction. | Texas--Fiction. | Christian fiction. | BISAC

FICTION / Christian / Contemporary | FICTION / Christian / Women

Classification: LCC PS3619 .I66 R45 2025 | DDC 813.6--dc23

To my mother, who has always been my biggest fan

AUTHOR'S NOTE

DO NOT SKIP THIS!

W riting Rejected has been both rewarding and challenging. Human trafficking is a devastating reality that affects millions of people worldwide, and I felt strongly about telling a story that doesn't shy away from that truth. At the same time, I know many of my readers come from a Christian background. My goal was to strike a balance by naming the reality of exploitation without sensationalizing it, and writing with honesty, care, and hope at the center.

The biblical story of Hagar is brief but powerful. Scripture tells us she was "an Egyptian" and a servant in Sarai's household, but it does not give us her history before that moment (Genesis 16, 21). Scholars generally agree her early life is unknown. Some Jewish traditions imagine her as an Egyptian princess given to Sarai, while other interpretations see her simply as a slave or handmaid. In every version, though, her story is one of being caught in systems of power beyond her control, yet she is also the first woman in the Bible to receive a direct promise from God and the only person to give God a name.

Because the text leaves her beginnings untold, this novel offers one possible way to imagine what Hagar's origins might look like if she lived today. In Rejected, that silence is re-imagined through the lens of modern trafficking and exploitation. It is not the only interpretation, but it is one attempt to bring her experience into a contemporary setting and ask how her story still speaks to us now.

Above all, this book is meant to give voice to those who are too often silenced. If you find some passages difficult to read, that is understandable. My hope is that the story also points toward resilience, compassion, and the God who sees.

Trigger warnings: This story contains themes portraying the realities of human trafficking and modern slavery, including child sexual exploitation, prostitution, sexual assault, and forced sexual experiences. It also depicts emotional abuse and trauma. Reader discretion is strongly advised.

Part One

Víctima de Trata

CHAPTER ONE

PUERTO CABEZAS, NICARAGUA

My stomach growled as I dug through a heaping trash pile in desperation. I hadn't eaten in two days, and the smell of rotting vegetables and moldy banana peels attacked my nose. My long hair fell into my face. I pushed it back behind my ears as I picked through the crumpled-up food wrappers. Flies buzzed past my ears mocking me, and I swatted them away.

This cafe was my first choice for leftovers. Most nights I could find a half-eaten tamal tossed out by a tourist or sailor. Midnight approached, and the full moon cast dark shadows over the spooky alleyway. I wanted to hurry home, but I didn't want to go empty-handed.

Papá died over a year ago. Before he died, he came home in the evenings from working at the dock, his face red, and weariness showing in his eyes. He would sit down, clutching his shirt. Mamá would run to him, saying something about his health. And then one day, he never returned home. I didn't see Mamá smile again after that day. Papá's strong arms would never hold me again. Mamá said he lives in my eyes and my smile, and that my big heart held his memory. But memories don't bring home dinner like Papá used to.

Now, at nine years old, I had to find our food. I helped because Mamá took care of my baby brother, Jose, in our tiny one-room shack farther in town. Mamá needed the most, since she still fed Jose with her milk. I was too big for that now. The last two nights, I found a half-eaten quesilla in this café dumpster and brought it home. It wasn't enough for both of us, so I told Mamá I'd already eaten. That way she and Jose could have it.

I hoped today's search would be better.

A crash sounded at the far end of the alley. Fear shot through me, and I pressed my thin body against the cold concrete wall, shrinking into the shadows. A tall man dug through the heaps of trash. I assumed he was trying to find his dinner too. He was stick-thin, but his belly stuck out like the bottom of a bowl. He must have found some food to fill his belly. I would try his spot once he left.

I hid in the shadows, watching and counting the minutes to myself as I waited. It took nearly thirty minutes before he moved on. Nothing worth bringing home was left in the scattered heaps of trash strewn about, so I headed toward the motel where the tourists stayed.

I squinted through the darkness to see if the coast was clear. The dark nights could be dangerous for a girl to be alone if I wasn't careful. Last week, Mamá told me about some kids going missing near the docks. Abril from my class at school hadn't been back since that day.

I hugged the shadows and crept down the street toward the hotel, scurrying like a rat between buildings. If I didn't find food and head home soon, Mamá would be worried.

I reached the motel and headed for the back alley where a kitchen filled the back side of the motel. It was one of the biggest motels in the city, big and so close to the beach that its pretty lights shone off the waves at night.

I rounded the corner and saw a pile of garbage. It was glorious! So many bags packed with rotting food. The smell of the old fruit, moldy vegetables, and rotting meat filled the air. There would be plenty to feed me and Mamá here!

I raced to the bags and heaved them around, searching for ones with food smashed against the sheer plastic. I shoved one bag, and it rolled, knocking over a tin garbage can. It clanged as it toppled to the pavement. I jumped and grimaced, hoping it hadn't been heard.

The back door of the restaurant banged open, and a plump man ran out, yelling in Spanish. He wore an apron smattered with food stains, and it made my mouth water. "¡Sal ya de aquí, rata!" he said. "¡Sale!" He called me an animal, but he ran at me with his teeth bared like a wild boar. He screamed at me again to go away. I ran back around the corner toward the front of the motel and smacked into a woman.

The woman wore nice clothes, so different from my brown, dirt-stained rags which barely held together. Soft hands landed on my shoulders, and I looked at her. She batted her long eyelashes at me and flipped her dark hair behind her back. She didn't seem disgusted as most people did when they saw my filth. She smiled at me with pity. There was something behind her smile I couldn't quite understand.

"Hello, sweetie," she said in Spanish. Her voice dripped with sweetness, too much sweetness. "Isn't it a little late for you to be out wandering the streets?" I stared up at her. I didn't know her, and she made me feel uncomfortable.

She took a puff of a cigarette and looked me up and down with a glint in her eye. I glanced around for a way to escape her. She blocked my way, and I couldn't go back since the man was still shouting at me from behind the motel. I didn't know what to do or how to get around her, so I said, "Excuse me. I think I'll go home now."

"She speaks!" the woman said drawing her hand to her mouth with mock shock. She smiled. "Are you hungry, dear?"

I nodded. My stomach growled in response, as if it heard her speaking. She waved her hand toward the door leading me on. It might have been my tummy doing the walking when I followed her. I was so hungry.

She led the way toward the motel lobby. I paused at the door, feeling too ashamed to enter. It was much nicer than any place I had been to. "I shouldn't go in there. I'm going home."

"Nonsense," she said, turning to me. "I'll buy you a nice dinner, and you can bring the leftovers home with you." She waved at me again to follow her as she walked into the lobby. The click of her high heels echoed against the tile floor.

I hesitated, but she seemed nice enough. She must be a tourist, so maybe she felt sorry for me. I had heard of such things.

The lobby was painted in reds and yellows, and four chairs sat in a circle to the right. A simple opening in the far wall revealed an old man sleeping in a folding chair behind the counter.

"Excuse me. Is the kitchen closed?" the woman asked.

The man grunted and woke up. He was thin and looked unkept, much like the man I saw scrounging for food in the trash. He waved her off and growled, "Room service only."

"Even better!" she exclaimed to no one in particular, with glee in her voice. What was making her so happy? She turned to me and said, "You can come to my room, and I'll order some food."

It was getting late though. Mamá would start to worry if I didn't return soon. The latest I had been out was 2 a.m., and it was still a thirty-minute walk home. I bit my lip and thought about leaving, but only for a moment. My tummy won again.

I followed her up a staircase.

"The rooms aren't super nice," she said, "but they're nice enough. The food is good."

I wasn't paying much attention to what she said, as I fought inside about going with her or returning home empty-handed.

"I just came in on one of the ships yesterday, but I won't be staying long. I leave tomorrow morning," she said.

The doors to the rooms lined the outside corridor. She went down a long concrete walkway and stopped at the last door. Unlocking it with her key, she pushed it open with her bottom, leaving it wide for me to enter. She smiled and waved me in.

I inched into the room. It was bigger than our entire house! A large metal box by the window blew cool air into the heat and humidity of the night, soothing my sweaty skin.

A single table stood in between two beds with a phone sitting on top of it. The table was bigger than our only table at home. The phone was like one the principal in my school used.

A fancy bathroom appeared through another door. A bathroom, with running water! Our house didn't have any running water. I fetched water from a well down the street every morning, and we peed and pooped in a hole in the small backyard.

The two beds were so big, one of them could fit my entire family. Clean white blankets that smelled like wildflowers covered the beds, along with pillows that felt like giant clouds. We didn't even have a bed in our house. We slept on blankets on the dirt floor.

I had never seen a place so fancy in all my life. I skimmed the bed-sheets with my finger. They felt so soft, so inviting. I imagined curling

up and going to sleep on top of the soft mattress. I almost forgot my
hunger. Almost. My tummy hadn't though, and it roared, reminding
me I hadn't eaten in two days.

The strange woman picked up the phone and ordered food. "We'll
have a little of everything on the menu."

The woman continued to chatter away about this and that, and
waved at the bed, urging me to climb up. Feeling embarrassed and
fearful, I paused and looked at her. She smiled and nodded toward the
bed, inviting me on.

I climbed on the bed, leaving dirty streaks on the white cotton where
my clothes touched, and propped myself up on the pillows. They were
soft like a stuffed animal but for your head. I pressed my face into one
of the pillows, and it didn't scratch or poke. It hugged me back. I didn't
even know you could sleep with something so soft under your head. At
home, I used my arm or a rolled-up shirt.

I felt like a princess. Nothing I knew was as comfortable as this
bed. I closed my eyes, content and amazed at my luck. I wasn't still
scrounging around in trash heaps in the heat and humidity but was
comfortable in the soft, cool motel bed.

It didn't take long for the food to come. Someone rapped on the
door, and the woman opened it to a young man carrying a tray. She
took it from him and placed it on the table next to the phone. The
smells of the earthy steamed banana leaf and smoky gallo pinto filled
the room.

I rubbed my eyes and stared in awe. It was a feast! Gallo pinto,
nacatamal, vigorón. The woman invited me to eat, and I dug in, stuff-
ing food into my mouth with my hands, trying to appease my hungry
belly. The flavors mixed in my mouth: salty, garlicky, tangy, nutty.

She watched me, not eating. Maybe she was waiting for me to finish before she started. I didn't know. I didn't care. I ate the fresh, delicious food, not leftover scraps from the trash.

It didn't take long for me to eat so much I almost made myself sick. There were plenty of leftovers to take home to Mamá, and she would have her fill too. But...maybe Mamá could wait a minute. I needed a little rest. My tummy was so full, I couldn't think straight.

My tired body was so heavy as I sank into the soft pillows, yawning. My eyes fluttered, shutting out the room around me. I could take the leftovers home to Mamá after a short, little nap...

* * *

When I woke up, I was no longer on the soft princess bed. I wasn't even on my dirt floor at home. I was on a hard surface in a dark room. The room was moving back and forth, like it was swaying in the wind...or on the sea.

CHAPTER TWO

GULF OF MEXICO

Darkness surrounded me like a thick blanket. I sat up, rubbing my eyes, in search of light that wasn't there. The ground I sat on moved, swaying or bobbing up and down. A musty smell surrounded me, like dirt mixed with sweat.

Movement around me sounded like other people, coughing and silent crying. They didn't say anything. Maybe they were scared to talk like I was. Where was I? Why was I here? How did I get here? My chest tightened, and my heart raced inside it. I started to sweat, and it wasn't because of the heat and humidity. The salty, fishy scent of the ocean filled the air. The port must be close by.

The dark never bothered me before. We didn't have electricity at our house, and the town didn't have many lights. Often, I walked in the dark or by the light of the moon to search for food. I was always more afraid of not finding food than running into a monster.

But the fear of starving was nothing compared to this new darkness that surrounded me. I shivered, drew my knees up toward my chest, and hugged myself.

I tried to clear my throat. The woman never told me her name, so I couldn't call out for her. She seemed so nice, like she wanted to help me. She bought all that food for me. But was she the one who brought me here? Did she put me in this scary dark place?

"Mamá?" I cried out.

Giggles rose up around me, a scared and sarcastic laughter. Some of the noise sounded like sobs. I couldn't be sure in the dark.

Someone moved next to me. Something touched my shoulder, and I jerked away from it, hitting my head on a hard surface beside me. I held one hand up to my aching head and the other hand out to touch a metal surface—hard, cold, and crusty.

Reaching beneath me, I felt wood. A splinter stuck in my finger. I jerked my hand up and rubbed the sore spot.

Not knowing where I was made my head throb more. That and the splinter in my hand made tears prickle at my eyes and run down my cheeks. It felt like my heart was trying to jump out of my skin. I couldn't catch my breath, like I'd been running even though I hadn't moved. My hands got all sweaty, and the sounds around me seemed loud and fuzzy at the same time.

Where is my mamá? I sobbed to myself as I tried to figure out what to do.

Someone that seemed ten meters away heaved and threw up. The room was large. Someone else exclaimed in disgust and moved away from the noise of the puking. The smell in the room thickened, the vomit mixing with the dirt and sweaty smells. I hid my nose in my filthy shirt to shield it from the stench, not wanting to be the next person to throw up.

"Who's in charge here?" a young boy's voice said in Spanish from the other end of the room. His words echoed off the wall, the only one brave enough to speak up.

Silence.

After what felt like hours, the same voice said, "Are there any adults here?"

Still, no one answered.

Someone said, "Ow!"

Another young voice said, "Sorry."

"My name is Juan," the boy from earlier said, his voice closer now, near the middle of the room. No one answered. "Does anyone know where we are or what's going on?"

No one said a word, but curiosity gnawed at me too. I needed to go home to Mamá, even though I would go home empty-handed. Where did the rest of the food go? Did the woman from the motel eat it all? I felt around me to see if it was nearby, but all I felt was the cold wall, wood, and another person. I jerked my hand back.

The room rocked up and down. I started to get a little sick to my stomach and hoped I wouldn't be the next person to add to the stench. The thick air made the dark room stuffy. The cool air of the motel room was long gone.

Pulling my feet close to my body, I sat with my back against the wall and wrapped my arms around my knees. I put my face on my knees, closing my eyes, trying to hide from the darkness. I let the tears flow down my cheeks onto my skirt. At least, curled up in this ball, it would be less likely for me to get hurt. I made myself as small as possible and waited.

* * *

After some time, faint light started seeping through small holes in the room from all directions, eating up the darkness. I lifted my chin and squinted.

Children filled the room. There must have been fifty kids of all different ages. Some looked as young as five and some as old as twelve. We all wore dirty clothes with smudges on our skin and scared looks on our faces. A girl sat on my right, a boy to my left, and two more girls in front of me, but facing away. Beyond that, it was a sea of dark hair.

The room wasn't really a room. It was a long, skinny metal box. Rust made holes in the gray walls, and light came through. The floor was cracked and rotting at the edges, letting more light in. On both ends I could see doors, but they had no handles or doorknobs.

Kids were the only things locked in here. No food. No water. No place to go to the bathroom. The puddle of puke from earlier in the night had dried in the middle of the floor on the far side.

I stretched my legs out as far as I could without kicking someone else. Pins and needles felt like they were sticking into my feet. I wiggled my toes to feel them again.

The boy a few years younger, sitting to the left of me, leaned up against the back corner of the space. As the morning light grew stronger, he gazed around with scared eyes, like he was seeing a ghost. His body shivered, though the stale air was warm. I knew how he felt inside—lonely, frightened, and nervous. I suspected all of us felt the same way.

When he caught me staring, I whispered, "Hola," low enough for only the two of us to hear.

He nodded back with big, terrified eyes. I could see his tear-stained face where the tears streaked away some of the filth on his cheeks.

"Are you scared?" I whispered. He nodded. "Me too. My name is Helena. What's yours?"

"Alessandro." He wasn't much of a talker. He spoke with quiet uncertainty, as if he were asking the question instead of giving an answer.

"Let's stick together and try to help each other," I suggested.

He nodded.

"How old are you?"

He held out his hand, fingers up. Five.

I held nine fingers up. "I'm nine."

He nodded.

"Where are you from?"

"Bilwi," he said, talking about what the native Miskito people call Puerto Cabezas. It made more sense now why he wasn't talking much. Miskito people spoke a different language, although it seemed he understood some Spanish.

I held out my hand to comfort him, and he put his hand in mine. The warm feeling of another person, on my side, calmed me too. We sat, holding hands, and waited.

I felt a tap on my right shoulder and jumped, moving closer to Alessandro. The finger belonged to the girl sitting next to me. She wore raggedy clothes like mine, a long skirt and tank top in a brownish color, due to the dirt on it. She looked a year or two older than me.

"Hola," she said, peering at me with big brown eyes. "How long do you think they will keep us here?" She pulled her shoulder-length dark hair into a ponytail behind her back, lifting sweaty wisps off her neck.

"I don't know," I said. "They put me here when I was still sleeping. I don't even know who did it or where we are."

"I saw when they put you in here. We were tricked. They told us we were going to get jobs at the dock, and they put us all in a truck and brought us to the port. Then they made us go in here and shut us in."

"What? Who were you with?"

"A bunch of these kids." She waved her hand toward the others. "There was probably ten of us."

"Where was your mamá? Wouldn't she stop them?"

"I don't have parents anymore. They're both dead. I was living on the street."

"Oh." I couldn't imagine trying to live on the streets on my own. I had to find food on my own, but at least I had Mamá and Jose to go home to. "Did the other kids have parents?"

"I don't know. I think they rounded up all the kids who were living on the street and told us about the job, then stuck us all in here. I'm guessing we won't be getting the jobs they were promising," she said, her voice echoing against the rusted walls. "I'm Adriana."

"Helena. When did they put you in here?"

"It was yesterday afternoon," she said. "We were the first group they brought here. Then they came a couple of hours later with another group."

I stared in disbelief, imagining the kids getting herded into the box.

"They kept bringing more kids until the middle of the night. I could tell because the light was long gone at that point, and when they opened the door, it was dark outside. You were one of the last ones they brought. They carried you in through that door and set you down next to me." She pointed toward the door near Alessandro.

"Was it a woman?"

"No, it was a man."

"A woman bought me food at the motel, and I ate it and fell asleep on the bed. When I woke up, I was here."

"That was lucky. At least you got a last meal."

"Where do you think they're taking us, and what do they want with us?" I opened my eyes so big it felt like they might fall out.

"I don't know, but whatever they have planned for us can't be good. After they put you in here, they shut the door and a few minutes later the entire box moved and swayed, like it was being picked up. I don't know how you slept through that. We were falling all over each other!" Adriana chuckled at the thought. I didn't know how she could find any of this even the least bit funny. "I think we're on a ship right now."

I felt the heat drain from my face. "They're taking us away from Puerto Cabezas?"

"It seems so."

"No!" I shouted. "That can't be!" I jumped up and banged on the rusty metal door with my fists, again and again. "Let us out of here!"

My shouts and the banging echoed through the cargo container. We can't leave Puerto Cabezas! What about Mamá and Jose? They can't take me away from them! They need me!

CHAPTER THREE

Tears streamed down my face as I continued to bang on the door. A boy came and stood next to me, pounding his fists against the door and yelling with me. Then another, and another. Soon eight of us, shoulder to shoulder, banged on the door together. The sound echoed through the room.

But nothing happened. No matter how much noise we made, no one came. My hands trailed down the metal surface of the door as I slid onto my knees in a sobbing heap.

The light, seeping in through the rusty holes during the day, disappeared. Day turned to night, and we still chugged onward, further and further away from Puerto Cabezas. My mind raced with questions I couldn't answer. *How long will we be here? What do I do? Why isn't anyone coming to help us?* I hunched over my knees on the floor, my muscles tense, and picked at the skin around my fingernails.

The stench of urine spread through the already musty, dirty room. I didn't want to add to it, but I had no choice. I had to pee so bad. Some decided to use the corner near the vomit as the official bathroom and walked over to pee on the wall. I was too scared to walk all the way across the space, walking around so many other children. I ended up peeing in my underwear and sat in the pool of warm liquid, embarrassed. My long, raggedy skirt and the wood floor soaked it up.

My stomach growled. Although it was usual for me to go several days without food, my body still resisted it. I heard grumbles from other children nearby. We were all hungry.

We were in that dark, musty room for two days, scared, weak, hungry, and in some cases sick. I felt like the world had dropped onto my back. My muscles ached from being tense for so long. Every blink of my eyes was slow, taking as much energy as I could muster. I had given up hope by the time the gentle up and down motion stopped, and the room became still.

I froze. A loud whirring and hissing sound interrupted the silence, coming from outside. The room jerked with a loud ping. I jumped at the noise, my body shaking. I felt the room jerked up into the air with a loud grinding sound. It swung back and forth. I fell on top of someone on the floor and scrambled to find my own space. Terror stole my breath away. The room reversed direction, moving downward, and hit the ground with a thud. The younger kids started crying.

Metal scraped the door near me, and I scrambled backwards, running into someone. The door creaked open.

It was night, but light from a nearby streetlamp poured into the room, blinding me. I blinked my eyes to adjust. Fresh air mingled with the musty smell, and I inhaled to welcome it. But the welcome feeling didn't last.

A scary-looking man walked in. He held a long black gun. We all gasped. I moved back fast, pressing against the other side of the container. He pointed the gun at us. I didn't want to look at the gun, but I couldn't help myself. The handle looked like burnt wood, but thick and bent, like Papá's machete. The hole in the front was round and deep, like a dark, narrow tunnel made of cold metal.

Another man came in. He had a gun too. He held it at his waist and moved it side to side.

I couldn't breathe. I couldn't move. Time felt like it stopped.

"Hands on your heads!" the first man ordered.

All of us that spoke Spanish obeyed, but the kids that spoke Miskito hesitated. Most looked around at the rest of us and copied what we did. One of the boys huddled against the side didn't react fast enough, and a third man pushed between the two gunmen and started beating the boy with his fists.

We all jumped back, too scared to move. I heard the smack, and the heavy thump when he hit the floor. The boy lay there, not moving, blood pouring from his nose.

"Is he dead?" someone whispered.

"No, look, he's breathing," someone else whispered.

His chest rose and fell, but the movement was shallow.

I moved further back and pressed my body against the metal wall. Sweat popped out on my forehead, and I started to feel dizzy.

The second gunman scolded the man who beat the boy. He waved the barrel of the gun at him and yelled, "Be more careful! El jefe needs this group. The numbers in the field are down to a hundred, and his girls are getting worn out."

A few of the smaller children started wailing.

"Shut up!" the second gunman yelled, swinging his gun back and forth at us.

The first gunman said, "If anyone disobeys, they will end up as he did," pointing to the unconscious boy.

Everyone quieted down, although I could hear muffled sobs. The three men divided us in half and made us go up a plank into the back of two large box-like trucks. I tried to walk without falling. My feet could move, but my body felt numb. I stumbled up the ramp into the truck. The rolling door clattered down with a bang, again into darkness. Once the door closed, most of us burst into tears.

We didn't know what was ahead for us, but we would never forget what was behind.

Locked in the dark again, I started counting to guess how many minutes we drove. I got to one hundred minutes when the delivery truck lurched to a stop. We cowered at the side of the space farthest from the door.

The door rolled up. Dim light from somewhere nearby showed the same men with their guns. The truck stood beside a house that looked like a castle from a fairy tale. So many windows I couldn't count them all. Each one lit up like stars against the dark night. Thick stone pillars, like on the church back home, stood in the front.

The men yelled at us to get out of the truck and into two lines in front of the house. I wobbled, and my whole body trembled.

They walked us around the side of the house, lined us up in one long line, and told us to undress. I clutched my skirt against me, but they raised their guns to point them at us. I dropped my dirty, urine-soaked skirt to the cobblestone sidewalk and struggled out of my ratty tank top. I covered myself as best I could with my hands. I didn't want to be the next one beaten, or worse yet—shot.

The man had said "el jefe" needed us, but who was this boss, and what did he need us for?

The men hosed us off with thick hoses, soaking us from head to toe. They sprayed water into my face, and for a moment, I couldn't breathe.

The water came out cold and fast, causing me to jump and shiver. It knocked the dirt, mud, vomit, and urine off of us. A brown river of grime flowed down the sidewalk to a large drainage grate. After about three passes, the river ran clear. I squirmed, covering my exposed body with my hands.

The gunmen directed us through the back door and down a hall. Towels lined the floor to catch the water dripping off us. The cool, crisp air in the house chilled my wet, naked skin, and goosebumps formed on my arms. The house smelled of flowers, and I breathed in the scent, trying to calm my nerves.

They led us into a huge room. The ceiling loomed high above us, with lights that sparkled like tiny stars. The windows were tall, way up on the far wall. The floor had stripes of dark and light wood, like a zebra I once saw in a torn-up book. One side was all mirrors, and made the room feel like it never ended. Across from the glass, big wooden panels stood in long rows. They made small rooms, like boxes inside the big one. People sat in them wearing white coats. Their eyes watched us when we walked in. I didn't know where to look. The room felt too big, too bright, too quiet.

I stood, naked, between a boy and a girl awaiting our next instruction.

The first gunman commanded, "Hands at your sides!"

We dropped our hands to our sides, and I pinched my knees together. A man with a camera started taking pictures of each of us, from the front and back. I stood there like a statue hoping the click of the camera was all I would hear and not a gun going off.

I squeezed my eyes shut, thinking if I couldn't see them, they couldn't see me. When the camera man came to me, he told me to open my eyes and look at the camera. I did as he said and saw the man with the gun following the camera man and pointing the gun at me so I would obey. He took pictures of me from the front and back and moved on to the next child.

Once the camera man finished, the gunmen directed the ten kids at the front of the line into the sectioned-off spaces. The rest of us waited in line for our turn.

A woman in a long, white coat checked me over. Her hands moved fast, like someone who didn't want to get yelled at. She kept looking over her shoulder, as if she was waiting for someone to come in and hit her or shout at her. Her back stayed hunched the whole time, like she was trying to be smaller, unseen. She didn't look happy, but it seemed she didn't want to hurt me. Her face said she wished things were different. She handed me a cup, and her hand shook. I was scared too, but I took the cup.

"I need you to pee in this cup," she said, her voice quiet. I think she wanted to be kind, but kindness seemed dangerous in this place.

"Right here?" I whispered.

She nodded. My hand shook as I placed the cup below me and tried to catch the pee that refused to come out.

"If you can't do it, they will get mad," she whispered.

I nodded, and a single tear slid down my cheek as I tried to relax. At last, my body let go and filled the cup.

She poked and prodded me as I held my breath and tensed at her touch. I winced as she stuck me with several different needles, tears prickling my eyes, threatening to fall. I held it all in, though, not wanting to draw the attention of the men with the guns who moved back and forth along the dividers.

When the exams finished, the gunmen lined us back up along the long wall, while the people in the white coats talked among themselves in a huddle. One of them came and stood in front of us. They split us up into two groups. Looking at his clipboard, one of the men in the white coats pointed at us with his pen and said "field" or "house." When he gave the command, the men with the guns directed us.

The field group was the largest, and most of the boys and all of the older girls were put in that bunch. Both Adriana and Alessandro were put in the field group, along with the beaten boy who had regained consciousness. I tried to tell Alessandro I was sorry with my eyes. I couldn't keep him safe here. He nodded, his scared face set in a frown.

Twelve of us were put in the house group, eight girls and four boys, and we all appeared to be under ten years old. Two ladies in black and white servant uniforms came into the room and motioned for our house group to follow them. One servant was tall, and the other shorter. Both had pretty faces and thin bodies with dark hair pulled back into buns at the bottom of their heads, olive-colored skin, and dark, sad eyes. They marched us in a line down the hall through a small room and out the back door into the night.

The shadows of the dark outside concealed our naked bodies. A cool breeze blew against the sweat on my skin, giving me chills, and I crossed my arms against my chest to keep warm.

They took us past a pool and down a cobblestone path to a large square building with double doors. The cobblestones felt cool to my feet. Through the double doors stood a security desk and a lobby area with couches on one side and a wooden table with matching chairs on the other. The servants took us down a hallway to the right, which curved around toward the back of the building, and we stopped at a door at the end of the hallway. The first servant led us in, and the second brought up the rear.

It was a large bathroom. Five silver sticks grew from the wall, like pipes with tiny holes at the end. The shorter servant turned a knob, and it rained inside the house! The rain was clean, not muddy like when it stormed back home. The water came down in little strings, like magic.

"Well, get under the water now and get cleaned up," the shorter servant said as we stared in amazement.

The pipes lined up together with no separators and one big drain. The servants gave us towels, a bottle, and soap and told us to scrub clean. Most of the dirt and grime had been washed away outside, but the stench still clung to us. The shower water warmed my body, unlike the cold river at home. Washing like this was new, and the water felt refreshing spraying against my dirty, sweaty skin. The river in Puerto Cabezas where I took baths was low due to the drought, and I hadn't bathed in weeks. The white soap turned brown in my grimy hands as I tried to scrub the layers of dirt off my body.

The servants stepped over to the door to guard the exit. A thought ran through my head. The men with the guns weren't here. The twelve of us could probably all run in different directions so the two servants couldn't catch us all. But where would we go? It wasn't like I could go home anymore. I was somewhere far away from Puerto Cabezas now.

My body still trembled, but my anxiety subsided the moment we stepped away from the gunmen. These servants looked nice enough, almost motherly. How long had they been here, and was it by choice? Or did they arrive like we did?

The servants came over to show us how to use the stuff in the bottle. I didn't have any at home and had no idea what it was for. They helped us make bubbles on our heads and showed us how to rinse it out.

Once we finished and toweled off, they gave us clothes to wear, frilly dresses for the girls and nice shirts and shorts for the boys. The servants stepped back and looked at each other with pride, nodding.

"This group has lots of potential," the taller one said.

"Yes, once they have some meat on their bones, they will do quite well," the shorter one said.

"I'm just glad it's not me anymore," the tall one said under her breath.

I shuddered. She didn't mean for us to hear it, but I had.

CHAPTER FOUR

NEAR TAMPICO, MEXICO

"Follow me," the shorter servant said after we showered and dressed.

Short Servant opened the bathroom door and led us down the long hall to the lobby, with Tall Servant taking up the rear. Retracing our earlier steps, we returned to the house and around to the front entrance. When we passed the big room, where they took our pictures and made me pee in a cup, silence filled it now. The "field" group had gone somewhere else, maybe getting washed up too.

Short Servant led us up the long staircase and turned left down the hallway to the last door. Before opening the door, she stopped and turned around to look at us. Her eyes looked big and sad, like the dog that begged for food in our village. Her mouth pulled into a frown.

Tall Servant cleared her throat from the back of the line. Short Servant nodded and started to separate us into twos, two girls in the first group, two in the next, and so on. She put me in the third group of girls. They put the boys together also, two to a group.

Short Servant gave us our room assignments. Each group got a room to share. "Breakfast will be at seven in the morning, sharp. When you hear the alarm, meet outside in the hallway, and we will lead you down to breakfast."

The other girl in my group seemed to be around my age and height with similar dark hair, hazel eyes, and olive skin. We were both dressed in frilly green dresses, making us appear even more alike. Looking at my roommate felt like staring into a mirror.

I walked into the room, followed by my "twin," and my mouth dropped open. The walls were the color of milk with shiny gold lines at the edges, like someone drew with treasure. Soft carpets that seemed too fancy to step on covered the floor, green and yellow and sand-colored. Across the room stood two big drawers made from dark wood that looked strong and expensive, made from the trees rich people must have. Near the door, where you could see it from the bed, a huge black rectangle hung on the wall.

I felt much more like a princess now, even more than in the motel room. Why would they clean us up and put us in these fancy rooms? Why did the servants appear nervous about everything?

"Wow!" the other girl exclaimed, eyes wide.

The huge bed stood in the center of the room. She ran the ten steps to the bed and hopped up. The girl jumped up and down on the thick, white comforter, its gold stitching sparkling in the light of bedside tall lamps. She sighed as she sank back onto the dark green, cream, and gold pillows, disappearing.

The door shut behind us, and I heard a click. I went to the door and tried to open it. Locked. We were stuck in this room until, I assumed, our 7 a.m. breakfast.

"Yeah, it's like a princess castle," I commented, taking in the beauty of the room. I thought about the locked door behind me. "But like Rapunzel though, since we're locked in."

We looked at each other.

"I'm Sofia," she said. "I guess we're going to be mejores amigas from now on."

I walked over to the bed and leaned against the dark wooden nightstand. "Yeah, looks like it. I'm Helena."

"Are you from Puerto Cabezas?"

"Yes, near Rio Cocal," Sofia said. "You?"

"Yes, near the airport. How old are you?"

"Nine."

"Me too. You look a lot like me."

She nodded. "I was just thinking the same thing. I wonder if they put us together because of that. What do you think they're going to do to us?"

I shivered. "No idea. But I don't want to be anywhere near the men with the guns."

"I know! Can you believe they beat that boy?" Her eyes got big, and her eyebrows rose.

"I don't want to be next."

"It's late, and I'm starving. I wish they fed us first. I don't want to wait until seven to eat," she complained. The clock on the nightstand said 3:48 a.m.

"Yeah, they starved us for two days, beat that boy in front of us, and expect us to sleep after that? I'm going to have nightmares the second I go to sleep." My stomach growled as I flopped on the bed and leaned against the soft pillows.

"What's in that room?" she asked, pointing to an open door.

I shrugged.

She hopped off the bed and walked through the door. "Wow!"

"What is it?" I dashed around the foot of the bed toward the door.

The bathroom was as big as my whole house back home. I'd never seen any room like it. In one corner a glass box stood, big enough for a man to stand in. Silver pipes grew out of the wall, like the bathroom earlier. Next to it, a giant white bowl with high sides sat alone, like the bowl Mamá used to wash clothes and baby Jose but bigger. Two sinks sat side by side, both with shiny handles and mirrors above them.

Three more doors were inside the bathroom. One opened to a tiny room with soft, white cloths stacked in neat piles. The toilet had a little room with a door, like it was too special to share space with the rest of the bathroom. But the last door led to a room full of clothes and shoes. So many, it looked like a store inside the house. I didn't even know someone could own that many clothes. The clothes all appeared our size.

"We could play make-believe all night long with these fancy clothes!" she exclaimed from inside the closet, clapping her hands and bouncing up and down.

Was she serious? I didn't want to be here at all. I wanted my mamá. I wanted to go home to Puerto Cabezas. I was tired and scared and anxious and... I sat on the soft carpet in the middle of the closet and started crying.

"What's wrong?" Sofia asked, holding a dress on a hanger.

"Don't you see? There's got to be more to it than this," I started between sobs. "Why would they bring us on a ship with all those other kids to set us up in a castle room to play make-believe? Something's not right. They're messing with us."

"Well, there's nothing we can do about it right now. And they're not bothering us. So why not make the best of the little time we have left?" Sofia reasoned.

The little time we have left. Her last phrase swirled around in my head. I tried to sniffle up my tears. My whole body trembled. I stood up and ran into the bedroom, pulling out drawers, looking for anything I could use as a weapon in case I needed it. The drawers in the night-stands were empty, and the dresser held nothing but more clothes.

"I miss my mamá. I want to go home." I walked back into the closet, eyes down at the floor, shoulders slumped, tears leaking down my cheeks.

"Crying isn't going to get you any closer to home right now."

She was right, but I'd never played "make-believe" with fancy clothes. Mamá would never buy play clothes. The closet was full of fancy dresses. The frilly one they gave me was the nicest thing I'd ever worn.

"I'm going to ask the servants what's going on the next time we see them," I said.

"I'm sure they'll tell us when they're ready. Nothing's going to happen tonight anyway."

I scooted to the back corner of the closet, under a row of clothes hanging in my face, and pulled my knees to my chest, sobbing. Sofia tried on an outfit, shrieking with delight as she saw herself in the large mirror covering one wall of the bedroom. She changed clothes and did it again. Clothes started piling up everywhere, hangers thrown to the side.

All I could do was think about Mamá and Jose. What were they doing? Did they find food without me? My thoughts drifted to the warmth of Mamá's body next to me at night. The floor in the closet reminded me of home, although the carpet was more comfortable than our dirt floor. I lay down on the soft carpet of the closet, curled up in the back corner, and fell asleep.

* * *

Beep! Beep! Beep! The alarm clock jerked me awake. The beeping continued.

I moved, and something brushed up against my leg. Thinking it was a gunman, I kicked at it and screamed, scooting further into the corner. When my eyes adjusted, I noticed it was only a dress lying near me on the floor. Every piece of clothing lay in piles around me. I couldn't walk without stepping on them.

"Sofia?" I asked, rubbing the sleep from my eyes. I stood and waded through the clothes to the bedroom.

Sofia fumbled with the alarm clock next to the bed, trying to turn it off. The sheets on the bed were messy, so she must have gone to sleep last night.

She slapped the alarm button off. "It says six-fifty. I thought we were supposed to go down at seven," she complained. "Why can't we sleep another ten minutes?"

"Maybe they want us to get ready?" I had no idea what "ready" would mean to them. "We just washed in the middle of the night, so I don't know what they expect of us now."

She put the alarm clock down on the nightstand and stretched out on the bed. "You should have come to bed. It was super comfy," she said, yawning.

I shrugged.

I walked to the door and tried the knob. It opened, and I peeked out. Several other kids in the rooms beside ours were doing the same thing. I heard footsteps and saw Tall Servant's head as she walked up the stairs to meet us. Short Servant was not far behind. I stepped out into the hallway and Sofia followed me, both of us hungry and ready to eat.

When all of us came out of our rooms, Tall Servant said, "My name is Crystal."

"I'm Ruby," Short Servant said. "I hope you had a nice night's sleep."

"We're going to help you get ready for your new jobs," Crystal said. "But first thing's first. Let's get breakfast."

"Follow us," Ruby said.

We followed her down the stairs, down a hall, and into a dining room. The biggest table I'd ever seen stood in the middle, dark and shiny like glass on the top. All of us could sit there and still have room. A white cloth ran down the middle, with silver lines that sparkled like stars. The chilaquiles and eggs on the table smelled so good. My stomach growled, but so did everyone else's. I didn't know which sound was mine.

Above us, a light hung from the ceiling, gold and glass and glowing like magic. Light bounced off it like glitter. The walls were covered with pictures of flying creatures and swirls that looked like smoke. The ceiling was soft gold and cream, so high a bird could fly inside.

At the end of the room, tall windows went all the way up to the ceiling. The red curtains looked like heavy blankets, with gold in them too. Outside, green gardens went for kilometers with little rivers jumping from fountains.

The room was clean. Beautiful. It felt like a dream.

Crystal waved for us to sit at the large table, and we scrambled into our chairs, ready to dig into the chilaquiles. I ate until I couldn't take another bite, almost feeling sick to my stomach. It reminded me of my last meal in Puerto Cabezas. Was this another trick like the woman from the motel?

Once everyone ate their fill, Crystal and Ruby led us back up to the bedrooms. They locked us back in and said they would see us at lunchtime. Our new prison was nice, but it was still a prison. We couldn't leave, and they left us nothing to do. No dolls or balls. Just clothes to play "make-believe."

I decided it wouldn't hurt to join in, since nothing bad happened to us last night. I still wondered what our "new jobs" would be but put that aside and joined Sofia. We tried on different outfits, showed each other, and gazed at ourselves in the mirror. It was fun! A little bit of fun in this strange new world.

At around nine o'clock, we were still in the walk-in closet when we heard the bedroom door open and shut. We froze and glanced at each other with wide eyes. The short servant, Ruby, came into the room carrying a stack of thin books. I let out a breath. No guns. No danger.

"You girls look very cute," she said with a big smile as she walked into the bathroom. "We should take some pictures of you...like the models in these magazines."

She held up the books, then walked into the bedroom and placed them on the nightstand beside the bed. She went to the huge, arched windows and pulled back the thick, dark green velvet drapes. Sunlight spilled into the room.

She pulled a camera from her apron pocket and walked to the bathroom to aim it as us. Snapping a photo, she said, "Come out into the better lighting."

We did as she suggested.

"Pose for me, girls," she said, camera to her eyes. Click. Click. "Show me how cute those outfits are." Click. Click.

She stayed for thirty minutes taking pictures. We changed clothes a few times, choosing the cutest outfits we could find: dresses, short skirts, crop tops, short shorts. It was fun to be able to play and not worry. Ruby seemed nice and treated us well, like a friend we could trust.

"Very cute, girls. Why don't you look at these magazines and find some more poses you might want to do later," she suggested. "I'll see you at eleven."

She put the camera away in her apron and walked out of the room. I heard the click of the lock behind her.

"That was super fun!" Sofia said, her mouth wide in a smile. She clapped her hands together in front of her face, bobbing on the bed. "I like Ruby a lot."

"Maybe that will be the 'job' she's talking about helping us learn," I said.

"Let's look at the magazines," Sofia said. She jumped up on the bed and pulled them off the nightstand, laying them out on the bed. She pulled one from the pile, opened it up, and started flipping through it.

I glanced over her shoulder.

"I could do these poses," she said, flipping her dark hair over her shoulder. She made a look, imitating the model in the magazine, as if she was gazing into the camera.

"That's pretty close," I noted, nodding.

I picked up another magazine and flipped through it. The girls' clothes barely covered their bodies. We always wore long skirts in Nicaragua, never even showing our knees in public. I wasn't sure why, but that was how the women dressed. Nothing like these girls.

I pulled out another magazine. A bunch of women in tiny swimsuits with only straps posed for the camera.

"Did you see any bathing suits in the closet?" I asked.

Sofia looked over my shoulder at the swimsuit magazine. Her eyes went wide, then she grinned like she just found treasure. She hopped off the bed and skipped to the closet, coming back out with some strings in her hand.

"Is that what these are?" she asked. I shrugged. "I didn't know what they were, so I didn't do anything with them. Let me see that magazine."

I showed it to her. She undressed and shimmied into the swimsuit. It seemed like it would fall off because it was made with only strings.

"I think you have it on backwards," I said about the string underwear, giggling.

Sofia had put it on with the wider part over her bottom and the string in front.

"The string goes in your butt," I said. She looked at the photos in the magazine, then took the string underwear off and turned it around. "Yup, that's it."

She struck a pose like the girl in the magazine. "What do you think?" I giggled.

"What?" she asked. Her eyebrows creased together, and her bottom lip jutted out.

"You look naked! It's worse than wearing just underwear!" I said, and she and I both burst into laughter.

I spread all the magazines out on the bed and froze when I moved to the last one. "Whoa!" I gasped. "These women are naked! They really don't have any clothes on!"

"What?" Sofia asked, looking over my shoulder. "Wow! And their breasts are so big!" she said, grabbing the swimsuit top with her flat chest in both hands. "Wait," she said and danced back into the bathroom. She came back out with socks stuffed into the swimsuit top to make her breasts look bigger.

I laughed. "You have very bumpy breasts."

It was nice to laugh a little, despite what happened. I decided I liked Sofia, and we could become good friends.

CHAPTER FIVE

Eleven o'clock came, and I lined up with the other children in the hallway to go down to lunch. I knew the way now, and things didn't seem as scary. I hadn't seen the gunmen all day, only Crystal and Ruby.

Torta de chicharron with salsa verde lined the dining table. Smoky, earthy smells filled the room as we sat and dug into the messy sandwiches. Juices from the beans and jalapeños dripped onto my plate. The spicy chorizo and melty cheese tasted so yummy.,I closed my eyes. I gobbled them up.

When we finished eating lunch, they led us down the hall to another huge room with high ceilings. It was a playground inside the house! Bright, colorful tubes ran across the ceiling like snakes. Five slides curved down to soft mats on the floor. Up high, a wobbly bridge hung in the air. It looked scary, but fun. A pit full of balls sat near one slide. A pretend rock wall made of plastic went up to more tubes. On the side, a huge box spilled over with toys. So many toys. I had never seen that many in one place. It looked like a dream, like a place from a picture book.

None of this made sense. People kidnapped us, took us away from our city on a ship, and brought us to this castle. They gave us clothes, a comfortable bed to sleep on, and delicious food to eat. And now they were letting us play. Why?

We stood at the door of the playroom, eyes wide and mouths open. The other kids seemed afraid to go play as well.

"It's okay. We have an hour to play," Ruby said, waving us into the room.

I stopped. Sofia glanced at me and shrugged. She smiled wide, tossed her hair behind her shoulders, and ran toward the rock wall.

Why were we here? I was sure it wasn't because Ruby and Crystal were bored and needing someone to take care of. We hadn't met the owner of this giant house, only servants, gunmen, and doctors.

Sofia slid down the slide and squealed with delight. Another girl pushed past me to join her, then another and another. For now I wanted to be like Sofia. Might as well have fun while we still could.

I squatted and crawled into the orange tube to join them.

***

An hour flew by.Crystal and Ruby led us back to our fancy rooms and locked the door. The bed was made, and the clothes hung back in the closet.

"Probably won't let us out until dinner," Sofia said as she kicked the bed post. We decided to look at the magazines and see who could find an outfit like the models in the pictures. We giggled and played until the clothes were all over the floor again.

The lock clicked and the door opened. A pleased smile grew on Crystal's face when she spotted us on the floor with the open magazines spread around us.

"I've come to show you how to use makeup," she said.

"Ooh, like the girls in the magazines?" Sofia asked, bouncing up and down and clapping her hands.

"Yes, exactly like that. I see you girls have been enjoying the magazines and the clothes. I'm so glad to see that," Crystal said, her hands pressed together.

She walked over to the bathroom, and we followed her. She opened one of the drawers and started pulling bottles and brushes out of it, placing them on the counter.

"Who wants to go first?" she asked.

"Me, me!" Sofia said raising her hand high in the air. She hopped up onto the counter and sat facing away from the mirror so Crystal could put makeup on her.

"You'll need to do this yourselves after today, so pay good attention," Crystal said as she picked up a sponge and small box.

She showed us the makeup. I stood beside her watching as she put it on Sofia's face. She explained the steps as she did it. Dipping a sponge into a box, she wiped thick, brown liquid on Sofia's tan cheeks. It was like magic. Sofia's face appeared smooth, not sweaty or dusty like mine did.

Crystal added pink to her cheeks with a brush and blue over her eyelids with a different brush.

"Does it hurt?" I asked Sofia when she blinked as Crystal drew around her eyes with a sharp little pencil.

"Not really. It just feels weird."

A little round brush from a tube made her eyelashes long and black, like the lady with the long eyelashes that tricked me at the motel. I shuddered when I thought of that woman trapping me in the motel room. She seemed like someone to trust, but maybe she was no different than Crystal and Ruby, trapping us in here.

In a matter of minutes, Sofia changed from a grubby Nicaraguan child off the streets into a beautiful princess twice her age.

Crystal put on the finishing touches to her lipstick and stood back to admire her work. "There! Now you look like a teenager."

Sofia turned around to gaze at herself in the mirror and gasped, putting her hands on her face. Mascara smeared onto the side of her eye.

"No, no!" Crystal exclaimed. "You can't touch your face. It will mess things up." She took a sponge and tried to wipe it away and put more brown liquid over the smudge to hide it. "There. All better."

We switched places, and Sofia watched me while Crystal put on my makeup, again explaining each step. Sofia stared with interest as I transformed into a "teenager," as Crystal called it.

"Okay, now pick out your favorite outfit to wear, and we'll take some pictures," she said.

We had played with the clothes so much already, we knew which ones we wanted.

I brought my outfit over to her, a modest dress, not too short, but with enough frills to make me feel pretty.

"Oh no, dear," Crystal said, holding it up. "That won't do. Find something shorter that shows your knees. Here, let me help."

Crystal dug through the clothes heap on the ground. She pulled up a red satin cropped tank top with a strap that crossed in front and then around the back of the neck. She dug through the messy pile until she found the matching shorts, so short they hit the top of my leg.

"Try these on," she said.

I pulled them on with a sigh, and she helped to get the neck strap right.

"You look exactly like that model in the magazine," Sofia said, running to grab one of the magazines and flipping it open. She brought it over to us. "See. Here," she said, pointing to one of the girls with an identical outfit.

I nodded and gazed into the mirror. I felt exposed, but I did look like the model in the magazine.

Sofia picked a fuzzy white crop top with short sleeves and a short white skirt with a flower right in the middle at the front. The skirt was almost as short as my shorts, showing the bottom of her butt.

Crystal stepped back and admired her work. "You are both very pretty girls. You will get a lot of attention here."

I didn't like the way she said "attention." Something in her tone was not right.

Crystal pulled out her camera and told us to copy the poses of the magazine girls. Click. Click. She moved around, snapping photos of each of us alone and then together. At one point, she had us face away and glance back over our shoulders towards the camera. Another pose called for us to stand facing the camera, blowing it a kiss with our hands on our hips. For another setup, we held hands facing each other with one of our legs up in the air behind us.

"That's enough for today, girls. It's siesta time." She put the camera back in her apron. "We've got a television show for you to watch this afternoon while you rest, and dinner is at five sharp." She waved bye and went out the door.

The giant black screen hanging next to the door lit up. We froze and stared at it, mesmerized. I had never seen anything like it. People were in the box, beautiful women, but tiny. They weren't real, but they seemed real. They walked down a long path wearing all kinds of outfits. Some looked ridiculous, others appeared very pretty. It was like a play but trapped inside a box.

"What's that?" I asked in amazement.

"I don't know," Sofia said, eyes wide. "It looks like a magic window."

"Or a moving picture book that talks," I said. I got close to see if I could touch the people, but I felt a glass screen. I tried to look behind it to see where they hid, but I saw dusty wires.

"I wonder if they're stuck in there like we're stuck in here," Sofia said.

All of the women wore very high shoes, making them appear tall and thin. Makeup, like we wore now, covered their faces. They had smooth skin, bright lipstick, and long eyelashes.

After a few minutes of watching the screen, Sofia said, "We should play make-believe like they are."

I nodded in agreement, still mesmerized by the television and the models in their skimpy outfits.

Life was so different here. No one could wear these types of outfits at home. Mamá would not let me wear clothes that showed my stomach or my legs. Only a few girls near the hotels in the middle of the night dressed like this, and Mamá always told me to stay away from them. She said they carried diseases and were up to no good. The clothes seemed wrong.

But this was a different place, and they had a different way of thinking here. The girls in the magazines, the girls on the shows, they all showed a lot of skin, and it seemed natural and acceptable.

Crystal said we would get a lot of "attention" in our skimpy outfits. I'd spent the last year of my life trying to avoid attention. The more I got, the less chance I could find food to bring home for Mamá and baby Jose. Mamá told me to never tell anyone where I lived or that Papá died or we would lose our house. Was attention supposed to be good or bad here?

The show ended, and another one started. More pretty girls, showing their stomachs and legs and wearing tall shoes.

"Let's try to be like them," Sofia said. She jumped off the bed and walked, hips wagging, across the room.

"You need tall shoes on," I said looking at her bare feet and giggling at her silly walk.

"You're right!" She dashed into the bathroom and came back with white heels matching her outfit. She teetered on the heels and almost twisted her ankle. "How do they walk in these?"

"Practice?" I said, laughing at her attempt.

"You try! I bet you can't do any better!" she said.

I knew I couldn't, but she didn't give me a break.

"Go on. Find a pair and try," she said, pushing me off the bed onto my feet. She almost tripped in the process, grabbing onto the bedspread at the last minute so she wouldn't hit the floor.

"With all the trouble you're having, I don't know if I want to try," I said, laughing again.

She frowned hard and squinted at me. I raised my hands in surrender.

I walked into the closet and looked at all the different pairs of shoes. I grabbed a pair of black heels lower than most but still higher than I'd like, hoping they would be easier to walk in.

I hobbled into the bedroom, walking on my tiptoes the entire time. I was not any better than Sofia at walking in heels.

"See," she said. "It's hard! How do those girls walk without falling down the hall?"

She pointed to the television showing the fashion show. On the screen, a lady walked down the hall with really, really tall shoes and a super long dress. The dress was cut way down in the front, had a big slit up the side, and the tummy part was kind of see-through. She walked with ease, as if she did this every day.

"And those girls in the bathing suits are all dressed in tall shoes, too," Sofia pointed out. She pulled the swimsuit magazine out of the pile and flipped it open. "How do you wear these shoes in the sand?"

"No idea," I said. I glanced at the clock. 4:56 p.m. "It's almost dinnertime." I took off the heels and put them back in the closet, thankful to be out of them.

We went to the door and noticed it was unlocked. I peeked out into the hallway and saw some of the others emerging from their rooms too. We lined up as Crystal and Ruby appeared out of nowhere.

They led us back down the stairs to the dining room for dinner. Food filled the long table, as usual. The smells of the carne a la tampiqueña and shrimp empanadas covered with salsa and melted cheese filled the room. The fishy empanadas reminded me of the boats at the dock back home. The crust smelled fresh-baked and buttery, like our yard when Mamá made corn tortillas over the fire. I got a whiff of the beans too, all mashed up and warm, and that little green sauce on the side gave off a scent of sour leaves but tasted good.

I took a bite of the soft, chewy meat. I used the folded tortilla to scoop up the meat and beans before crunching into the empanadas. They made the sound of stepping on dry leaves, and my tongue tingled with the spices. I wanted to eat it slow so it would last longer, but my hungry tummy urged me on.

After we finished eating, Crystal said, "We have some instructions for all of you. Today was a typical day for you for this week. Breakfast at seven, lunch at eleven, dinner at five. You don't have to be ready when you come down to breakfast, but you must be dressed your best for lunch and dinner, girls with makeup on. Your doors will be unlocked shortly before, and you can come down on your own at those times."

Ruby jumped in to continue. "Each of you will be given a new name. You will only go by those names from now on while you are here. You will call each other by your new names. You answer to your new name. You introduce yourself to others by your new name."

"Ruby or I will visit you tonight to give you your new names and show you what things you might need to get ready for bed. We will provide you with entertainment in your rooms each afternoon and evening this week."

Ruby looked around at us. "Disobedience will come with severe consequences. If you follow the rules, you will survive and thrive here. If you don't follow the rules, well, I can't say what will happen to you."

"What happens after this week?" one of the girls asked.

"We'll give you new instructions at the beginning of next week," Crystal replied.

"I want to go home," one of the other girls whispered.

"This is your new home," Ruby said. She looked around the table, stopping to make eye contact with each of us in turn. "New home, new name, new way of living. Look around you. This is your family now. You're not going anywhere."

Crystal and Ruby seemed to pause for effect and to let their words sink in. My lips started quivering as the tears threatened to spill. I looked around the table at my new "family." They had the same looks on their faces as I felt I had on mine. Helplessness, sadness, and grief for the loss of our real families and the lives we knew back home. Tears fell from some of the younger kids' eyes, but they didn't dare cry out loud. I didn't either because I was afraid of what could happen here if I didn't follow directions.

My stomach tightened into knots, my appetite gone. Her words echoed in my mind: "You're not going anywhere." That meant I would never go home again. I would never see Mamá or Jose again. I would never climb the trees by my home or play with my dolls or go to school and play fútbol with my friends.

Crystal and Ruby led us back to our rooms. I dragged myself as though the weight of the world was on my shoulders. I couldn't look at anyone after what they just told us. I didn't think any of us expected to be able to go home, but the hope had always been there, in the back of our minds until someone said it out loud.

When we got to our room, I fell onto the bed, tears pouring down my face, smearing my mascara all over the white pillowcase. I sobbed into my pillow not caring what Sofia thought of me. I didn't want to be here. I wanted to go home.

Ruby came into our room carrying another stack of magazines. She came over to the bed and placed the magazines on the nightstand next to me. She put her hand on my back and rubbed it in circles.

"I know it's hard. I went through this when I was your age. But you'll get used to it."

I didn't want to hear it. I didn't want to know kidnapping was the way these people, this "jefe," got what they wanted. I didn't want to be comforted. I needed some time to think through this.

But she didn't give me time. When I didn't stop sobbing, she tried another tactic.

"Look, she isn't crying like a baby," Ruby said, pointing at Sofia. She turned to Sofia, saying, "You're sweet as azúcar, so your new name is going to be just that. Except in inglés. Your name is Sugar."

"Sugar," Sofia repeated.

Ruby rolled her eyes at me, tears still flowing down my cheeks. "I guess you're like liquid azúcar, so your new name will be miel in inglés. Your name is Honey."

"Sugar and Honey," Sofia said, nodding.

I sobbed too hard to talk or think straight.

"Yes, Sugar and Honey," Ruby confirmed above my sobs that filled the room. "You're both sweet and desirable.

"Now let's get down to business," Ruby said. She led Sofia-now-Sugar into the bathroom and started pulling drawers open. "You will take a shower or bath every night before bed. To properly wash off your makeup, you'll use…"

I didn't catch what she said to "Sugar." I buried my face in the pillow and kept crying until Ruby left the room. I wanted nothing to do with any of this anymore.

I calmed myself down enough to sit up in the bed.

"I know you're not happy about this, Helena…er…Honey," Sugar said. "But think of it this way: they're being nice to us and giving us what we need. I didn't even get to eat this great at home. We were barely scraping by."

"How can you be so quick to be okay with all this?" I said between sobs. "This can't be all they have in store for us. Why would they kidnap fifty kids so we could live like queens in this castle? It doesn't make any sense at all."

She thought for a moment. "I mean, you're not wrong. But they haven't done anything bad to us yet. It's all been good."

"Except the kid that was beat!" I reminded her. "One bad move, and our lives could be over."

"The kid that was beat survived, and I haven't seen those gunmen since we left the big room where they did the medical exam," Sugar said. "Maybe they went with the other kids, but they're not here."

"I wouldn't bet on them being away for good. Remember what Crystal said at dinner. 'We'll give you new instructions next week,'" I said mocking her voice. "I don't know what they have planned for us, but it isn't always going to be as good as we had it today."

"Let's look at the new magazines Ruby brought." Sugar picked up the stack and fanned them out on the bed.

We both glanced at each other in shock. Gone were the fashion magazines. The women in these new pictures wore nothing at all.

CHAPTER SIX

On the second morning at El Jefe's house, Ruby and Crystal left us on our own to come down to breakfast. The alarm still went off at six-fifty to wake us up and make sure we weren't late. We rolled out of bed and brushed our teeth the way Ruby taught Sugar last night. We headed down to the dining room and took our seats. Scrambled eggs, fried tortillas, sausage, and black bean dishes lined the table, filling the room with mouthwatering smells.

Most of the children sat around the table. When the clock hit seven, it looked like we were missing one.

"Where is your roommate, Coco?" Crystal asked.

The girl called "Coco" blushed and shrugged, looking down at her plate. "She was gone when I got up."

"I'm sure she will come soon. There are big consequences for being late," Ruby said with a smirk.

We dug into our food. It was different from home, but I liked it a lot. Of course, any food was better than leftover food from the trash heap. My body was still getting used to having three meals a day after having only one for so long.

"Why don't you all introduce yourself to everyone with your new names?" Ruby suggested while piling food onto her plate.

There was Spring and Autumn, Berry and August, Raven and Kitty, Angel and Gabriel, Honey and Sugar, and Coco. Candy was missing.

I heard the front door open and feet stomping in our direction. Two men appeared in the doorway to the dining room, guns hanging from straps around their waists. These were different men from the gunmen we saw when we first arrived, but they looked as strong and scary.

They drug the missing girl, Candy, between them. Sweat dripped from her face, and her hair tangled around her head. Grass stains and dirt covered her clothes, as if she had rolled around on the ground.

One of the men covered her mouth with his hand. It was so big it covered her entire face. Her tiny wrists were clamped in his other hand.

The man next to him said, "We found a runaway trying to sneak away out the front gate. She will now learn the necessary consequences. Send Beatriz in to clean up after we're finished."

He nodded in Crystal and Ruby's direction with an evil smile on his face. They dragged Candy out of the dining room dragging her toward the stairs.

We all looked at each other in horror. What were the "necessary consequences" for trying to run away? Were they going to beat her like they beat that boy in the cargo container?

A few minutes later we heard Candy's a loud scream. I covered my ears and put my head down, my eyes squeezed shut. I couldn't see how they were hurting her, but the screams from the room upstairs scared me. I wanted to run and hide, but that would only bring the same punishment on me. What were they doing to her? Was she going to live? I buried my face in my hands to hide my tears and tried to push the thoughts away.

The screaming stopped. I didn't hear any gunshots. Maybe she was still alive?

Crystal sighed. "We told you yesterday if you disobeyed the rules, you will suffer the consequences. Unfortunately, Candy didn't listen, and she paid the consequences. I suggest the rest of you follow the rules, so it doesn't happen to you too."

We all nodded, our faces pale, eyes wide, and tears rolling down our checks. First the beaten little boy, and now who knew what was happening to Candy. They gave us all this food, clothes, and the nice bedroom, but there was a price to pay – our freedom.

I didn't feel hungry after hearing Candy and couldn't finish my breakfast before we returned to our rooms. The bed was made, and the clothes in the closet had changed. New lacy lingerie sat in bins, and all the panties were now strings.

Crystal told us to be made up and dressed for lunch before she left us alone in the room. We got to work applying the makeup she left yesterday and tried to remember her instructions. After what we heard at breakfast, I was anxious to obey orders. When we finished our makeup, we didn't look quite as good as when Crystal did it yesterday, but we still looked pretty.

We picked our outfits for the day. I selected a strapless black and white striped crop top with a short jean skirt. Sugar chose a short red shirt shaped like an X in the back and short black shorts.

"What do you think they did to Candy?" I shivered just thinking about her screams.

"Something very terrible," Sugar said. "Did you hear her screams?"

"I covered my ears as soon as it started." I shuddered again.

"I think they wanted us to hear it. It scares us into obeying if we hear what could happen to us."

"Do you think she'll be at lunch?" I lowered my voice. "Do you think she's still alive?"

"I don't know. We'll be at an odd number if they kill her. I have no idea what they plan to do with us and if it matters," Sugar admitted. "I'm just going to keep doing what they ask."

"They could always get someone else to take her place," I said. "I mean, they kidnapped all of us; they could kidnap others."

"I suppose so. I guess we'll have to see."

Candy didn't show up to lunch, but Coco's face looked pale. She hugged her arms around her stomach. In the playroom after lunch, Sugar and I climbed into the playground tubing and found Coco. In hushed voices, we talked about Candy and her crying.

"When I got back to the room, Candy was curled into a ball on the floor of the closet, naked. She wouldn't let me get anywhere near her. She just rocked back and forth in the ball sobbing to herself."

"What do you think they did to her?" My eyes darted around the room to make sure no one heard us.

"I'm not sure. She wouldn't to talk to me. That's all I know."

"Whatever happened, I don't want it to happen to me," Sugar whispered. "I'm doing whatever they tell me to do."

I felt the same way. Those men looked happy about hurting her when they got the chance.

"I'm glad she's still alive," I said. "It could have been much worse."

"Why isn't she down here now?" Sugar whispered.

"They let her stay in the room for lunch to calm down, but she will have to come down for dinner.".

We slid down the slide to the bottom of the playground when Crystal yelled it was time to go, and we all headed back to our rooms together. Another show started on the black screen with a boy watching something on the television in his room at night. The picture was all fuzzy, and his nose was inches from the screen. He was acting really weird about it. The people spoke in English with Spanish words appearing at the bottom of the screen.

That was how the rest of the week went. Breakfast, new clothes in the closet, lunch, playtime, new nude magazines, a show with a lot of kissing and touching bare skin, dinner, a photo shoot with Ruby or Crystal, another show with more kissing and touching the other's pipí and cucú, and bedtime.

By the seventh day, lacy string underwear, string swimsuits, sexy lingerie, and skimpy outfits felt normal. We slept in lingerie, went to meals in skimpy outfits, and played in the pool on the fourth day wearing string swimsuits. They tried to make us look like the girls in the new magazines during the photo shoots. Often, we posed without clothes, without feeling like we had to cover ourselves.

On Sunday, I asked Sugar when we were back in our room, "What do you think the instructions for us will be next week? Do you think they will be hard? I don't want to disobey and end up like Candy."

On day five, Candy had told us what happened to her. The men did adult things with her, one after the other. After they were finished they beat her on her back and the back of her legs with a stick, telling her the next time she disobeyed, they would kill her.

"I don't know," Sugar said. "I don't want those men touching me." Since then, she wasn't the same. She didn't talk much. Most times, she just listened and did what she was told.

As if on cue, the television turned on. Soft music played in the background. A teenager, or at least she looked like a teenager, was on the screen. She sat without any clothes on a chair facing the camera and blew a kiss at us. Then she reached down and put something inside her.

I squinted at the screen and gasped. The bedspread was identical to the one in this room. I looked behind me at the headboard and back at the screen. It was the same. The nightstand beside the bed was the same.

On the screen, the naked girl was doing things I would never even consider, and she had done them in this bedroom.

CHAPTER SEVEN

The second week at el jefe's house, instead of leaving magazines, Ruby and Crystal left toys to put in our cucú. Instead of regular shows, the screen showed girls using the toys, many of which were filmed in the room we were locked in. They made it clear that our "job" was going to be making videos...naked. The photo shoots became more frequent, twice a day now. It was only a matter of time before they brought in video equipment.

Raven refused to do the naked photo shoots. The men laughed when they dragged her up the stairs. Her screams were worse than Candy's. I obeyed but felt sick to my stomach the entire time.

The third week, the screen showed two participants, some girl and boy, some both girls. During one evening after dinner, Crystal brought Berry into our room. We were both forced to play with him like in the shows. Crystal took photos the entire time. *Click. Click.*

When we came back from lunch the next day, a new camera hung from the ceiling right over the bed. It looked like a big black spider with one shiny eye. Tall sticks with three legs stood near the foot of the bed on either side.

Both Ruby and Crystal came in that afternoon, but they didn't have their cameras in their aprons. They carried bigger cameras over their shoulders that attached to the tall sticks. They brought Berry in again to play and told us what to do. At nine years old, I had sex for the first time with nine-year-old Berry, and it was all caught on camera. But this time, no clicking sounds came from them, only a whirring.

By the fourth week, we watched shows with two girls and one boy, and Berry was brought in again to play the boy part.

"It's Sugar and Honey-covered Berries for dessert," Ruby said as she told us what to do for the cameras.

Sex and being "sexy" for the camera became a part of our daily life. And they praised us for it. They told us how beautiful we looked, how sexy we were, how mature it made us, how grown-up we were.

"Don't tell any of the others, but you're our favorites," Ruby said.

"You're very special," Crystal told us. "I love you both as if you were my own daughters."

They cheered for us and gave us big hugs when we did well in the videos. It made us want to keep doing our best.

During the fifth week, Crystal took my hand after dinner and led me down the hall, past my usual room, to the second-to-the-last door on the left. I'd never seen anyone use that bedroom or the one at the end. We kids always figured those rooms belonged to Ruby and Crystal, but I guess we were wrong. ·

"You'll stay in this room tonight," Crystal said.

"Alone?" I asked, scared of what the answer might be.

"Without Sugar, yes," she said, not answering my question.

Sugar had been by my side since they paired us on day one. We'd stuck together through the changes, the bad stuff, the pain. She was like an older sister to me. She made me feel safer when we were together. It scared me to think I'd be without her.

Crystal and I stepped into the room. It looked a lot like the one Sugar and I stayed in, but instead of green, the colors in this room were red, gold, and white. A single dresser stood off to the side, and the room felt bigger than ours. In one corner, a plush armchair with a matching ottoman was next to a marble table in the corner. A vase with white orchids sat at the center of the small table, their sweet scent filling the air.

Crystal put her hands on my shoulders and turned me around to face her. "We will have guests tonight. Jefe Hernández and his tenientes will be staying tonight. Your job tonight is to make his teniente happy, with anything he asks of you. Wait on him, hand and foot. Nothing he wants is too much. Do what he tells you to do."

She gave me a big hug. "You will be judged on your hospitality toward the teniente." She paused and looked around before whispering, "You have a mother and brother, right?"

My eyes widened. "Yes," I whispered, nodding.

She got right up in my face, so close I could smell her shampoo and see the pores on her cheeks. She looked me in the eye and said, "If you mess this up, your mother and brother will pay dearly. Please don't let them down, or there will be necessary consequences."

My heart raced. I swallowed the lump in my throat. How did she know about my family? All we "learned" over the past four weeks would be put to the test. If we failed, it could be a severe beating or our lives and the lives of our family might be hurt.

"Please," she said with tears in her eyes. "I don't want to see you hurt, my little girl, and if you fail, they will also hurt me."

Crystal gave me another big hug, straightened up and backed away. "Your uniform is in the bathroom. Go put it on and fix your hair and makeup and wait here for the teniente."

She turned around and left the room, the lock clicking behind her.

I walked into the bathroom and saw my "uniform" lying on the counter between the sinks. Black and white, like Ruby and Crystal's. The top looked like a tiny shirt with strings to tie around my neck and back. Lace trimmed the edges, and a little black bow sat right in the middle at the neck. My shoulders and belly showed when I put it on.

The skirt was short and black with white lace at the bottom. Someone had sewn a shiny white cloth to the front, like a tiny apron. A pretend white bow was attached on the back.

Next to the skirt, long, net-like socks lay folded, black with white lace on top. The black part looked like the fishing nets I'd seen back home at the docks. A white lace headband with a small black bow sat beside them. The white shoes next to it had skinny straps that wrapped around the ankles.

I sighed and got dressed. This uniform didn't look like the modest servant outfits Crystal and Ruby wore. The skirt barely covered my bottom.

I opened the bathroom drawer with shaking hands and grabbed the makeup: lipsticks, powder, blush, mascara, and eye shadow. Enough to make me look five years older. I picked up the brush, pulled it through my hair, and started putting makeup to my face.

I kept thinking about what Crystal said. "Don't let us down...or else." Was the "or else" as bad as taking care of the teniente would be? The beating might be worth it if it didn't come coupled with the rape by the guards. I sighed again. There was no way out of this. Maybe if I behaved, the teniente would be kinder.

I didn't have to wait long before one of the servants brought up the teniente's luggage, set it inside the room, and left. I pulled the luggage stand from the closet and set it up between the armchair and the bathroom. I rolled the suitcase further into the room. It felt heavy, and I had trouble lifting it onto the stand. I laid it flat so my guest could open it with ease.

A few moments later, a man walked into the bedroom and locked the door behind him. He stood short with thick muscles and wide chest stretching his shirt like the buttons were going to pop open. Salt-and-pepper hair covered his head in a neat cut and continued down his face as a trimmed beard framed his square jaw. His almond-shaped eyes, deep and dark, locked onto me and scanned me from head to toe with delight.

I stood straight from my seat on the edge of the ottoman, head held high, eyes avoiding his burning gaze. "Hola, Señor," I mumbled.

His hungry smile showed his bright white teeth that lined up straight. One tooth glowed as gold in the light from the window, matching the gold chains around his thick neck.

"Hola, Señorita. They sure found me a pretty one this time," he said to himself.

"My name is Honey, and I'm here to make your night a little sweeter, Señor." I said my line.

He crept toward me in the room. I kept my head held high, eyes away from his. My body shook with fear, and he could see my trembling. He stood a foot taller than me even with the high heels. I looked up to see his face.

He put his arms around me and grabbed and squeezed my bare butt under my skirt, lifting me up so my legs wrapped around his thick body. He set me down on top of the ottoman, so I was closer to his height.

"Unbutton my shirt and take it off," he commanded.

My hands quivered as I tried to work the buttons, scared he would hurt me if I didn't go fast enough.

His shirt fell to the ground, revealing muscles so strong they caused the veins on his arms to bulge. His olive skin, dark from the sun, was covered with colorful tattoos and scars, on his arms, around the nape of his neck, and down his back. His tummy was tight and toned. He could break me in half if he wanted to.

He took off his belt, folded it in half, then snapped it in my face. I jumped back, almost falling off the ottoman. He laughed. "Jumpy, are we?"

I straightened up and stood straight and stiff on the ottoman. "Sorry, Señor," I said, still trembling.

He reached behind me and took off my bra, leaving me bare-chested in front of his bare chest. "I don't think you're really old enough to need that yet anyway. You don't have anything up here to hide yet," he said, rubbing his warm hand against me. I shivered. "Are you cold, Honey?"

Before I could respond, he reached his hands behind me and pressed me against him. I could smell cigarettes and alcohol on his breath. Close enough to feel me shaking in fear.

He picked me up, again his hands on my bare butt, squeezing as he lifted me off the ottoman onto the floor again. "Take off my pants."

I fumbled with the button. They slid to the floor, showing his tight briefs with a giant bulge. He uncovered his pipí in front of me.

I wanted to scream. I wanted to run. This man was not Berry. He was too old, too big for me.

But if I did either of those things, the "necessary consequences" would come, and it would be much worse than this. I just had to get through this night.

***

I kept my head down and avoided eye contact when I rejoined Sugar in our room after the weekend was over. She didn't look up when I walked in. I winced when I sat on the floor next to the bed, the soreness screaming at me from below.

I didn't say anything. I didn't know what to say. My throat felt swollen anyway.

After a minute, she said, "I guess we're back to our original job now. Like nothing happened."

I nodded, staring at the rug.

She picked at the edge of her skirt, then pulled her knees up to her chest and rested her chin on them.

"It was awful," she whispered, then burst into tears.

I swallowed hard, then climbed up on the bed next to her. I didn't touch her but sat next to her.

"I keep hearing it.," I choked out. "His voice. His breathing."

She sniffed and wiped at her tears. "Yeah."

I couldn't sleep that night. Sugar woke up twice, screaming and covered in sweat. Maybe staying awake was better than sleeping. I didn't want to relive the nightmare.

The next morning, I showered until the water turned cold, trying to wash the dirty feeling off me. But it didn't work. Being with Berry wasn't as bad as being with the teniente, a man three times my size. A man thirsting for power and dominance. A man who couldn't care less about women. A man who prided himself in being a criminal.

Ruby and Crystal gave us the next two days off, but they expected us to start making videos again mid-week, as if nothing was different.

But everything was different.

CHAPTER EIGHT

It had been four years since the first teniente visit, and I still couldn't stand the smell of cigarettes or the sight of tattoos. That weekend was only the first of many times we hosted them.

After I turned thirteen, I woke up feeling sticky and wet. I shot up and gasped. Blood soaked the sheet. My eyes darted around the room. It reminded me of the first time Berry and I had sex.

"Sugar," I cried. "Help! I'm bleeding!"

She rolled over and yawned. "What?" When she saw the blood on the sheet, her eyes widened, and she jerked away from the spot. "What happened?"

"I don't know!" I jumped out of bed and looked down. Blood was smeared across my shorts. Something was wrong.

"Do you have a cut?"

"I don't feel hurt at all." I jerked my shorts off and looked around my legs. No cuts or scrapes. A drop of blood fell out from between my legs onto the floor. "It's coming from inside me!" I dashed to the toilet. "There's blood in my pee!"

"I'll go get Ruby." I heard her dash out the door.

The doors weren't locked anymore. We had accepted our fate, our inability to run away, after several tried to escape and failed over the years. Especially after what happened to Coco two years ago. After her failed escape attempt, her body was covered in terrible bruises and welts. She disappeared for several weeks. We all thought she had died until she came back with several casts from broken bones.

Sugar returned with Ruby, who looked at the spot on the bed. "Ah. It's time."

Sugar and I looked at each other with raised eyebrows.

"You've grown up, Honey. This is normal for girls your age." She rummaged around in the bathroom drawers and pulled out a long, thin package. "This is a tampon. It catches the blood. Here." She opened the package. "Put this inside you."

Ruby showed me how to use the tampon applicator and explained the monthly period.

My heart rate slowed to normal. I wasn't injured. I was a woman.

"They will give you shots to stop it from happening. For now, take these three pills." Ruby pulled out a pill box from the drawer where the tampons were. I held the small, round pills in my hand, looking at them. "Just swallow them. They'll stop the bleeding."

My job changed after I started bleeding. Ruby led me out of the house and around the back to the servants' quarters. She stopped in front of a door. Iron numbers hung in the middle. 109.

Ruby knocked, and a girl in lacy lingerie opened the door and peered out, blinking to adjust to the light. She looked about two years older than me. Her hair shot out from her head in a wild mess. A sleeping mask rested on top of her head.

"Roxy, this is Honey. She just turned into a woman. Show her what to do." Ruby turned to me. "You'll be staying here from now on. Roxy will take care of you." She gave me a little hug and left me with Roxy.

Roxy stepped aside and waved me in. Light from the hallway spilled into the room, revealing three twin bunk beds arranged along the walls. Heavy curtains hung over the lone window, blocking out the morning light. Other girls slept with masks on in four of the beds.

Roxy rubbed her eyes and grabbed a satin robe from a hook on the end of a bunk bed. "Follow me."

I followed her out the bedroom door and down the hall to the last door on the left. She pushed it open, and I recognized the bathroom from my first night here. "Here's the bathroom. Tampons are over there. Shampoo over there. Towels over there. Makeup in those drawers." She pointed out each item as she talked. I noticed the vanity counters with chairs lined up along the mirror.

Roxy glanced at me as she showed me the items in the bathroom. She seemed annoyed at having to "train" me.

She motioned for me to follow her out the bathroom to the door across the hallway. It opened to a giant closet with skimpy dresses hanging around the perimeter, heels and boots on shelves, and lingerie in baskets. "Clothes are in here. You pick what you want each night."

Roxy closed the closet door and walked back down the hall to the front entrance. "There's the lobby. There's the lounge. There are things to do in both of them." She waved her hand toward another area that looked to be a break room.

She turned and returned to the bunk room. She paused in front of the door. "We sleep during the day because we're up all night. Since you're bleeding today, you get a break. Stay out of the room until at least two o'clock. We need our sleep."

With that, she went into the door and shut it, leaving me alone in the hallway.

I stood staring at the closed bunk room door, my mouth hanging open. I missed Sugar. Roxy seemed cold and distant, nothing like Sugar. Maybe she was tired. She said they slept during the day.

I walked toward the lobby and noticed the armed guards for the first time, sitting at a desk near the door. I hurried past into the lounge. Three girls sat around a table playing cards. They looked up when I entered.

"Hi," one said. "You must be new."

I smiled and looked at my feet.

"Join us. We need another to make it even. Do you know how to play chinchón?" another girl said.

"No."

"It's okay. We'll teach you. I'm Diamond."

I sat next to her at the table. "I'm Honey."

"Nice to meet you. This is Bambi and Peaches." She nodded toward the other two girls. They smiled at me. "You just start bleeding too?"

I nodded.

"Best day of the month," Peaches said, leaning back in her chair and cradling the back of her head with her hands.

"Did they give you the pills?" Diamond asked.

I nodded again.

"Don't worry then. They'll give you a shot, and you'll be back to work tomorrow," Bambi said, rolling her eyes.

"Back to making videos?" I asked.

They all looked at each other.

"Oh, no. If you're here, that means you've been 'upgraded,'" Peaches said with air quotes around the word "upgraded."

"What do you mean?"

"You're working the streets with us now. You're too 'worn out' to be of use as a house girl anymore," Peaches said, again using air quotes for "worn out."

"But we're not too worn out for the streets," Bambi said, rolling her eyes again.

"Better enjoy the one night you have off while it lasts," Diamond said, dealing seven cards to each of us.

***

That evening, a man in a white coat came by to give everyone a shot. They came every three weeks and gave us another shot. I still bled a few days each of the next two months before the bleeding stopped entirely. Each time they gave me pills on the first day, and I got the day off work. The bleeding would stop the next day.

Every night I wasn't bleeding, the gunmen took me and the other women into town. They took us near the port to a long street lined with doors leading to nothing but bedrooms.

They left us each in a different bedroom and growled, "Don't even think about trying to leave. We're right outside." They pointed their guns at us. "Wait inside until your first customer arrives."

And the men came, one by one, all night long. Most looked rich. They wore expensive suits and fancy watches. They came to have their fun, to satisfy themselves. Some nights I saw over five men.

One night, I got assigned the bedroom at the end of the row. The first man of the night was a bigger man, wide enough to fill the doorway.

Maybe this was my chance to escape. I had obeyed all these years, avoiding the threat of punishment. Several of the other girls had attempted escape unsuccessfully and had suffered the consequences. I never had a chance that I thought might work before now. While obeying didn't give me the pain of the beatings and rapes, what I was forced to do every night wasn't much better. I was tired, worn out, ready to be done with this life.

I gave the man what he wanted, and as he readied himself to leave, I stayed close by. When he opened the door to leave, I got as close to his back as I could get without touching him. He stepped out of the door onto the street. I followed, slid to the right behind him, and dashed around the corner before he even closed the door behind him.

I took off running, barefoot, breathing in the salt of the sea as I huffed through the street. Where I would go, I didn't know, but I ran until I couldn't go any longer. One block. Two blocks. I was doing it. I was getting away. The more space I put between me and the bedrooms, the more likely I was to be free from them.

Streetlamps lit up the darkness of the night. If I wasn't careful, I would be noticed. A girl running down the street at night couldn't be common.

A crowd of people mingled ahead, and I sprinted for them. Maybe I could lose myself in the crowd. It looked like a party was happening. Bright paper picado fluttered overhead, strung from balcony to balcony. They cast a warm glow below them, adding to the light from the streetlamps. Music pulsed from massive speakers sitting in a truck bed parked along the side of the cobbled street.

My lungs burned, and my legs felt like rubber, but I kept running until I reached the crowd. I pushed my way to the middle and gulped in the humid air. I wanted to bend over and gasp for breath but didn't want to draw too much attention.

A vendor called out, "Gorditas! Tres por veinte!"

I smelled the food for the first time as I tried to catch my breath. The smoky scent of carne asada filled my lungs, and my stomach growled.

A woman in the crowd gave me a dirty look and put her hand over her child's eyes. Then I realized I couldn't hide. I couldn't blend in. My skimpy red dress and heavy makeup gave me away. I smoothed down the skirt of my dress as long as I could make it, but it still barely covered my backside. I pulled the neckline up to try to cover my cleavage, but it was no use. The fabric was too short.

"¿Quieres compañía?" a man whispered in my ear, asking for my services.

I jumped and shrugged away from him. "No estoy trabajando," I said, letting him know I wasn't working. I pushed further into the crowd.

A hand grasped my shoulders from behind and pulled me backward. I screamed as I fell to the ground. I felt my hair being gathered on the top of my head, and my body dragged, by my hair, across the cobblestones. The ground tore through the bottom of my dress, leaving scrape marks on my butt and legs. I struggled against my assailant, withering like a snake, clawing at his hands around my hair.

He hauled me away from the crowd and into a dark alley. The music disappeared into the background. My screams echoed between the buildings. He covered my mouth. I tried to bite his hand, but it pressed so hard against my face that I couldn't open my mouth. I clawed at his hand, trying to pry it away from my mouth. He flipped me over onto my stomach, still holding my face with his massive hand. I could barely breathe through his fingers.

The first strike bit into my back, tearing the skin between my shoulder blades. The pain burned deep and hot, like a fire racing up my skin. A rod of some sort was striking my back, over and over. I covered my head with my hands and tried to curl into a ball to make myself smaller. It struck me again, this time hitting my legs.

"This is for running away," a male voice said as he hit the back of my calf with the stick. My muscles burned. "No...one...runs...from...el...jefe."

The pain radiated up my legs. I struggled, trying to distance myself from the rod's strikes. My muscles locked up. I couldn't run if I wanted to. My legs ached and bled. I could feel the blood dripping down the back of them. My heart hammered in my chest. I felt like throwing up, as if my body was rejecting the pain.

I couldn't see my attacker, but it didn't matter. The pain overwhelmed me. My vision blurred, graying out at the edges. The alley spun. A heaviness set in, and my body went limp.

Then the world went dark.

CHAPTER NINE

I woke up to darkness. Memories of the cargo container flooded my mind, and I bolted upright, feeling the surfaces around me. I sat on an elevated cloth surface that gave in the middle like a hammock. Pain seared through my legs as I tried to stand. They buckled beneath me, and I landed in a heap. I could feel the welts in the back of my legs, sticky with puss.

I ran my hands over the cold, smooth floor. It reminded me of my room in the servants' quarters at Jefe Hernández's house. Did they bring me back? I felt the surface I had been lying on behind me. It was thin, without a mattress, and low to the ground. More like a cot than a bed.

The door opened, spilling light into the small windowless room. It blinded me, and I blinked to adjust. Ruby walked in rolling a cart in front of her. Her face twisted into a frown, her eyes sad.

"Why would you run?" she whispered, glancing over her shoulder. She couldn't shut the door. The small windowless room was too dark for her to see what she came to do.

"I..." My voice sounded weak and horse. I tried to clear my throat, but it was too dry and swollen.

"Running now is just as bad or worse than running when you were younger," she said as she helped me to my feet and back into the cot. "Lie on your stomach."

She helped turn me over. She winced when she examined my wounds for the first time.

"You're going to be out of commission for at least a week to heal," she said as she applied a thick, clear cream to my scrapes. It stung, and I cried out in pain. She pressed hard on the wound, trying to press the pain away. It didn't work.

I gritted my teeth as she dressed my wounds.

"You'll be stuck here in this cell until you're well enough to work again," she said. "They aren't going to feed you while you're in here."

"I've been hungry before," I said through gritted teeth. My voice came out like a growl through my dry throat.

"Here, drink this." She gave me some water from the cart. I drank it down, feeling the cool liquid soothe my throat. "Don't try to run again. The next time will be twice as bad as this time. I've seen them do much worse. You're lucky they didn't break any bones."

She finished dressing my wounds in silence. While she worked, I looked around the small room. The cot took up most of the space. In the corner, a small hole served as the only toilet I'd get. Concrete walls boxed me in, with no windows to let in light. The narrow door that Ruby walked through stood as the only break in the solid gray walls.

"Where am I?" I asked before she could leave.

"The basement below the servants' quarters," she answered. "It's basically a prison, a dungeon. Left empty, mostly, until servants try to escape."

I sighed.

"You should be back to work by next Monday," she said when she finished. "Rest up." She turned and rolled the cart out, closing me into the darkness again.

***

The next week felt like the worst of my life. Every time I moved, pain shot through my bruises and cuts. I couldn't even tell if it was day or night. The room stayed pitch-black. It reminded me of the nights back home in Nicaragua, when the moon didn't shine and the night felt quiet. But at least back then, Mamá lay beside me. I felt safe. I felt loved.

Now, I lay alone. No one touched me with kindness. No one cared if I cried. Sometimes, they slid a bottle of water into the room, once a day, maybe. I never knew when it would come. The door cracked open enough for a hand to shove it through, then slam shut again.

I was only thirteen, but my body hurt like it was a hundred years old. I felt used up. My head wouldn't stop spinning. I kept thinking about the container. The videos. The tenientes. The men, the ones they called my "customers," even though I never got to keep any of their money. I should've been in school. I should've been laughing with my friends. Or helping my family, like other girls back home who got jobs and helped out. But this? This wasn't helping. This wasn't normal.

I cried, but only in whispers. Quiet tears in the dark. It didn't matter. No one listened. How did I end up here? I wasn't supposed to run. But they planned to sell me again. I couldn't do it anymore. I had to try to get away.

I thought I could escape, but it made my life even worse. Why did I think they wouldn't find me? Of course they would. Maybe the next man had already been waiting for me, and he got mad when I didn't show up.

Maybe I deserved this. Maybe I was ruined. Dirty. They always told us we were nothing without them. That we'd never survive on our own. And maybe...maybe they were right.

My mind played tricks on me. I replayed the past. Every mistake. Every time I "messed up." I obeyed so I wouldn't get punished. But it never made a difference. And for what? They gave us food and shelter. I couldn't find that on my own here in this strange country. Maybe that was all I needed. Maybe I owed them for that.

No! He hit me. They sold me. They told me lies. I wasn't born for this, I told myself. I did the right thing. I tried to get away. Even if no one helped me, even if I died in here, I still ran.

But what other choice did I have?

"Helena." I whispered, reminding myself of my real name. Not Honey. "Helena Downs."

I had to hold on to the girl I was before they took me. Before they used me. Before they destroyed me.

I didn't know how long I would have to do what they said to stay alive, but I would survive. I was stronger than they thought. I'd figure something out. Even if I had to pretend a little longer until I found a way out.

***

I didn't try to run away again.

After I resolved to play along, knowing I didn't have a choice, I got quite good at my job. I still resented every new customer that came into my room, but accepting my situation seemed to be the easiest way. I played with the minds of every disgusting male that decided to buy his pleasure. Many of them requested me multiple times. I built up a repeat customer base, and they rewarded me for it. Better clothes, better meals, better living quarters. I learned to play the game.

By the time I turned eighteen, they no longer wanted me to play the game. I was old, used up. The men all wanted younger girls.

Instead, they put me in the kitchen to cook for the new girls and the field slaves. I jumped for joy the first night they didn't call for me to go to the row of bedrooms in the city. I had played along and done what they told me to do for five years, entertaining twenty to thirty men a week, every week. It had finally paid off.

Though I cooked for them in the kitchen of the mansion, I didn't see the children. We prepared the food before they came down to eat and cleaned their rooms while they ate. I didn't want to get beaten for being seen, so I followed orders. This new job made me an excellent cook. The house cooks made food for el jefe himself when he visited, so they knew how to make the most magnificent meals. I learned to cook like them.

Late one night, the television in the kitchen showed the Miss Teen Tamaulipas pageant. I gathered with the other cooks as Aitana Bernal was crowned Miss Teen Tamaulipas. Food for the field slaves, leftovers from the day, simmered on the stove as we watched the final decision being revealed. At sixteen, Aitana had risen through the beauty pageant ranks quickly. Her beauty shone beyond any I had seen before.

El jefe was in town with his tenientes. He must have been watching from the television in his study. As soon as they announced Aitana as the winner, he burst into the hallway and yelled, "Maria!"

I heard Maria, the head servant, scurrying to the study. We all moved closer to the kitchen door to find out what the yelling was about.

"Get her for me," Jefe Hernández said.

Maria hesitated. "As a wife, Señor?"

Jefe Hernández had several wives already. Each wife controlled one of his mansions across his empire. The Tampico mansion did not have a wife living here. Instead, it entertained the making of child pornography and holidays for his highest officials. But Jefe Hernández got what he wanted, and Tampico was the only place to house a new wife.

On a rainy Tuesday after the pageant, rumors flew around the house. Aitana's family had been summoned to the house. We worked overtime to ensure a successful visit. Jefe Hernández sent the house girls to the servants' quarters, and we cleaned all eight bedrooms from top to bottom. We prepared fancy dishes of carne a la tampiqueña and torta de la barda with mangos a la canela for dessert.

After lunch, the family met with Jefe Hernández in his study to make the deal. I wiped the rag over the dining table when Maria came in and pulled me away.

"You will now be servant to Señorita Aitana," Maria said. "You are to prepare her for the wedding. It will happen tonight."

"Tonight? That's too soon," I said. "How can we prepare her so quickly?"

"You will do it...or else."

I knew what that meant, and I would not fail.

Maria gave me instructions: "Wash, wax, pluck, makeup, dress. She's a beauty queen, so there probably won't be that much to do, really."

I followed Maria into the study where Señorita Aitana's family gathered with Jefe Hernández. She lowered her beautiful face and picked at a painted fingernail. I reached out my hand to her, and she eased up. Her mother rose and hugged her, tears staining her cheeks. Señorita Aitana went to her father and hugged him. She looked at him as if begging him to somehow stop this arrangement. But he nodded, a sad nod, and let her go.

I took her sweaty palm in my hand and led her out of the study, up the staircase, and to the bedroom next to Jefe Hernández's room. She trudged along behind me. When I stepped into the room, my mind jumped back to the first time the teniente visited me in this same bedroom. That moment traumatized me then, but so many more terrible things had happened since. Part of me almost wished I could go back to those days.

I guided her to the bathroom and got her ready for the wedding night. Maria gave me specific instructions, and I did what she said. I helped Señorita Aitana with her hair, her makeup, the dress.

"I can't believe Papá let him take me." She huffed and pouted as I brushed her hair. "I can do this myself, you know." Rolling her eyes, she snatched the brush out of my hands and ran it through her hair.

"I'm just trying to help, Señorita."

"If you want to help, tell me how to get out of this place."

"I've been trying to do that for ten years now. You can't escape el jefe. He has spies everywhere. And they use violence and mind games to control us."

I felt sorry for her. But she was better off than the new girls or the other teens working the streets. At least she would only be forced to be with el jefe himself.

Two hours later, she walked out into the backyard for the ceremony. As she started down the aisle, Maria pulled me aside "You will be her personal servant from now on."

I nodded.

For the next three months, I attended to Señora Aitana, helping her adjust to a life at La Mansión de Tampico. Jefe Hernández came to town more often than he had been in years past, doting on his newest wife.

But Señora Aitana loathed Jefe Hernández. For taking her away from her family. For taking her away from her first love, her preparatoria boyfriend, Santiago.

When Jefe Hernández left on his many business trips or to one of his other homes with another wife, Señora Aitana snuck out to be with Santiago. I would come looking for her at night, and her room would be empty. One night she managed to sneak Santiago into her room, and I caught them under the Egyptian cotton sheets of her luxurious bed. I left them alone, embarrassed by what I saw.

Jefe Hernández knew of Señora Aitana's extracurricular activities. The halcones watched out for him throughout the country, and espías watched the house as well. It didn't take long for the news to get back to him that his wife messed around with another man.

"How dare you bring another man into our home, our bed?" I heard Jefe Hernández yell at Señora Aitana through the thick oak door of her bedroom.

"You have how many wives?" Señora Aitana yelled back.

"He is not your husband. I am," Jefe Hernández growled back at her. "This will be taken care of immediately."

He stormed out of the room, down the stairs, and out the door.

Señora Aitana dashed out of the room after him, but she couldn't stop him. He jumped in his car and headed down the driveway. She raced back to her room and called Santiago from her cell phone, trying to warn him about el jefe's anger and sudden exit after their heated argument.

I never saw Santiago after that night.

The next time Hernández left town, Señora Aitana called the police. They pulled up to the front of the mansion, and she met them at the door. She took them into the study to tell them about Santiago having gone missing. She told them all about Hernández' drug operations and his sex slaves living in the servants' quarters. She told them everything she learned about Hernández' empire since she arrived. They thanked her for her information and promised to investigate Santiago's disappearance.

Two nights later, Señora Aitana also disappeared.

CHAPTER TEN

None of us questioned what happened to Señora Aitana. We all knew. Working in the cartel was a dangerous job. For us. For anyone who talked too much. We didn't choose to work here, but I wasn't going to say anything.

Jefe Hernández would not be played. He would get his way. Soon, he started looking for a new wife to replace Aitana and run his Tampico mansion.

I spent the next six months back in the kitchen with the other cooks, trying to stay out of sight. But when a record-breaking hurricane headed for South Texas and the east coast of Mexico, my job changed again.

Around that time, Isabelle Serug and her family evacuated from Texas to Mexico. I never would have known her story, but one of the halcones spotted her as she crossed the border. He told Jefe Hernández about her beauty, and from that moment on, her fate was sealed.

As with Señora Aitana, Jefe Hernández summoned Señorita Isabelle's family to La Mansión de Tampico and took her to replace his wife. Like Señora Aitana's parents, Señor Abe could do nothing about it. You didn't piss off el jefe and live to talk about it, as Señora Aitana found out the hard way.

When Señorita Isabelle and her large family arrived at the house, Maria summoned me to the study to welcome our new guests. Jefe Hernández gave Señor Abe and Isabelle's brother Louis lots of gifts: a Range Rover, two new RVs, horses, money. Once Jefe Hernández shook hands with Señor Abe, I took Señorita Isabelle up to the bedroom next to Jefe Hernández's room.

She looked young, about to turn seventeen, two years younger than me. Her beauty shone brighter than even Señora Aitana's. The most beautiful of all Jefe Hernández's wives. Her shoulder-length black hair caught the bathroom light as I styled it, shiny like polished obsidian. Her rich, copper-brown skin reminded me of the earth as I brushed on the wedding makeup. The dress hugged her narrow waist and full chest. She seemed like the perfect choice to replace Señora Aitana as Jefe Hernández's Tampico wife.

The day after the wedding, rain poured and the wind battered against the windows, whistling through the house. During siesta time, I rested in the back sitting room with several of the other servants.

All of a sudden, I heard Teniente Romero shout in panic from the foyer, "¡Rápido! ¡Necesitamos un médico!" His voice echoed through the house. "¡Ayuda! ¡Ayuda!"

I jumped up from my nap and rushed out of the sitting room to see what happened. Every servant in the house did the same thing, and I joined the crowd near the foyer.

Jefe Hernández lay sprawled on the floor. His body twitched, his face was pale, and his breath came in shallow gasps. Three of the male servants picked him up and carried him up the stairs to his room. Señora Isa stood by the door to the study asking something in English that I didn't understand. She was pale and trembling.

The doctor came and hurried upstairs to Jefe Hernández's room. Shortly afterwards, Señora Isa went up to see him. I hid in the shadows awaiting orders from her. She and the doctor left Jefe Hernández's room and went into her bedroom. I approached her door to listen. The doctor examined her to see if she had gotten the same sickness as Jefe Hernández, and I heard the doctor tell her she was healthy.

"What about Helena, my personal servant? She was in and out of this room too," I heard Señora Isa say.

"We should check her as well," I heard the doctor say.

I nudged my way into the room.

"Is this Helena?" the doctor asked. Señora Isa nodded. "I'm going to examine everyone in the house to ensure everyone is healthy, Helena. We're going to start with you, since you were potentially exposed to Jefe Hernández's germs here in this room."

I could feel my eyes widen and my eyebrows shoot to the top of my forehead.

"I'm fine. I'm healthy. Hopefully you are too. I'll step out so he can examine you," Señora Isa said. She slipped out the door.

When she left, the doctor did a thorough examination, checking my whole body. I felt a little uncomfortable, but the exam was nothing compared to the other things that happened to me in this same room. My eyes fluttered, trying to blink away the memories.

"You're completely healthy. No symptoms or concerns," the doctor concluded.

I let out a breath.

Over the next day, reports came in from Monterrey, Mexico City, Guadalajara, Chihuahua, and Hermosillo that all of the servants, mules, halcones, and tenientes broke out with the same boils Jefe Hernández and Teniente Romero had. Everyone in his massive cartel empire, except for the servants caring for Señora Isa and her family, were sick.

Señor Abe revealed to Jefe Hernández that the disease was inflicted upon him and his empire by Jehovah, Señor Abe's god, because Jefe Hernández had taken a married woman to be his own.

From downstairs in the kitchen, I heard the shouts coming from Jefe Hernández's bedroom.

"What is this you've done to me?" he bellowed. "Why didn't you tell me she was your wife? Why did you say, 'She is my sister,' and let me take her as my wife?"

His voice shook the entire house.

He summoned Maria to his room, and she dashed up the stairs. Shortly afterwards, an alarm blared throughout the house indicating a house-wide servants' meeting. I shuffled to the ballroom with everyone else.

"It seems La Mansión de Tampico was never meant to have a wife running it," Maria said when all the servants appeared to gather in the large room. "El jefe has sent Señora Isa and her family away." She lowered her voice. "Not in the same way he sent Señora Aitana away."

A collective breath came out of us, the heat warming the room. I liked Señora Isa. She was nothing like Señora Aitana—cold, manipulative, and distant. No. Señora Isa seemed kind. She showed me how to talk to her through the translate app on her phone. I even learned how to say "bath" in English when I helped her wash up in the morning.

"Eddy, Honey, Berry, and Daniel."

My head jerked up when Maria said my name. I met her eyes. She smiled, and her eyes almost did too. I could tell she was happy for me, but a tiny spark flickered there, like she wished it was her instead. She tried to hide it, but I saw.

"You will go with them. To Texas."

To Texas? To the United States of America? Eddy was doing some sort of happy dance. His eyes sparkled. He didn't question the new assignment.

I couldn't believe it. Maria had to be lying. This was some trick. Some test. Maybe she wanted to see if I'd run, so they could drag me back and punish me for "disobedience."

People like me didn't get to walk away.

I stared at Maria, waiting for the catch. Waiting for the smirk, the slap, the command to get back to work. But she said nothing.

I blinked. Maria still stared at me, waiting for me to say something or do something. She said I was free to go with Señora Isa to Texas. Just like that.

My heart pounded, but not with hope. Hope got people like me killed. It pounded with fear. What if someone was waiting outside? What if we took a step out and they shot us in the back for fun? Or worse. What if they let us leave, then tracked us down later, to remind us of who was in control?

He did that to Señora Aitana. No servants' meeting was called, though, when she disappeared. Maybe this was different, but I didn't know what was real anymore.

Who was I without them? I'd been in this place for ten years. I didn't know any differently anymore. What if the outside world hurt more than this one? That was what they wanted me to believe. They told me I was safer here, that I needed them.

No. I couldn't think like that. Señora Isa would take care of me.

What if this was my only chance? What if it was real? What if I never got another door out of this hell?

Eddy sensed my hesitation and came over to me, putting his arm around me. I jerked away. No man touching me felt right, even someone as nice as Eddy.

He raised his hands and backed away. "It's okay, Honey. They're taking us with them. Away from here."

But I was still frozen. My legs wouldn't move, and my hands shook. My body remembered too much.

"We will be their servants. They will take care of us," he said.

Maria pushed her way through the crowd to me. She took my trembling hand in hers and led me to the side of the room, out of earshot of the others.

"This is your chance, child, to escape all of this," she whispered. "The entire cartel is out of commission. El Jefe is sending you away with Señora Isa. They won't follow you. Once you're in the United States, you'll be free." She handed me a little green book.

I took it and stared at the cover: México Pasaporte. When I opened it, a photo of me started back, but the shirt I wore in the picture was one I didn't recognize. Hillary Morales. That was who it said I was. They were giving me a new identity. I wasn't truly Mexican. They erased my Nicaraguan roots, my Nicaraguan name, and replaced them with a country I lived in for most of my life but never chose. Still, it didn't matter. This passport was my way out.

I looked into Maria's eyes. Tears glistened in them. She seemed sincere. She seemed full of hope for me.

"You're getting out. Walk away, and don't ever speak a word about your experience here. Everything will be okay."

Part Two

Madre Sustituta

CHAPTER ELEVEN

SOUTH TEXAS

"Disculpe, Señorita," a woman said to me.

I pulled my shopping cart to the side of the grocery store aisle to allow her to pass. From her accent, she seemed Nicaraguan also. Her little baby, snuggled close to her breast in the wraparound sling, reminded me of baby Jose, sparking the memories of my last night in Nicaragua.

How was Jose now, twenty years later? What about Mamá? Did they survive? My heart ached for them. I hoped that once I got to the United States, I might be able to find them, but my limited resources prevented me from doing so.

I shook my head to shake off the memories. I was shopping for the weekly groceries, and I needed to focus. Consulting my list, I added some rice to the cart before moving to the next aisle. I inhaled a lungful of coffee-flavored air. I added some coffee grounds to the cart for Amo Abe and checked them off the list.

When I finished with my selections, I rolled the cart to the checkout.

"Good morning, Hillary," the cashier said.

"Hello, Jack," I said.

"It's a beautiful day today," he said in a singsong voice as he started ringing up my items. The town was small, and Jack usually worked on the days I got groceries. He always smiled, sometimes with way too much enthusiasm.

"Yes. A very nice day in South Texas," I said, smiling at him.

"Do you have plans for the weekend?"

"The weekend? Today is...Tuesday, no? I don't think about that yet." I laughed.

"Well, you should. Maybe we can do something one of these days."

I froze. Jack's friendliness always shone through, but I had no idea he liked me as more than a customer.

"I...eh...lo siento," I stammered. My English had improved over the past ten years, but I still forgot my words when faced with an embarrassing or anxious situation.

"It's okay. If this weekend isn't good, maybe we can try some other time," he said. He smiled at me, and the smile appeared genuine.

I felt bad, but I didn't want any men in my life. Not after all I'd been through.

I paid with Patrona Isa's credit card and heaved the grocery cart out to the Range Rover. The car served as payment from Jefe Hernández to Amo Abe in exchange for Patrona Isa ten years ago. Both of them had new cars now, so they designated it for me to use while I was working for them.

The humid air smelled of wild grasses and mesquite trees. The sun shone down, beating against the black pavement and radiating heat as I piled the groceries in the back of the car. The wind whipped my long, dark hair across my face and into my eyes.

Canaan Ranch sprawled in the rural land ten minutes away from the grocery store. Once I left town, I felt the wind pushing against the car as I drove on the four-lane divided highway. When I exited the highway, the car bounced through narrow gravel roads, the dust billowing behind me. I passed by ranch land and oil rigs, and a few houses here and there. Our ranch was in one of the few subdivisions in the area.

I pulled into the subdivision and drove past one-story, modest houses to the end of the road. A large Canaan Ranch sign arched over the entrance to the long driveway. I drove to the front door and parked.

As I unloaded the groceries and carried them to the kitchen, I thought about Jack's invitation. I lived a lonely life on the ranch. Patrona Isa was my only friend and also happened to be my boss. Over the past ten years, I had gotten to know her well. She didn't work, so she often sat with me while I cleaned the house. We'd talk for hours about her life on the reservation, her family, her adventures in Houston and South Texas, and all the fertility treatments she tried. She loved to talk. I didn't mind. Her stories filled the silence and saved me from having to share my past. I felt too ashamed to go there. I didn't want to relive it, not when it already haunted me every day.

I put the groceries away and cleaned up the kitchen. I did my job well. I'd been working for Patrona Isa since she brought me back with her from Mexico. Even before, at my last job, I did my best...after the beating. Though back then, I worked out of fear and blackmail. Now, I worked with loyalty and pride.

Amo Abe applied for my H-2B visa so I could work for him as a "nanny," thinking he and Patrona Isa would have children soon. But even after multiple fertility treatments, no children came. So instead, I took care of the house and cooked their meals. They gave me a place to live and paid me well. I never made a single dollar until I started working for them. Their sponsorship kept me in the United States, and I never forgot that. I owed them more than I could say.

In all the years working here, I never thought to date. I never ventured far from the ranch. I didn't want any more men in my life. I was damaged goods.

Patrona Isa came in the front door as I finished cleaning the kitchen. I poked my head out the kitchen door toward the dining room. She smiled at me and held up the fresh flowers in her hand. They filled the house with their rich fragrance.

"Hi, Hillary," Patrona Isa called from the dining room when she saw me. She traded out the old, faded flowers on the table for the fresh ones in her hand.

"Hi," I said. I took the old flowers from her and carried them to the trash. The smell of the rotting flowers reminded me of the trash piles I used to dig through to find food. I turned up my nose to avoid the smell.

"How was your morning?" she asked, following me into the kitchen.

"Was good. I see Jack in the market when I pay."

"I think he has the hots for you, girl," Patrona Isa said, teasing me. "He always asks how you are whenever I see him."

"Sí...ugh. He ask me out today."

Patrona Isa's face lit up. "Really? That's great!" She bounced up and down, giddy like a schoolgirl, her long braid bobbing behind her.

"I say no."

"What? Why? You've been here for ten years now, and I've never seen you date."

"I just...I don't want."

"He seems like a nice guy."

"Yes, he look like a good man," I said and sighed. I tried to think up an excuse as to why I didn't want to date any guy. "But I don't feel...how you say...connection."

"Okay, that's fair."

She was going to let it go.

"How was your morning?" I asked her, changing the subject.

"It was great. I went to yoga and then stopped by the florist on the way back."

"You have more things today, or you stay here with me?" I still had the shared spaces to clean—the living room, dining room, and kitchen.

"I wish I could stay here and hang out with you, but I have tennis lessons at the country club today," she said. "You should come sometime. I bet you'd like it."

"I don't know. I don't do sport much. I think I fall down or hit the ball far, far away," I said, laughing. She laughed with me. "Also, the wind is very strong today. Maybe the ball fly away."

"The fences should break it up a little. I'm not too worried," she said. "I'm going to go change into my tennis clothes. I'll see you later." She waved as she walked out of the room toward her bedroom.

* * *

By the time I finished cleaning the other rooms, dinner time had crept up on me. Patrona Isa came home from tennis and joined me in the kitchen to help. She loved to cook. Sometimes she handled the whole meal herself, but most nights, we worked side by side. Together, we chopped vegetables and stirred the pots. Once the food started simmering, I grabbed the plates and silverware and set the table in the dining room.

A few minutes before the food finished cooking, Amo Abe walked through the front door. He said a quick hello and headed straight to the dining room with a book in hand. At thirty-five, he carried himself with quiet confidence. High cheekbones, a sharp jawline, and warm-toned skin gave him a natural charm, and his tall, athletic build only added to it.

The sun dipped low through the kitchen window, casting gold light across the countertops. The scent of roasted squash and whitefish filled the house. I carried the platter of food into the dining room and placed it in the middle of the table. Patrona Isa followed and took her seat to Amo Abe's right.

"Would you like to join us for dinner, Hillary?" Amo Abe asked. He always invited me. "Please?" he added, motioning to the chair on his left. His brown eyes sparkled with warmth.

Amo Abe carried a kindness I hadn't seen since my childhood. Unlike the ones from my past, men who used fear and power like weapons, Amo Abe offered honesty and kindness. With the exception of my father, every other man in my life had treated me like an object. But not Amo Abe. He cared about people, no matter their story or situation. And that showed in the way he practiced radical hospitality.

"Yes, please join us," Patrona Isa said, smiling.

"I didn't plan that, but if you want, okay," I said. I felt like an intruder with as many times as I ate with them, but they never showed any concern.

I sat at Amo Abe's left side but scooted my chair away from him to give him space.

"How was work, dear?" Patrona Isa asked.

"My company landed another big client today, a big bank out in California," Amo Abe said. He owned his own company, a company using artificial intelligence to find fraud and cybercrime at banks. The company had thrived over the past ten years. His office tower now stood as the tallest building in the area, around the block from the neighborhood where we lived. Amo Abe often shared stories about his journey and the wins along the way. He loved every part of his work.

"That's great! I bet Elijah is ecstatic," Patrona Isa said. Elijah managed the sales team at Amo Abe's company.

"We finally surpassed a billion dollars in revenue last year," Amo Abe said.

My eyes widened in amazement. A billion dollars! I couldn't even imagine that much money. Despite Abe's great wealth, the Serug family never flaunted it. They lived in the small, unincorporated community of Canaan between Benavidas and Alice, Texas. Everyone on the street knew everyone else, and they all worked at Abe's company. The Serugs didn't own their land but built their ranch and company building on land owned by a close friend of the family. The Serugs' ranch included a horse stable, community pool, RV park, and pow-wow arena.

"That's wonderful! Everyone has worked so hard to get there. You've come a long way," Patrona Isa said, touching his hand. Despite their arranged marriage many years ago, Patrona Isa and Amo Abe loved each other.

The lights flickered, and we all glanced up toward the chandelier and back to each other in confusion.

"Hmm," Amo Abe wondered. "That's strange."

They flickered again, and darkness enveloped us.

CHAPTER TWELVE

As the darkness settled into the dining room, I felt my chest tighten. I went from being unable to breathe at all to panting like a dog. The memories of the dark cargo container flooded my mind, and beads of sweat peppered my forehead. I hadn't been afraid of the dark before that night, but ever since, the darkness stirred fear inside me.

"The wind must have knocked the power out," Abe said.

I heard his chair scrape against the floor as he stood. He turned his phone flashlight on as he went in search of a lighter for the candles in the middle of the table. Relief flooded me when he lit them, and the candlelight ate up the darkness.

Why was I so afraid? Nothing would happen to me in the safety of the Serug house, even in the dark. But I didn't like being so close to a man in a dark room, even if it was a man as kind as Amo Abe.

"I'm glad the power went out after dinner was ready. It's been a while since I've cooked over the open fire," Patrona Isa said and laughed.

I was glad she didn't notice my discomfort. I took two deep breaths, in through my nose and out through my mouth, to calm my racing heart.

"We have a lot to be thankful for, living in this country and this time. Electricity is such a blessing," Amo Abe said.

After dinner, the power still hadn't returned. Patrona Isa held the flashlight while I washed the dishes and cleaned up the kitchen.

"Here, take this with you," Patrona Isa offered, handing me the flashlight as I prepared to walk the distance to my RV. "You might need it tonight if the power doesn't come back on."

I smiled and thanked her, taking it from her as I walked to the back door in the kitchen. "I see you Thursday."

"Have a good day off," Patrona Isa said, giving me a quick hug.

I made my way through their backyard to the path leading to the back of the RV park.

Amo Abe set up our living arrangements when Eddy and I came here with him and Patrona Isa from Mexico to South Texas. It took a year to build the house and another three months to set up their RV park. Amo Abe allowed us to stay in his RVs and provided food and new clothes.

The RV park welcomed the public and offered twenty spaces. The Serugs kept two RVs permanently set up, one in the back where I lived, and one in the front which housed three other servants. Daniel and Diego managed the horse stables, caring for the four horses and leading riding lessons and horseback tours for visitors. Eddy, Amo Abe's servant, oversaw the rest of the Serugs' house and property. He managed the RV park and kept the community pool clean.

I reached my RV and went inside, careful to lock the door behind me. Darkness pressed in on me from every direction. My breath came fast, too fast, and my heart pounded hard in my chest. I backed against the wall near the door and checked the lock again. For a moment, I became that nine-year-old girl, trapped in a dark space with fifty other kids. My eyes darted across the room, scanning for danger. I raised the flashlight and swept it through each shadowy corner.

Nothing moved. No kids. No armed men. No rusty cargo container.

Canaan felt safe, but I took no chances. I felt grateful for the long-awaited quiet, although the aloneness often brought back the memories. I still couldn't shake them after all this time. Would I ever be able to?

I sat on the couch and put my head between my knees trying to calm my breathing. I should feel safe, but fear clung to me like it always did. Irrational or not, it refused to let go. Ten years had passed since I served Jefe Hernández in Mexico, but the impacts of those years cut deep. I couldn't erase them.

The RV smelled of the cranberry scent of a candle I burned that morning. The small place allowed for any scent to linger. I rose from the couch and rummaged in a cabinet until I found my lighter and lavender candle. I liked the lavender at night. The scent calmed me. Without it, the nightmares clawed deeper. With it, I drifted into sleep for a little while most nights.

I lit the candle and set it on the dining table, watching the flickering glow settle over the room. My eyes wandered around the lonely RV, and Jack's invitation surfaced in my mind again.

Would dating be so terrible? I shivered at the thought of letting a man hold me. A memory of a teniente forcing himself upon me flashed in my mind, and a wave of nausea surged up my throat. I swallowed hard, gripping the table to steady myself. No, I couldn't be with another man. Not even a kind one.

I sat back down on the couch, eyes closed, and breathed in the lavender scent. Deep breaths, in through my nose and out through my mouth, helped calm my nerves and settle me down. I never chose this life. Papá set it into motion when he left us alone.

"Papá! Why did you have to leave us?" I cried into the darkness.

I balled my fists up and shook them into the darkness at my father. Did I play a role in his death? Tears flooded my eyes and threatened to fall. He worked so hard trying to feed us, even if his meager earnings only bought one meal a day. Did I add to his stress? Did I cause his heart to stop?

Demons haunted me every night. Ten years of safety and security on Canaan Ranch hadn't stopped them from coming. Would they ever stop?

***

"Hillary!"

I heard my name being called from the front of the house. The smell of lemon cleaner hung thick in the air, so thick I could taste the lemon on my tongue. I set my scrub brush on the edge of the free-standing bathtub in Patrona Isa's bathroom.

"In here, Señora!" I called back.

Patrona Isa walked into the bathroom looking stunning, as she always did. She wore a green string bikini top that brought out the green in her hazel eyes, a long black wraparound coverup skirt, and black flip-flops showing her emerald-green toenails. Her hair knotted into a long braid down her back. She must have been returning from the community pool.

"There you are, Hillary," she said, out of breath. "I'm going to make dinner tonight, so don't worry about that." Her almond-shaped eyes sparkled when she smiled at me, radiating kindness.

"Yes, Señora."

"I'm surprised you're still in here. You're usually done with the bathrooms by now." She tilted her head to the side. Her brows pulled together, and her mouth pressed into a thin line. "Is everything alright?"

"Sorry. I got distracted. I finish the other bathrooms and bedrooms. Just this and your bedroom left."

"It's okay. Take your time. Like I said, I'm going to make dinner tonight. You're welcome to stay," she offered.

"Yes, thank you. That's great," I replied, thankful for the offer tonight. I didn't have many groceries left at home and needed to get to the store. With tonight's invitation, I could wait until tomorrow to go shopping.

"I'll change in the guest bathroom and then get started on dinner," Patrona Isa said. She grabbed some clothes out of the closet and left the room, closing the door behind her.

I stepped back to admire my work. The faucets in the double vanity sinks and stand-up shower sparkled in the light. The granite counters shone, and the marble tiles in the shower and on the floor glistened. The free-standing jacuzzi tub stood as the last remaining task in the bathroom.

When I finished cleaning, I put the supplies away under the sink. I picked up my feather duster and walked out the bathroom door into Patrona Isa and Amo Abe's bedroom.

I picked up one of the framed photos sitting on the dresser and dusted it off. Patrona Isa smiled back at me from the picture. She must have been about nine years old, holding up a rabbit by the ears. Her older sister, Mickie, and her older brother, Louis, stood by her side. Her parents beamed with pride behind them, their hands on their youngest child congratulating her on her first catch. Snow covered the ground around them.

Originally from northern Minnesota, the Serugs grew up on a Native American reservation. Patrona Isa's parents met a heartbreaking death when she was only sixteen, forcing her into an early marriage to Amo Abe. They left the reservation together, at the calling of their god Jehovah, to build a new tribe in South Texas.

Patrona Isa's dark eyes stared back at me from the photo frame. Her features looked so similar to my dark hair and eyes. Peering into the face of the little nine-year-old girl in the photo, with her family beside her, reminded me of when I lived with Mamá and Jose in Nicaragua. It seemed like everything around here brought back memories.

I tried to shake them off and picked up the next photo to dust it off. Patrona Isa and Amo Abe danced at one of his company's functions. She wore a long sequined green dress, bringing out the green flecks in her eyes. Her thick black hair hung in a single braid down her back to the curve of her rounded butt. Amo Abe's black suit included a green tie matching Patrona Isa's dress. His long dark hair also hung in a single braid down his back, about as long as his wife's.

I put down the now dust-free photo of the Serugs and hurried to dust the rest of the photos on the dresser. The sheets for the bed were in the laundry room, so I headed in that direction. When Patrona Isa passed by the laundry room to go to the kitchen, I grabbed the laundry basket and went back to the bedroom to make the bed.

Patrona Isa was gone, but her green string bikini hung in the bathroom and caught my eye. As I tucked the sheets and bedspread under the mattress, my thoughts drifted back to the first time I saw a bikini.

The memories never let up. They came in waves, crashing over me without warning. I wanted to forget those years of my life now that I had found safety here in South Texas, but I couldn't shake them.

By the time I finished cleaning the master bedroom, dinner had rolled around. I stashed the cleaning supplies and headed to the half bath off the living room to wash my hands. When I walked into the dining room, Amo Abe already sat at the table reading.

He glanced up from his book and smiled at me, the smile reaching his eyes. Sitting at the head of the six-person oak table, he greeted me. "Hello, Hillary, dear. I'm so glad you could join us for dinner. How was your day?"

"Good, thank you for asking, Señor," I replied, taking the seat to his left and scooting down the table.

Patrona Isa walked in carrying a large round platter by the handles and placed it in the center of the table. On the platter, a green and white ceramic plate with red flowers held a stack of fried fish. Next to it sat a matching green bowl filled with wild rice.

She always turned to this meal, fried fish and wild rice, when something was bothering her. She and Amo Abe grew up eating it on the reservation. It was her comfort food.

"This looks wonderful, Princess," Amo Abe said, using her Native name.

She sat next to him on the opposite side of the table from me and put her hand on his in a gesture of love. "I have my last fertility treatment tomorrow in Houston. If this doesn't work, we're out of options."

"Last time you went for your treatment, I went to the altar at the same time as the appointment," Amo Abe said. When they first arrived in South Texas, he built an altar out of stones in the middle of the woods. "I hunted a deer, made a sacrifice, and called on the name of Jehovah. But I never heard a response. No dream, no vision, no sun shining down on the altar from between the clouds. Nothing. The deer was completely consumed, and there was still no answer."

"Maybe it wasn't the right time," Patrona Isa said. "Maybe tomorrow it will happen."

"It's getting frustrating. Jehovah had promised that I would 'become a great tribe' and that 'my name would be great,'" Amo Abe complained. "How exactly is that going to happen if we can't have children?"

Patrona Isa's face fell. She confided in me several times about not being able to give Amo Abe any children after her endometriosis treatment. She always wanted to be a mother. Amo Abe's words, no matter how true they seemed, were difficult for her to take. I felt sorry for her and awkward being a part of this conversation.

Amo Abe huffed. "I even told Jehovah that if we don't have a child to carry on our name, we might as well adopt Eddy. At least this 'tribe' could continue through him."

"Well, that would make for an interesting family, especially since Eddy is older than I am," Patrona Isa sneered.

"Your appointment is tomorrow at eleven?" Amo Abe asked, ignoring her snide remark and getting the conversation back on track.

"Yes, I leave for Houston at seven," Patrona Isa replied. "I tried to relax as much as possible today to relieve any stress. Hopefully this time it works. They are going to be transferring two embryos this time. It's our last chance."

"I'll be at the altar at eleven then. I'm going to do as much as I can. I want to hear from Jehovah," Amo Abe said. "I feel like we've done exactly what Jehovah has asked of us, and I haven't heard anything from him in a while." He tilted his head and thought. "The last time I heard from him was...When I had to rescue Louis from that mess he got himself into."

Patrona Isa's older brother, Louis, ran into some problems recently. I didn't know all the details. I only knew Amo Abe went away with a friend of the family for about a month trying to settle the issue.

When Amo Abe came back, he said Louis was back where he belonged. During his adventure some great priest blessed Amo Abe after the incident for what he did to save Louis.

"Jehovah had told me then that he would be my shield and that I would be greatly rewarded. Since then, I've heard nothing," Amo Abe said, frustration clear in his voice. "Where's this reward he spoke of?"

"I don't know, dear," Patrona Isa moaned. "You know I'm as frustrated as you are, maybe more. I feel like it's all my fault that nothing is working. I want a baby more than you do." She lowered her head and picked at her fish.

"I'm sorry, honey," Amo Abe said, reaching out to touch her hand.

I jerked my head up from my meal at the term of endearment he used for his wife. I felt out of place. I didn't belong in the middle of their couple time, especially when they were talking about this.

"Hillary?" Patrona Isa said.

I snapped back to the present, the memory of my name change in Jefe Hernández's house tucked deep inside my head, hopefully never to come back again.

"Sorry, Señora. What you say?" I asked, embarrassed.

She squinted at me. "Are you okay? You seem a little...off...today."

"I'm fine. Just a little...how you say...distracted."

"Okay then. If you ever need to talk about anything, I'm here for you," Patrona Isa said with a caring smile.

"Yes, Señora. Thank you." I picked at my rice. My food lay untouched, and I didn't want to appear ungrateful.

I never told Patrona Isa my background. Despite our friendship, as much as an employee and employer could have, over the past ten years, I kept my past buried deep in my memories, as Maria had instructed me to.

After dinner finished, I walked through the back door and across the backyard toward my RV. It was awkward at dinner to listen to Amo Abe and Patrona Isa's dilemma of lack of children and fertility treatments. She drove to Houston and back countless times now trying treatments from ovulation induction to intrauterine insemination to in-vitro fertilization. This trip would be her third time trying IVF.

I wanted this day to be over so I could start fresh tomorrow. Hopefully the memories wouldn't come up again. It would no longer be the anniversary of the first day in my previous master's house.

The walk to the RV didn't take long. The South Texas heat still lingered, but the sun already set, so the air felt more bearable. A near-full moon lit the path, casting long shadows from the oaks lining the path.

When I reached the RV park, I spotted Eddy emptying the trash cans near the picnic tables by my site. I gave him a quick wave, and he returned it. I closed my eyes in appreciation for the Serugs for giving me my own RV. I couldn't imagine sharing one with Eddy, Daniel, or Diego.

I didn't carry the same history with Eddy and Daniel as I did with Diego. Eddy joined Jefe Hernández's operation under different circumstances. His father worked as a mule in the organization, smuggling drugs across the Mexico-Texas border. After his father died, Eddy volunteered to join the cartel and earned his place in the crew.

Diego and Daniel suffered through the same misery I had, back when we were part of the "house group." I didn't cross paths with Daniel, though. Only Diego, who went by "Berry," stayed in the same group of kids I belonged to. Daniel came after I started bleeding, so I didn't know him the same way. Seeing Diego still triggered flashes of pain, terror, and memories I couldn't forget. Their RV sat at a safe distance near the front of the park by the main road, so we encountered each other only a handful of times.

I felt exhausted by the time I got home, so I locked the door behind me and went straight into my bedtime routine. I lay in bed, staring at the ceiling, trying to allow sleep to overtake me. Yet I worried what dreams might come after all the memories and thoughts of the past haunted me over the course of the day. I didn't have much choice in the matter, and as sleep pulled me under, the dreams hit me hard like a vivid movie.

CHAPTER THIRTEEN

I shot up in bed, my heart beating out of my chest, sweat pouring down my face and neck. My bedsheets twisted around me. I trembled, the fear from the dream still alive inside me. The images wouldn't leave me alone. They kept coming back, night after night. The horrors of my childhood continued to haunt me, after almost two decades.

I needed therapy, maybe some sort of prescription, something to suppress these memories.

The clock read 2:34 a.m. I feared going back to sleep right away, too scared the vivid dreams would continue to come back. The first time hurt enough. I didn't need to relive them every night.

I shook my head back and forth. Despite the late time, I decided a shower might help forget the dream and the memories that generated it. I let the hot water wash over my head and back, washing the painful memories away. Think about the present, not the past.

The cartel no longer enslaved me. I called myself a free woman, sort of. The work visa still tied me to the Serug family. If I left, I'd have to either find another employer willing to sponsor me or risk deportation. If that happened, where would I even go? I wasn't Mexican, no matter what the fake passport from the cartel claimed. I didn't have any papers proving my Nicaraguan origin, and I didn't know if I could prove it if I tried to go back. Did any hospital there even record my birth? For all I knew, I hadn't been born in one.

Where did that leave me? Free in name, yet the chains remained.

Even so, life here in South Texas treated me better than any other place I'd known. The Serugs offered kindness, respect, and stability. They treated us like part of their family. Their warmth sometimes overwhelmed me. I should've been able to relax here, to live in peace and let go of the past.

But every time I saw the others who came back with me from Mexico, especially Diego, the memories came back in full force. He had been my first sexual partner, but not by choice. Did he feel the same way when he saw me? Did the memories hit him like they hit me? What had those years in the house group done to him? Did it affect boys the same way it broke girls?

I shook the thought away. Forgetting was the only way I'd get back to sleep. Hot water streamed over me one last time before I turned off the shower.

I reminded myself: I was safe now. The Serugs took care of me. No one here made me act against my will.

***

I had finished cleaning the kitchen when Patrona Isa walked in the front door after her appointment in Houston. The light from the afternoon sun shone through the window.

"How was your appointment, Señora?" I asked when she walked into the kitchen.

"We'll find out in two weeks. I hope it works this time. I'm so tired of driving back and forth. And today was the worst with all the rain this morning." Her shoulders slumped as she sank into the chair, eyelids heavy, voice dragging.

"You need rest. Too much stress is not good," I cautioned. "You want something? I bring it."

"A glass of water would be great," she said. "You're right. I'm going to the living room to put my feet up and rest." She left the kitchen and headed for the living room.

I got a glass out of the cupboard and filled it with ice and water and brought it out to her. "I make the dinner, Señora. You rest now and don't worry," I said, handing her the water.

"Thank you, Hillary," she replied, weariness in her voice. "I'm so glad to have you here with us."

"You want something special for dinner?" I asked, wanting to make her as relaxed and comfortable as possible.

"Anything you make will be amazing, I'm sure. I'm glad I don't have to do it tonight," she said, smiling.

I smiled back and headed to the kitchen to figure out what to make for dinner.

This morning, I went grocery shopping, both for myself and for the Serug house. The sky stayed cloudy, heavy with mist that clung to the windshield. Rain seldom came this time of year, but the damp air forced the windshield wipers to slice through the wet film on the glass. I had rushed in and out of the store, trying not to get soaked.

The rest of the day, I stayed inside. I finished cleaning the shared areas of the house and got dinner started. I left Mexican food behind when I left Mexico. I didn't want reminders. I couldn't handle them. Still, I used the techniques I learned in that kitchen to teach myself how to make the foods from the reservation where Patrona Isa and Amo Abe grew up. I also learned some American-style recipes from the Food Network, which helped me get creative.

Tonight, I chose roast venison and squash with wild rice. It would be familiar to her with an American twist. I hummed while I worked, rubbing seasoning into the roast before sliding it in the oven. Ten minutes before it finished, I added the squash to the pan.

Amo Abe walked in the door as dinner neared completion. He went straight to Patrona Isa to ask about her appointment. Anyone could see how she lived at the center of his heart. And how much he ached for a child.

"How did it go?" I heard him ask her from the kitchen.

"The usual," she replied. "Now we wait. They said we would know in two weeks, you know, same as before. I go back on the fifteenth."

"I went hunting this morning and found the most perfect deer. I was at the altar right at eleven o'clock," Abe said. His voice got faster, more animated as he continued. "Do you remember that first time you and Louis saw me build the altar and offer a sacrifice to Jehovah?"

"Yeah," Patrona Isa replied. "The sun came out from between the clouds while you worshiped, shining right on the altar."

"Yes!" Abe said, his excitement almost unable to be contained. His energy filled the house, and I peeked around the corner, being careful to stay as concealed as I could. "It happened again! I didn't know if I was going to be able to light the sacrifice—the wood was wet from the rain—but I finally got it going. I asked again about the promise of offspring, saying that a servant of my household will have to be my heir if he doesn't intervene and we don't have a child. And then, the sun broke through the clouds and shone down right on the altar, like before! It was amazing!"

"Did you hear anything from him?" Patrona Isa asked, excitement now coming from her voice as well. She pressed her hands together in front of her in anticipation.

"Yes, actually! How could I forget that part?" Abe said. "Jehovah spoke through the sunshine and said, 'This man shall not be your heir.'" He paused, taking her hand in his and looking her deep in the eye. "He said, 'Your very own son shall be your heir.'" He brushed his lips against her hand, and she jumped out of the chair and flung her arms around him.

"It's going to happen!" Patrona Isa said with excitement. "This has to be it! This treatment is going to work!" She pressed her lips against his, and he kissed her back.

I ducked back into the kitchen before they noticed me eavesdropping. I felt happy to hear this might be the last treatment Patrona Isa would need. She'd been trying for eight years now to get pregnant without any luck. She would make a great mother, and she deserved to have a baby of her own.

I put the food on serving dishes and brought it out to the dining room. I peeked my head into the living room. The happy couple was cuddled up on the couch together. I hated to interrupt.

"Excuse me," I said. "Dinner is served, Señora."

"Thank you, Hillary," Patrona Isa purred. She gave Amo Abe one last squeeze and kiss and got up to follow me to the dining room, with Amo Abe close behind her.

"Are you going to join us, Hillary?" Patrona Isa asked. "We have a lot to celebrate, and we'd love for you to celebrate with us."

"Thank you. I'd love to. What we celebrate?" I asked, trying to pretend I hadn't overheard the conversation.

"Abe heard from Jehovah that we're going to have a son!" she exclaimed, her face shining with pride and elation. "This treatment must have worked."

"Is wonderful!" I said, holding my arms out to her for a hug. "You try for so long. You really deserve this." I hugged her. "I bring the champagne, but no, that's bad for the baby." I giggled, and she laughed with me. When she felt happy like this, she became such a pleasant person.

We sat to eat, and Patrona Isa couldn't stop talking about the nursery, the timing of the baby, and how my duties as a nanny would soon begin. She beamed with excitement. Becoming a mom had been her dream since she was a little girl.

I didn't feel even a hint of jealousy. Joy welled up in me for her. As for me, I wanted nothing to do with men, dating, or the activities it took to get pregnant. I'd experienced more than enough sexual activity to last a lifetime. Loving someone the way normal people did felt out of reach. I didn't think I could ever see sex the right way again. Girls who went through what I had ended up on one of two paths: some chased attention, others avoided all touch. I had shut down.

Dinner flew by. I cleared the dishes and cleaned the kitchen. Tomorrow was my day off, so I wanted to leave the house spotless so Patrona Isa wouldn't have to worry about cleaning.

When I finished, I stepped into the living room to say goodbye. The happy couple cuddled on the couch, watching a movie and stealing kisses like newlyweds. The love in their eyes made it clear how much they cared for each other.

"I finish for today, Señora," I said, waving from the doorway. "See you Thursday," I added, reminding her I had the next day off.

"Okay, Hillary. Have a good day off," she said, waving me away with a smile.

I slipped out the back door, grateful to leave the house and the lovebirds behind. The sun hovered above the horizon, not quite ready to set. I passed the oak trees in the backyard and walked through the gate between the Serugs' yard and the small backyard behind my RV. Since I'd already eaten dinner with them, I didn't have to make my own. I had the whole evening to relax.

I turned on the Food Network to watch my favorite chefs battle it out and pressed the button on the side of the couch to pop out the footrest. The sound of the TV helped me relax, and for once, I felt content. Before long, I dozed off.

A noise woke me.

The sun had set, and the moonlight streamed through the wide window on the side of the RV facing the Serugs' house. The hands of the clock neared midnight. I turned off the TV and lights and started toward the bathroom to get ready for bed.

But something moved outside the window. I froze. My body tensed as I stepped back, staying out of view. I leaned toward the edge of the window and peeked out, trying to figure out what I'd seen.

It might be a deer. They sometimes wandered near the houses at night. The waning moon cast a dim light across the yard. I could see enough to know it wasn't a deer. Faint light glowed through the kitchen window and the back door of the Serugs' house, blending with the moonlight, and outlined the shape of a man.

An intruder.

My heart thumped in my chest. The beating echoed in my ears. I shivered, even though the RV wasn't cold. I glanced at my door. Locked.

I peered out the window toward the figure standing near the oaks on the other side of the fence from me. I couldn't tell if the man was facing my direction or away from me. Could he see me looking out the window at him? I shrunk back, hiding myself from view.

What could he be doing this late at night in the Serugs' backyard? Should I try to warn Patrona Isa somehow? They were probably asleep by now, and I didn't have a phone.

I squinted into the darkness. From here, the man didn't appear armed, but this was Texas. Everyone carried a gun.

That thought reminded me. I had a gun too.

I ducked away from the window and crept to the compartment under my bed. I pulled out the .38 revolver and tiptoed back to the window.

Should I handle this myself? That felt reckless, but I might have the element of surprise on my side. I didn't think he had seen me peering out, but if I opened my door, even a small sound might alert him.

The man hadn't budged. He stood, frozen like a statue, the entire time. Maybe he had seen me. A chill crawled up my spine. I backed away from the window again.

I still hadn't decided what to do when the clouds shifted, and the moonlight hit his face. He stared straight at me.

CHAPTER FOURTEEN

I set the gun on the table and ran to the door to unlock it. I sprinted through the gate and toward the man.

"Amo Abe!" I shouted from a distance, my breath coming in spurts.

He stood in the dark, arms outstretched to the sky. He dropped his arms to his side and seemed to notice me for the first time.

"You okay? Are you walking in sleep?" I asked, gasping for breath when I reached him.

"I'm fine, Hillary," Amo Abe said. He spoke with a faraway look in his eyes, but his words sounded firm. I felt embarrassed at my sudden worry, and he seemed to notice. "It's okay. I know this must look strange."

"Yes! At first, I thought you a robber!"

"No, it's just me...and Jehovah."

I felt even more embarrassed to have interrupted a moment between him and his god. He talked about Jehovah as if they were best friends, as if they talked often. I didn't quite understand it.

"I'm sorry," I mumbled. "I...I didn't know."

"It's okay," he said, forgiving me at once. "I had a dream. Jehovah told me to come outside and look at the stars. He told me to count them, if I could. He said that would be the number of my offspring."

My brows furrowed in disbelief. "He tell you that? In a dream?"

"Yes." He paused, thinking. "I doubt he means Princess and I will have that many kids. If we do, we'd have to give you a raise!" He chuckled.

I wanted to laugh, but I couldn't bring myself to do so. I stood there, amazed at what he said. His dream caused him to get up in the middle of the night and come outside to look at the stars...count the stars.

"Patrona Isa know you are here?" I asked.

"I don't think so. She seemed fast asleep when I woke up from my dream."

"You scare me so bad, I almost take out my gun!"

"I'm so sorry, Hillary. I certainly didn't mean to scare you." He smiled, but it didn't reach his eyes. "The whole day, and night, have been surreal. I hadn't heard from Jehovah in so long, and then, in a matter of twenty-four hours, he speaks to me at the altar and through a dream."

I smiled because he appeared happy, but I still wondered about his mental state. I guessed we would find out in two weeks whether the visions and dreams would become reality.

"Okay, now I know you are not a robber, I go home now. Good night, Señor," I said.

"Good night, Hillary," he responded.

I turned and walked through the gate and back into my RV to get ready for bed, still wondering about what all this meant for them.

* * *

Two weeks flew by, and the day of Patrona Isa's follow-up appointment arrived. She had taken it easy the entire time, letting me take care of her while she spent most of her days on the couch or relaxing by the pool. I didn't blame her. This was her last chance. Even though Jehovah spoke to Amo Abe at the altar and in the dream, I figured a little cooperation from Patrona Isa couldn't hurt. Sometimes even miracles needed a nudge.

Since it was Tuesday, I focused on grocery shopping and cleaning the shared spaces. I also needed to scrub the baseboards today. It had been a month since the last deep cleaning. I had plenty to keep me busy.

The air hung warm and humid, as usual. I drove the old Range Rover to the grocery store and pulled into the parking lot.

I wandered the aisles for almost two hours shopping, checking off every item, and making sure the cupboards would teem with essentials in the Serugs' kitchen. They could select whatever meals they wanted this week. With our monthly powwow coming up Friday, I grabbed extra food to make for that as well.

When Jehovah called Amo Abe to leave the reservation and move to South Texas to build a "new tribe," he brought his employees from the Houston office. Eighteen people came. Once he settled at Canaan Ranch and finished building the neighborhood and powwow arena, he taught everyone about his Native American culture. The six children learned how to dance and play the drums, and they loved dressing up in the regalia and playing in the arena. The adults also joined, learning how to play the big drum in the center and perform the traditional dances.

Every month, Amo Abe hosted a powwow, and the whole neighborhood showed up to celebrate. He changed some of the traditions to focus more on Jehovah rather than the spirits of his original tribe, blending Native practice with church service. It always ended with a big potluck dinner.

After I finished loading the groceries into the back of the SUV, I headed back to the ranch. By the time I put the food away, lunchtime had rolled around. I grabbed a quick bite before starting my cleaning.

Later that afternoon, while I finished wiping down the baseboards in the living room, Patrona Isa walked through the front door. Her eyes looked puffy and red, and her makeup was smeared down her face.

Her expression stopped me cold. This wasn't the return I expected.

"Señora?" I spoke in a hush. I stood and walked toward her, resting a hand on her arm.

"Oh, Hillary," she cried. Tears spilled from her eyes. "It didn't work. There's no baby."

I wrapped my arms around her and held her while she cried into my shoulder.

"I so sorry, Señora," I whispered as I rubbed her back. Her sobs continued. "Does Amo Abe know?"

"No, I couldn't get a hold of him. He must have been busy at work all day. I didn't want to tell him over the phone anyway," she said between sobs. "Although maybe I should have. He's going to know as soon as he sees me." She stepped back out of my arms. "Look at me. I must look like a hot mess."

"You beautiful as always, Señora," I confessed. Patrona Isa was the most beautiful woman I'd ever known. Even through her tears and puffy red eyes, her beauty shone through.

"You're too sweet, Hillary," she scoffed, not believing me. I didn't hold it against her. She felt upset, and today's news of no baby shook her faith.

I guided her to the couch so she could sit down and compose herself. She sat and put her face in her hands and continued to cry. I brought her some tissues so she could wipe her tears and get herself together before Amo Abe came home.

"You want something? I get it, Señora," I said.

"You've been so great already, Hillary," she responded. "Thank you."

I left the room to get a glass of water for her from the kitchen. She must be dehydrated with all the crying she'd been doing.

"I make dinner tonight, Señora," I said, handing her the water once I returned to the living room.

She thanked me again. With tissues, water, and a soft place to sit, she didn't need me there now. I left her alone to start dinner.

I bustled around the kitchen, taking my time to get dinner ready. Amo Abe would be home soon, but I didn't want the food to get cold if he was delayed for some reason. While I waited, I wiped down the counters and cleaned the microwave and refrigerator, the few things I had to do for today's work.

Once the kitchen sparkled, I pulled out the food to make dinner. By the time the clock neared seven, I started to worry. Amo Abe almost never returned home this late from work. I glanced out the kitchen window. The sky still held a faint orange glow, but darkness had taken over. Patrona Isa mentioned she hadn't heard from him at all on her way home, and now he still hadn't shown up.

I tried to push the thought out of my head. The news about the baby already hit Patrona Isa hard enough. The last thing she needed tonight was another heartbreak.

My life before coming here had been difficult, but hers hadn't been easy either. After a car accident killed her parents, her grandfather, the man who became her guardian, suffered a stroke. He ended up in a rehab center, leaving her and her two siblings more or less orphaned. Around that same time, doctors diagnosed her with endometriosis. After marrying Amo Abe, he moved her away from the reservation to a strange town. She told me about the battles she fought trying to figure out who she was and where she belonged. Life on the reservation didn't prepare her for life beyond it.

Hearing that the fertility treatment failed must have crushed her, especially after the promises from their god. Why would a god give someone hope, whisper promises of children, but rip away their last chance to have them? It didn't make sense. I felt grateful I never trusted in this god. All he seemed to give was disappointment. How would Amo Abe take the news?

The front door opened and slammed shut. Heavy footsteps stomped on the front rug. I peeked my head around the corner, and I froze. Patrona Isa turned too, catching sight of Amo Abe and gasping.

His hair stuck out in all directions, tangled and messy. Dirt streaked across the left side of his face. His brown eyes were wide and wild, full of shock or awe. His clothes clung to his body, caked in mud, dust, and splashes of something that appeared a little like blood.

Chapter Fifteen

A fter stomping several times, Amo Abe took his shoes off. They weren't going to get clean enough by stomping the dirt and mud onto the rug.

"Um, Señor, what happen?" I asked, coming into the living room after seeing the way he looked.

Patrona Isa stood and dashed over to the entrance. "You're a mess!" she exclaimed, forgetting her bad news and looking him up and down. "We need to get you out of these clothes before they track dirt all through the newly cleaned house!" She glanced at me.

"You ladies aren't going to believe what happened," he started, ignoring the comment about his clothes and moving further into the living room.

"Wait! Don't sit yet!" I said. I ran to the closet and pulled a blanket out to lay on the chair for him to sit on.

Once we all sat, Amo Abe sitting on the blanket draped over the chair and Patrona Isa and me on the couch, we turned to him to hear his story.

"I went to the altar today to seek Jehovah about your follow-up appointment," Amo Abe said. "I did the usual, hunted a deer with my bow, put it on the altar, and burned it. The sky was blue, so the clouds couldn't part for the sunshine today like they did last time. Instead, I heard a voice from heaven, Jehovah's voice. Clear as day."

He paused, whether for dramatic effect or to collect his thoughts, I wasn't sure, but both of us hung on every word.

"The voice said, 'I am Jehovah who brought you out from Ur Street of the Chaldeans to give you this land.' So, I asked Him, 'How am I to know that I will own it?' And He said, 'Bring me three animals and two birds.' So, I went hunting. I cut the animals in half, but didn't cut the birds in half."

I must have made a disgusted face because he explained before he continued with the story. "A long time ago, one of our Native traditions was to cut animals in half, let their blood pool in the middle, and walk through to seal a contract with someone. We haven't done that in ages, probably since before Princess was born, but that's how it used to be. The person who was making the promise would walk through the blood first, essentially saying they would rather die than break the contract. If they broke the contract, the other person could kill them. Then the other person would walk it to say they would fulfill their side of the contract."

It didn't make any more sense to me. It still sounded gross, but I listened as he went on.

"Anyway, He told me to get the animals. So, I went hunting again and got exactly what He asked for. It took a while. It isn't easy to hunt that many animals in a day's time. Most people wouldn't be able to find the one deer I found initially for the altar, let alone the other three. But I was able to do it. Probably with Jehovah's help. I kept bringing the dead animals back to the clearing with the altar so I could go back for more. I had to shoo away vultures each time I came back. They were flying in circles above me, waiting for the animals. Once I had all that Jehovah had asked for, I laid them out in the clearing near the altar just as He told me to. And then I waited to see what He would do."

"You didn't walk through the blood?" Patrona Isa asked. "You sure look like you did with all the blood on your clothes!"

"No! I couldn't do that! I can't hold up my end of the bargain!" he exclaimed. "I'm just a mere human. How could I promise to do what Jehovah wanted me to do perfectly? If I walked that bloodbath, I would essentially be signing my own death certificate."

"So, what happen next?" I asked, enthralled by his story.

"I was waiting to hear from Him again, and the vultures kept flying down and trying to eat the dead animals," he said.

We gaped at each other, both wearing disgusted grimaces. The whole thing seemed bizarre and gross to me, yet Amo Abe told it as if he was amazed at the experience. I think I would have run away the minute some voice came out of the sky and told me to go kill animals.

"Anyway, so I shooed them away, making sure not to walk on the blood path while I was doing it. I certainly wasn't going to get into a contract that I knew I couldn't uphold. Then I sat against the altar and waited," Amo Abe said. He ran his had through is long hair. "I waited so long that the sun started setting, and I fell asleep!"

"Oh, no!" Patrona Isa exclaimed. "Did He get mad at you?"

"He didn't seem mad. When I fell asleep, I felt this thick, dark presence all around me. Jehovah's voice said, 'Your kids and grandkids will end up living in a land that's not theirs. They'll serve the locals and be treated poorly there for four hundred years. But I'll deal with the nation that enslaves them, and when it's over, your family will walk out loaded with wealth. As for you, you'll live a long life, die in peace, and be buried at a good old age. Then, four generations later, your people will come back here, because the Klebergs' wrongdoing hasn't piled up enough yet.'"

"That's bizarre," Patrona Isa said.

I raised my eyebrows. "Who are the Klebergs?"

"Oh, they own part of the land near Kingsville. They let us stay at one of their RV parks when we were RVing around South Texas before you joined us. They were so nice to us. I wonder what sin He's talking about."

"I don't know, but when I was asleep, I had the weirdest dream," Abe started. "There was a smoking fire pot, like the one we used for the smudging at powwows on the reservation."

I interrupted him, "Smudging? What that?"

"We don't do it at our powwows here," Patrona Isa said. "In Minnesota at our powwows—and sometimes other ceremonies—we used prairie sage. We put it in a small pot that an elder held. Then we lit the sage on fire. Smoke rose from the pot, and the elder used a feather to blow the smoke around the arena. It helped clear away bad spirits and thoughts. That's called smudging."

"Oh."

"Yeah, so a smoking fire pot, like in a smudging ceremony, appeared in my dream and floated through the blood path," Amo Abe continued. "Then a sword, flaming with fire, twirled through the blood path. It was as if Jehovah was saying, 'I know you can't hold up your end of the bargain, but I can. And I will do it for you.'"

"So, what was the 'bargain' He was committing to?" Patrona Isa asked.

"He said, 'To your descendants I give this land, from the Nueces River to the great river, the Rio Grande River—the land of the Klebergs, Hebbronvilleites, Falfurriasites, Edinburgites, Raymondvilleites, Aliceites, Harlingenites, McAllenites, Brownsvillites, and Encinoites,'" Amo Abe said, his eyes wide.

Patrona Isa burst out crying at his words. "Descendants?" she asked, eyes wide. "We can't even have *one* child. How are we going to have descendant*s*?"

I moved closer and put my arm around her sobbing shoulders.

That was when Amo Abe realized the follow-up appointment hadn't gone as well as they thought it would go. I could see the confusion turn to sorrow on his face. He left his chair and knelt in front of Patrona Isa, taking her hands and looking into her tear-filled eyes.

"The treatment didn't work." He said it as more of a statement than a question, even though he hadn't heard the results from her yet.

"No. I'm not pregnant. The embryos didn't implant. The treatment didn't work," she said between sobs.

"I'm so sorry, Princess," he said, rubbing his thumbs over the backs of her hands. He pulled her up into a hug, his dirty clothes against her crisp clean ones, holding her close.

I caught his eye, pointed toward the kitchen, and mouthed that I was going there to leave them alone. I rose without a sound and slipped out of the room. This was too much.

None of this was my business. I worked as their housekeeper, focused on keeping the place clean and making sure there was food on the table when they wanted it. Sure, being a nanny and helping raise their kids would've been nice, but I'd gone without that for ten years. It wasn't my dream. It was Patrona Isa's.

Always the optimist, Amo Abe said from the living room, his voice low but still reaching the kitchen, "It's going to happen. I don't know when or how, but it's going to happen."

"Stop it!" I heard Patrona Isa yell.

I peeked back in the living room, staying as hidden as I could from their view.

She stood and pushed him away, her face red with anger. "Stop saying that! You can't know that. It's been *eight years* since we started trying. We've done *everything*! *Nothing* has worked." She paced the living room floor, fists clenched, arms straight down by her sides, looking at the floor. She stopped and glared at him. "I'm broken! There is *nothing* your Jehovah can do for me now. The doctors said if this treatment didn't work, we're out of options. I would *think* they'd know."

Abe tried to pull her into a hug, compassion and hurt in his eyes, but she pushed him away again.

"I'm tired of you always getting my hopes up. Of *Jehovah* always getting my hopes up," she said. "I can't keep doing this, Abe! I can't deal with this emotional roller coaster!"

"Honey, please," Abe said, reaching out to her.

Patrona Isa pushed him away, refusing to be comforted. My stomach turned at the word he used.

"If you're so convinced that you're going to be a great tribe, why did you even marry me? You knew it wasn't going to happen with me! You knew that before we got married. So much for 'Loving you is more important to me than having kids. If Jehovah wants us to have children, He'll make a way,'" she said, impersonating his voice. "You didn't actually mean it, did you?"

"Of course I meant it, Princess," he begged. "I meant every word. But things have changed. Jehovah has promised us descendants now, which means He will make a way."

"Well, then where are they?" she spat back at him. "What way?"

"I don't know, honey. Please, just calm down for a minute and let's talk about it," Amo Abe pleaded.

Ugh, that word again.

"I don't want to calm down!" she yelled. "There's nothing to talk about! Your stupid Jehovah is lying to you, making you think there's hope when there's none. Putting too much pressure on me to produce when I can't."

The compassion drained from Amo Abe's face, and anger replaced his usual calm demeanor. "Do *not* call Jehovah stupid!"

"What else am I supposed to think? He's giving you all these promises that can't be fulfilled. It's a good thing you didn't walk that blood path, because you can't give Him the tribe He wants!"

She sat on the couch and put her face in her hands, crying.

He let out a long sigh and stared down at her as if trying to figure out what to do or say next. Sobs filled the silence as Patrona Isa sat on the couch, face in her hands, refusing to look at Abe. She resembled a deflated small child being reprimanded by her father.

After a long silence, Amo Abe sat next to Patrona Isa and put his arm around her shoulders. She seemed to have calmed down a little; at least her anger disappeared. Her sobs slowed, but her breathing still came in gasps as she tried to calm herself.

Patrona Isa looked up at Amo Abe, desperation and sadness written all over her face. She took a deep breath and said, "I'm sorry. I shouldn't have said that about Jehovah."

She drew in a long breath and released it in a steady exhale. "I know how much you want this. How much you believe this. I just don't know how any of his promises can be fulfilled through me." She looked down at her hands. "Maybe the reason Jehovah had Hillary come back from Mexico with us was to give us a child to start our tribe.

Since Jehovah has kept me from having children, have sex with Hillary. Perhaps we can build a family through her."

CHAPTER SIXTEEN

I about passed out at her words. Patrona Isa was suggesting Amo Abe have a baby with *me*? What an absurd suggestion! I was not his wife! I might not be any healthier than Patrona Isa, after all the cartel put me through. No way would I have forced or coerced sex again. Never ever.

All the memories of the men from my past came flooding back at the same time. Diego, all seven of the tenientes, the customers. Ten years of forced relationships. Patrona Isa didn't know the details of my past. She never would have suggested that if she knew.

Blood rushed to my head. My chest tightened. Black spots started invading my vision. I backed up to the kitchen counter and leaned up against it, trying to get myself together.

She couldn't be serious. Surely, she didn't expect Amo Abe to do that. I tried to calm down. I took a deep breath, in through my nose and out through my mouth. *Calm down, Hillary. She has to be joking.*

With all my panicking, I didn't even catch what Amo Abe said in response. I peeked back into the living room. They sat side by side on the couch, elbows on their knees, eyes fixed on the floor. Patrona Isa slumped in place, like the weight of the world had crushed her, like she had given up on life altogether. Amo Abe didn't look much better.

The oven timer buzzed, breaking the silence. I pulled the casserole out and set it on a hot pad on the counter. My hands shook. I didn't want to call them to dinner. I didn't want to see Patrona Isa, not after what she suggested. Cooking meals was part of my job, but I didn't have to stay for dinner.

"Excuse me," I mumbled into the living room. "Dinner is ready."

They both looked up at me, a strange look in their eyes.

Patrona Isa spoke first. "Do you want to stay for dinner, Hillary?"

I shook my head. I wasn't the least bit hungry, not after what I'd overheard. How could she say something like that? We were friends. Or at least, we had a respectful working relationship. My job was housekeeping, not prostitution.

"No, thank you, Señora. Not today," I blurted. "I come clean up after though, since tomorrow my day off."

"That would be great," Patrona Isa said. A hint of sadness tinged her voice. I couldn't tell if she felt that way because of the argument, the failed treatment, my decision not to join them for dinner, or maybe all of it wrapped into one.

I brought the casserole to the dining room and set it on the table runner with a serving spoon. I left without a sound through the back door to head to my RV.

I was glad to be away from that house. I needed a hot shower to try to wash the events of the past hour out of my head.

* * *

When I finished my shower and walked back to the Serugs' house, I found Patrona Isa waiting for me in the kitchen. I gave her a small sideways smile, but I didn't feel glad to see her. The whole thing felt off, like she had planned to corner me.

"Hello, Hillary," she said in a sweet voice, smiling, though the smile didn't reach her eyes. Something was up.

"Hi, Señora," I replied.

"I need to talk about your work visa. It's expiring soon, and I wanted to make sure you still wanted to work for us before I renewed it," she said, matter-of-factly.

"Um, yes," I choked out. "I work for you for ten years. I stay, if is okay."

"We'd love for you to keep working for us too," she started. "But we did originally hire you to be a nanny, and well... Unfortunately, with this last fertility treatment not working, we aren't going to need you for that service any longer."

"But Señora," I protested. Panic was in my voice, and I couldn't help it. "I clean the house. I cook for you. Ten years. I buy the food. I help with everything you need. I can do more. Please!"

I couldn't lose my job. I didn't have anywhere else to go.

"Well, there is one thing you could do that would secure your job..." Her voice trailed off.

"What is it? Anything!" I said.

"You know how we've been trying to get pregnant unsuccessfully," she said and paused, trying to find the right words. "If you were to help us with that, your job would be secure."

So, this was how she planned to play it? Give her a baby or get kicked out of the country? Dios mío!

"What...what do you mean, exactly?" I stammered.

"You know how Hernández had multiple wives?" she asked.

"Yes."

"I would give you to Abe, sort of as a second wife."

"Señora, I don't think that is a good idea."

"You said you'd do anything."

"Please...not that."

"Okay, then." She started walking away and responded over her shoulder, "Your visa expires end of next month. You can work for us until—"

I grabbed her arm. "No, please!"

She stopped and looked at me, down to my hand around her arm, and back at me. I jerked my hand away.

"I'm sorry, Señora," I said, looking toward the ground.

"So, you will, or you won't?" Patrona Isa asked.

I sighed. My heart dropped. I felt the weight of the world on my shoulders. I had nowhere to go. I was nobody. What choice did I have?

"Yes, Señora. I do what you want," I said, tears prickling my eyes and threatening to fall.

"Then it's settled. I'll sleep in the guest room tonight, and you can sleep in our room with him."

I swallowed hard. "Yes, Señora."

She turned on her heels and left the kitchen.

She had no idea what she was asking me to do. The fact that this arrangement existed to make a baby instead of to produce dark web porn did little to help. I still felt used. Like a pawn in their twisted game of Let's Make a Tribe. They were dragging me back into the same abuse as at Jefe Hernández's house. I escaped modern slavery when I left Mexico with the Serugs. I was supposed to be safe now. No one should ever force me into another sexual encounter again.

Yet here I stood, in their kitchen, awaiting an arrangement that felt similar. Wrong. Familiar.

My stomach twisted into knots. My heart pounded so hard it felt like it would tear through my chest. Sweat broke out across my forehead. All the feelings I had worked so hard to bury came flooding back. I couldn't stop them now. I couldn't run. I had no choice but to revisit them.

My fear turned to anger. She was blackmailing me. Holding me hostage with the work visa. This had to be illegal in the States. What if I turned her in? She wasn't Jefe Hernández with the police in her back pocket. I bet she could get in some serious trouble.

But would it help me? If I reported her, I still wouldn't get my work visa renewed. Would they deport me because of my fake Mexican documents? Or worse, could I get arrested for fraud because of them?

From every angle I looked at this situation, I lost.

I took a deep breath and started scrubbing the dishes. I couldn't believe she dropped this on me without any warning. Tonight. She wanted this to happen tonight. I didn't even know if I was on the fertile part of my cycle. What would be the point if I wasn't? If I had to go through with this, maybe I could at least get her to talk about it more and plan it out, so the timing made sense. After eight years of trying, she knew how to track those things.

I peeked into the living room, but it was empty. Amo Abe must have already agreed to the arrangement, or else Patrona Isa wouldn't have brought it up to me. Maybe she was talking to Amo Abe about it, letting him know I'd said yes.

"Señora?" I called down the hall once I finished the dishes.

"In here," I heard her say from the guest room. I went down the hallway and tapped on the door. "Come in."

"Señora," I started. "If we do this...maybe we need to plan? Make sure I'm in the right time...of my cycle?"

"Good point, Hillary," she said. "When was the end of your last moon...er...period?"

"I finish last Saturday," I said.

"Oh, perfect. So, you should be the most fertile starting next week on Thursday," she said.

I let out a silent sigh of relief. Not tonight.

She rummaged through the closet and pulled out a calendar. "Let's see..." She flipped to the right month. "You can stay in our room for a week and half, just to be sure. From Thursday to the next week on Sunday."

My spirit fell. An entire week and a half of hell all over again. It wasn't one time. Of course, it took many tries to get pregnant. I would have been lucky if I got pregnant from one time.

"Yes, Señora," I mumbled. "The dishes are finished. Can I go now?"

"Yes, Hillary. Have a good day off tomorrow, and we'll see you on Thursday."

I turned around and headed for the back door, relieved tonight wasn't the night, but unhappy and unsure about a full week and a half sleeping in Amo Abe's bed.

When I reached the RV, I flopped down on my bed and let it all out. Without even brushing my teeth, I cried myself to sleep.

* * *

The following day, my day off, I decided to look for another job. Surely some family needed an au pair. If I found another job before next week, I would be off the hook.

The problem with living in South Texas, though, was that the towns and neighborhoods were spread out. I didn't have a car of my own to use when I was off work or even a phone to get an Uber or call a cab. And the nearest town took a ten-minute drive.

I decided to take one of the horses. They weren't mine either, but it would be missed less than the Range Rover would be. I put on my riding boots and cowgirl hat to shade me from the sun and headed out the RV door.

I walked to the front of the RV park and down the street to the horse ranch entrance. Daniel greeted me, and I felt relieved not to see Diego anywhere in sight.

"Can I take one of the horses for a little while?" I asked Daniel.

"We have a tour starting at three, but you can have him if you return him by noon," Daniel replied.

My watch read nine, leaving me three solid hours. "Thanks. Is he ready to go?"

"Give me a few minutes, and I'll bring him out," he said.

I waited at the front of the stable area. He brought the horse, Pegasus, out of the stable, and I swung myself into the saddle.

"Thanks, Daniel. I'll see you at noon."

I kicked it up to a nice canter, and Pegasus and I made our way to town to the library. I figured they would have computers so I could look up some jobs. We passed by trees and open land, a few oil rigs, and a cattle ranch before I made it to town. I secured Pegasus to a post outside of the library and gave him a pat on the neck before heading inside.

The library did have computers I could use to search for childcare or housekeeping jobs. My best bet would be childcare since often times nannies could live with the family. I hadn't heard of a live-in housekeeper other than myself.

Three postings for nannies came up in the search, all starting in the summer, still months away. Ugh. I tried housekeepers, but as I suspected, every listing offered only day jobs. Leaving the Serugs meant finding a new place to live, and the money I'd saved wouldn't go very far.

No luck. I guess I would be doing the Serugs' bidding after all.

Deflated, I headed back home.

CHAPTER SEVENTEEN

The week slipped away before I was ready. I refused Patrona Isa's invitation to eat dinner with the Serugs all week, choosing to come back after dinner to clean the dishes instead. I no longer felt comfortable being around after her manipulation tactics. On Thursday after dinner, I washed the dishes and put them away when Patrona Isa walked into the kitchen.

"You haven't forgotten our deal, have you?" she asked with a smirk on her face.

"No, Señora. I come tonight." I forced the words out. She wasn't going to let this go.

"Good," she said. "Then I'll send in the paperwork to renew your work visa after you've finished the week and a half."

"I still get Sundays and Wednesday off, like always, Señora?" I asked.

"Yes, of course, Hillary. You can come over only for the evening and leave right after Abe's finished on those days. I'll pay you overtime."

Great. I got paid overtime to have sex with Amo Abe. Now I felt like a prostitute again. Sex for money. Oh, and for a work visa. At least I got to keep the money this time. But it was still wrong, and I could do nothing about it.

I nodded at her. "Do I have to sleep there all night on my work days, or can I go home after he...finished with me?"

"I suppose you could go home, if that's what you want."

"Señora, with respect...he is your husband," I said. "I shouldn't do this. And I don't want to stay. This is not...something I enjoy."

"Hmph. Fine. Yes. You can leave when he's done."

I put the last dish away and wiped down the counters. "He ready now?"

"I'll find out," Patrona Isa said and left the room.

I shifted my weight in the kitchen and wrung my hands, tension twisting in my chest as I waited for her to return. She came back around the corner five minutes later and waved me to follow her. I complied, because I didn't have a choice. She led me to the master bedroom and walked through the door. Amo Abe sat in the armchair in the far corner of the room.

"Here, Abe. Take Hillary as if she were your wife," Patrona Isa said and moved aside to reveal me in the doorway. Abe nodded and rose from the chair. "You two enjoy."

Patrona Isa smiled at me before she left the room, closing the door behind her.

"Hillary," Amo Abe said, nodding.

"Amo Abe," I replied, copying his nod.

I didn't know what else to do. Patrona Isa put me in an awkward position. I didn't dislike Amo Abe, but I never saw him as someone I liked either. He was Patrona Isa's husband, nothing more, nothing less. I shifted my weight and looked down at my hands clenched in front of me, knuckles white.

Amo Abe waved toward the bed. I sat on the edge of the bed facing him. Instead of approaching me, he also sat, but back in the armchair.

"Hillary, I know this is awkward and uncomfortable," he started, reading my mind. "Princess means well. We have tried so hard to have children of our own. You know this as well as I do. You've been here through all the fertility treatments. You've seen the emotional toll it's taken on her. She feels she's out of options.

"Jehovah has promised us descendants, but they haven't come," Amo Abe continued. "No matter how hard we've tried, we have failed. Now Princess has given you to me to try this last possibility. I don't know that I agree with it, but we've exhausted all other options, so I am listening to her voice. This is far from ideal. and there's no guarantee that it will work, but *if* this works, your child will be my child. Your child will be the beginning of our new tribe."

He paused. I blinked, keeping my face blank. It didn't matter what he said or how kind he tried to be in explaining the situation. The premise didn't change. They had forced me into a situation I never would have chosen. Knowing he didn't agree with it gave me some comfort, but it didn't change what he planned to do.

He stood from the chair and approached me. I rose to my feet, and he pulled me into an embrace, pressing his lips against mine. My whole body tensed, and the kiss spiraled me down into a memory I never wanted to revisit.

I shook the memory of the teniente away and jerked backwards out of Amo Abe's arms.

I'd never experienced a real relationship. The trauma ran deep. Amo Abe became the first man to kiss me since leaving Mexico.

He seemed to sense my hesitation and pulled away, holding the sides of my arms and looking me in the eyes. "You don't want to do this." He stated it as a fact rather than a question.

I pursed my lips into a tight straight line and inched my head from side to side.

"Princess is forcing you to." Again, a statement rather than a question.

I offered a hesitant nod.

He dropped his arms to his side and sighed. "This isn't going to work."

"But...the work visa," I protested. Panic started to well up inside me. I couldn't stay in the United States without it. What if Patrona Isa refused to renew it because Amo Abe sensed my fear?

"Is that what she's offering you?" Amo Abe asked. Patrona Isa must not have told him the full deal.

I swallowed hard and nodded.

"Do you like playing card games, Hillary?"

What a bizarre question in this moment. I shrugged. "I don't play much. No one to play with."

Amo Abe went to the desk at the side of the room and pulled out a deck of cards. "Here's what we're going to do tonight. We're going to play cards. Nothing more. We'll stay in here long enough to make Princess think we procreated, and then you can go. Come back tomorrow, same time, same place, and we'll do the same. I won't tell if you won't tell," he said with a wink.

I raised my eyebrows in surprise. "Really?"

"Really." He climbed up onto the bed and leaned the pillows up against the headboard. Turning himself toward the center of the bed, he shuffled the cards.

I stood in shock next to the bed, watching. He dealt eight cards to each of us, putting the rest of the pile in the center.

That night, we played cards and talked. Once we started playing the game, I became more comfortable with him and climbed onto the other side of the bed, cards between us. He taught me how to play Crazy Eights.

After I got the hang of the game, he started telling me stories about growing up on the reservation. I told him stories about my childhood, before being taken from my home and brought to Mexico. It was the first time I had talked to someone else about my childhood, and it felt good.

"What does your brother do now?" Amo Abe asked, after several stories about daytime at home.

I paused, unsure of what to say. It seemed so long ago. If he was even still alive, Jose would be twenty-two by now. "I don't know," I mumbled. "I didn't stay in contact."

Amo Abe seemed to sense my hesitation again and changed the subject, asking about the school I went to growing up. We continued casual, comfortable conversation, and before long, two hours passed.

"I think that's enough for tonight, Hillary," Amo Abe said after I won the third game in a row. "You're just too good!"

I smiled. "Thank you, Amo Abe."

He cut me off. "Please, it's just Abe."

I nodded. "Thank you, Abe. This night...it was more nice than I thought. Thank you for understanding me."

"You're welcome, Hillary. Come back tomorrow. I need a rematch," he said with a wink.

I smiled back at him.

This same pattern, playing cards and chatting, went on the following evening. I learned so much about Abe and Princess. I dodged talking about my younger years at Jefe Hernández's house but talked about

as much as I could remember of my childhood. I became more comfortable around Abe through our card game meetings, feeling like I
knew him in a way I never had before. He became a friend to me, like
no one else. He took an interest in me, though I deflected many of his
questions.

During the third evening, the night before my day off, we started as
usual, Abe dealing the cards between us on the bed. We chatted and
laughed as we played the first game of Crazy Eights. I felt much closer
to Abe than before.

When I won the game, he congratulated me by pulling me into a
hug. I stiffened at first, but he didn't try to go any further, and when I
realized that, I relaxed into his arms. We lay on the bed in each other's
arms. The cards lay untouched, ignored in the moment.

"What do you want out of life, Hillary?" he asked.

"Hmm." I thought about the question. "I want to feel safe. In my
job. In my home."

"That's not asking a lot. Everyone should feel safe. Do you feel safe
here?"

"Sometimes. More than other places I lived...until last week."

"When Princess threatened you about the work visa?"

"Yes, that part."

"Do you feel safe with me now?"

I paused. He had treated me like a gentleman all week, recogniz-
ing my negative reactions and changing the subject when I showed
discomfort. Even when he pulled me into his arms, the moment felt
almost comforting instead of threatening.

"Yes, I feel okay with you now."

"I'm glad," he whispered, soothing my hair. He kissed my forehead, and my shoulders tensed but relaxed back into his arms. I did feel safe with him.

He ran his fingers through my hair, pressing soft kisses down the side of my face. His breath brushed my cheek with each exhale. A strange warmth stirred inside me at his touch. No man had treated me with such care before. He traced his fingers along my arm, letting them glide to my wrist. Goosebumps rose across my skin, and a shiver ran down my spine.

The room seemed quiet now. The accelerating beat of my heart and the soft sound of his breathing near my ear replaced our chatting and laughter.

Abe tilted my chin up and brought my lips to his. My body reacted with a heat wave, shooting from where his lips caressed mine, down through my body. What was this confusing feeling? I spent my life building up walls against men who used and abused me. But Abe's gentle touch didn't seem like it needed to be shielded against. In fact, my body seemed to want more.

I gave into my body's desires and kissed him back. When I welcomed his kiss, he deepened it, igniting a fire inside me. I clung to him, and he hugged me tighter, our bodies pressing against each other. I channeled all my frustrations with Patrona Isa into this passionate moment with Abe, causing me to overflow with desire.

I felt his body heat radiating out from him, warming me. I thought about the work visa, the overtime pay, anything to keep me from flashing back to my past at Jefe Hernández's house.

As he kissed me, his hand explored my body, pausing to gage my reaction. I tensed, feeling violated, and memories of the teniente who rubbed his hand over me came rushing back.

My heart raced, and my mouth went dry. Tears welled in my eyes, and I couldn't stop them. Wrapping my arms around myself, I tried to shrink, to disappear. I tried to ground myself, but it was too late. Through the fog of panic, one desperate thought throbbed like a heartbeat: *Get out. Get out. Get out.*

Abe stopped mid-motion, pulling away from me.

"I'm sorry," I whispered. "I can't..."

I took a deep breath, inhaling his mint and woody scent, and backed away from him and off the bed. I stood looking at him, trying to see Abe and not the evil man from my memories.

He didn't look hurt. Instead, understanding filled his face. What he understood, I wasn't sure, because I hadn't revealed any of my time in Jefe Hernández's house with him.

He said, "It's okay, Hillary. I went too far. You can go for the night. I'll see you tomorrow. Thank you for your friendship."

I gave him a slight nod and turned and ran from the room, tears flowing down my cheeks.

CHAPTER EIGHTEEN

When I reached the RV, I flung myself on the bed and cried.

He said, "Thank you for your friendship" as I walked out. Friendships belonged to a distant past I struggled to recall. I left all my friends behind in Nicaragua. Sure, Sugar counted in some ways, but that connection came more from survival, not trust. I didn't even know how to be a friend anymore.

I sat in bed, taking deep breaths, in through my nose and out through my mouth, trying to calm my racing heart. I shook my head back and forth, shaking the awful memories from it. I reminded myself I was safe now. In my RV. No men lurked nearby to take advantage of me. No one owned me here.

But my heart still raced. My breath came in gulps. Sweat clung to my palms.

I couldn't get away from the memories, the nightmares. Even with Abe being so kind and gentle with me, he turned into a monster in my mind the second he started touching my body.

I was so broken.

That night, instead of the nightmares, my dreams were pleasant. I dreamt about a family. Abe, me, and a young boy who resembled Abe but had my eyes. The boy and I sat at the dinner table when Abe walked in the door. He walked up to me, a big smile on his face. I stood, and he hugged me. I lifted my lips to meet his, and we kissed, not a kiss of passion, but a kiss overflowing with love. A kiss like I never experienced in all my life. He went to the boy and kissed him on the head, resting his hands on the boy's shoulders.

"How was school, son?" Abe asked.

The boy smiled up at his daddy. "It was good."

"Did you learn anything new?"

"We learned about the solar system!" He started bouncing in his seat and singing, "Mercury, Venus, Earth, and Mars. Jupiter, Saturn. Uranus, Neptune."

"Very cute, buddy," I said smiling.

Abe took his seat at the head of the table and started dishing out the food onto the boy's plate. He passed the serving spoon to me before getting his own food.

"How was work, Daddy?" the boy asked.

"It was great, son. I got a new investor today. The company is growing. Someday maybe you can take over for me."

"Yes! I wanna be just like you when I grow up, Daddy!" The boy squealed and dug into his food.

I woke up, refreshed and feeling much calmer than when I fell asleep, but now my head spun. Thoughts ping-ponged around in my mind. Butterflies fluttered in my stomach. A feeling of longing filled me, a longing for the dream to be real.

I touched my lips, remembering the feeling of love radiating through me when Abe kissed me in the dream. I had never felt true love before.

Was that what love felt like? I couldn't feel that way about Abe. Regardless of the fact that Patrona Isa had wanted me to procreate, she didn't want me to fall in love with him.

I never felt love for anyone other than my parents and baby brother. Never for a man. But Abe seemed different. He was caring, patient, and kind. He wanted to get to know me at a deeper level. He shared stories and his life with me. And now the vision of him being such a sweet daddy to my baby boy ignited a different feeling inside me. This vision of a family I could never have—Abe was not mine to have—made me think about what the future could hold for me. Could I find love somewhere out there?

I spent the following day relaxing by the pool. The rush of the man-made waterfalls pouring into the side of the pool caused ripples along the surface of the water which sparkled in the sunlight. The smell of chlorine wafted toward me with the cool breeze and mixed with the coconut smell of my sunscreen. As I sat in the lounge chair under the umbrella, I tried to read my book, but my mind kept wandering back to thoughts of Abe. My stomach fluttered in anticipation when thinking about spending this evening with him again. What was wrong with me?

A few days ago, the day seemed to fly by, though I wanted time to stand still so I wouldn't have to be with Abe. Now, the day dragged on, every second seeming slower than the last.

At the same time, though, I felt worried...nervous. What if the memories came back again? What if his touch ignited darkness and fear instead of the love I felt through his kiss in my dream? What if I ran away from him again? If I couldn't keep myself together, would Patrona Isa be mad that we never procreated and kick me out onto the street?

I gave up on the book and gathered my things to go back to the RV for lunch. As I made nacatamales, I heard a knock at the door.

I froze. No one ever visited me, and I wasn't expecting anyone. I inched toward the door and peeked out the window. Abe stood near the steps.

I pulled the door open, blinking at him, my brows knitting together as my hand tightened on the knob.

"Hello, Hillary," Abe said. He saw my face and rushed on, "I thought I'd come over and see if you wanted to play cards at your place." He held up a deck of cards. "You mentioned you didn't have anyone to play with, and I had some free time."

"Uh...sure." My voice came out low and unsure as confusion churned inside me. Was he being friendly, or was he trying to trick me into doing more? The memory of the dream came back to me, and I looked at him in a whole different light, making the butterflies flutter in my stomach.

He smiled. "May I come in?"

"Uh...sorry," I said, stepping aside to let him through the doorway.

He looked around the RV. "I like what you've done to the place. Princess, Louis, and I spent nearly a year in this RV, and it never looked, or smelled, as nice as it does now."

I blushed at his compliment. I tried to make it my own, putting little touches like fresh flowers and girly accents around the small space.

"Do you want nacatamale?" I offered. "I'm making lunch. I can make some for you too."

"That's very kind of you, Hillary. Thank you for the offer." He sat at the dinette table and started shuffling the cards.

I finished assembling the nacatamales as the sound of shuffling cards filled the room. He must have shuffled them a hundred times while I prepared the food.

I sat across from him at the dinette with my plate of food and set one in front of him. He dealt out thirteen cards around the plates to both of us.

"What we play?" I asked, curious about the thirteen cards.

"I'm teaching you how to play Hearts. You're too good at Crazy Eights for me to play with anymore." He laughed and explained the rules to the new game.

We played and talked while we ate. I fumbled through this new game, not as skilled as the other game, and took three brutal losses. He shuffled the cards for round four and paused.

"You seem fairly comfortable right now," he observed. "But I sense some reservations. Like a wall, built up around you, keeping people out."

I paused, wondering how much I could reveal to him.

"There's a part of your life I'm missing," Abe continued. "I want to know all about you, Hillary. You told me stories of your childhood, but what about the rest of your life?" He studied me with interest. "You've been with us for ten years now. What about before that? How did you end up working for the cartel?"

I froze. My face fell, and I started to retreat into myself. The wall grew twice as high and twice as thick now. I couldn't speak. My mouth dried, and a lump formed in my throat. I tried to swallow but couldn't even manage that. I know he had no intention of setting off my panic, but thoughts of my ten years with the cartel flooded back. The cameras. The men. The skimpy outfits. The brutal beatings and rapes for the girls who didn't obey. The threats of harm to my family.

The silence seemed deafening, but Abe sat as if he welcomed it, staring at me. Waiting.

I looked up at him, eyes wide, and shook my head. I looked down at my hands, letting the silence win the day.

He looked at me, searching my eyes, my face. He broke the silence. "It was that bad, huh?"

I pursed my lips together and looked back down at my hands. I couldn't have this conversation.

He started shuffling the cards again. "Whatever it was, you didn't deserve it. You are a wonderful part of Jehovah's good creation."

I thought about that as he dealt the cards. Did Jefe Hernández also count as part of "Jehovah's good creation"? I couldn't see any good in him. In my mind, he and his men represented nothing but evil. They treated people like objects. They used people for money. They showed no regard for human life whatsoever. They traumatized me and countless others to the point where I couldn't function in a normal relationship.

I wanted to trust Abe. I wanted to like him. I wanted to think he wasn't like the men in the cartel. Abe hadn't acted like he wanted to only use me. He came over to my place on his day off to spend time with me. But was it all a means to an end? Was he doing it only so I would have his child?

The dream came flooding back to my mind. The perfect family where Patrona Isa didn't exist, and I lived with Abe and our little boy. The kiss felt so real and so full of love. The sweet way Abe smiled at me and talked to our son. My heart yearned for a life like that. A life where I forgot about my past, and the future looked bright. Could that be my life if I pushed my memories down to the depths of my mind and gave into him?

I was distracted, and Abe won yet another game.

"Next time we go back to Crazy Eights. This Hearts game...I don't understand it," I said. I didn't seem to get either the card game of Hearts or the reality of giving my heart to a man.

He stood and headed toward the door. "I'm glad I came over. Thank you for humoring me with the new game. Even if you avoided my topic of discussion."

Tears formed in my eyes. "I'm sorry, Abe. I just...I can't."

That seemed to be my theme when it came to Abe. He pulled me into a hug and rested his cheek on the top of my head. His mint and cedar scent washed over me. I relaxed onto his chest and let him hold me, trying to keep the tears from falling. It felt good to be in his arms, like no other man I'd ever been with. I didn't want it to end.

He pulled away and looked into my eyes. Tilting my chin up, he kissed me, a kiss so familiar, straight out of the dream. I allowed myself to be overwhelmed by the sensation of his love.

It ended too soon, and he left me desiring more. He nodded and turned to walk out the RV door toward his house.

"I'll see you later, Hillary," he said over his shoulder, smiling the sweet smile he used for our son in the dream. He walked through the gate, across the lawn, and disappeared into his back door.

Could I let go of the past and allow myself to feel life again?

* * *

I felt a strange anticipation as I walked to the Serugs' house that evening after dinner. Between the dream and the afternoon kiss, my world had been turned upside down. Finding kindness in a man gave me hope and left me wanting more. More of him.

I walked in the back door and through the kitchen to the living room. I didn't see Patrona Isa or Abe. I continued back into the house and knocked on the bedroom door.

"Come in," Abe said from inside.

I opened it and peeked my head in. He stood from the armchair, setting his book down on the nightstand, and walked in my direction. I entered the room and eased the door shut behind me.

When I turned around, he stood right in front of me.

"Hello, Hillary," he murmured, tucking a stray lock of hair behind my ear.

"Hello," I said back, smiling up at him. I ran the reel of the dream in my mind to keep the bad memories at bay. His loving kiss, the sweet way he talked to my son...our son.

Abe cradled my face, tilting my head back and bringing his lips down to mine. I closed my eyes and wrapped my arms around him, kissing him back. His mint scent calmed me, while his cedar scent ignited desire inside of me.

He pulled away, looking into my eyes, and raised his eyebrows. "Are you okay?"

I nodded, offering a small smile. The kiss lingered on my lips, and I wanted more.

He acquiesced and pulled me into another kiss, this one more passionate than the last. I kissed back, encouraging him to keep going. He picked me up, cradling me, and carried me to the bed, lowering me with care. He climbed up next to me, pulling me close to him. I could feel his warmth, his breath on my face as he put his hand on the back of my head, pulling us close into another kiss.

My body ignited at his touch as he ran his hand down the side of my torso and back up. He hesitated. I took his hand in mine and placed it on my chest, giving him permission to explore me. I suppressed the memories, deep inside me, and thought about the dream and the present moment as he cupped my breast and explored my mouth with his tongue.

I focused all my attention on Abe, on his gentleness, his love, his care and concern for me. The demons didn't come as I expected them to. Abe was sweet, gentle, caring the whole time as we surrendered to Patrona Isa's demand.

CHAPTER NINETEEN

Over the next few days, I finished my fertility window with Abe in a whirlwind of desire, anticipation, and ecstasy. My mind played tricks on me. I dreamt more of raising a family with Abe. Those dreams helped me to focus on the love I felt for him instead of memories of my past.

On Monday after the final day of my time with Abe, Patrona Isa walked into the kitchen while I prepared dinner.

"I turned in your paperwork today. Hopefully your time with Abe worked. If not, I'll have you do the same next month." She said it matter-of-factly, like she had finalized a business transaction. For her, that was all this arrangement ever meant.

She wouldn't have to coerce me next time. I held onto a silent wish that it hadn't worked, so I could have another week with Abe.

As dinner neared completion, Abe walked in the door from work. Both Patrona Isa and I walked to the doorway between the kitchen and the living room to welcome him. He gave Patrona Isa a kiss, the same kiss he gave me in my dream. In this moment, though, instead of a kiss, he gave me a side hug. Had our friendship ended now that my time with him had finished? My heart sank, and I tried to hide my disappointment and jealousy.

"Did you want to have dinner with us tonight, Hillary?" Abe asked.

My stomach fluttered when he said my name, and I smiled, gazing into his eyes.

"Yes, please," I choked out, clasping my hands in front of me.

Patrona Isa narrowed her eyes at me, and I dropped my hands to my side, straightened up, and stopped smiling.

Dinner felt awkward. Patrona Isa and I both seemed to vie for Abe's attention. I feared losing his friendship, love, and affection and went a little overboard trying to hold his attention. Patrona Isa's face didn't hide her annoyance. I didn't know what she expected when she asked me to have a baby with her husband. Did she expect me to separate my emotions from the "transaction"?

* * *

Four weeks later, I woke up from a dreamless sleep in my bed in the RV. My stomach churned, and I could taste the metallic taste of stomach acid rising in my throat. I tried to swallow it back down, jumped out of bed, and rushed to the bathroom, throwing open the toilet lid. My stomach jolted, and I dry-heaved into the toilet, but nothing came out. I sat on the floor in front of the toilet still feeling sick to my stomach, as if I could throw up at any moment. Sweat beaded on my forehead.

My period came on time a couple weeks ago, lighter and shorter than normal, but it showed up. Patrona Isa had tracked my cycle on her calendar. She asked me about it the day it should've started and kept pushing until I told her it did. Her disappointment showed all over her face.

Now, as I sat nauseated on the floor of my small bathroom, I started to wonder if the lighter, shorter period even counted.

I eased my way up, trying to calm the churning in my gut, and walked to the kitchen for some saltine crackers. They helped when I fought off the stomach virus, so I hoped they would work now. I pulled them out and sat at the dinette, taking slow, small bites, the salty scent of the crackers filling my nose. As the crackers hit my stomach, I expected the nausea to return, but instead it subsided, leaving me feeling strong enough to get ready for the day.

Before showering, I brewed my normal cup of coffee, but the second the coffee smell reached my nose, I felt the nausea return. I dumped the boiling liquid down the drain, washing warm water behind it to clear the scent. I opened the window to let fresh air into the RV and clear the coffee smell from the air. What was wrong with me?

Today my chores consisted of weeding the flower beds in the Serugs' yard. I dressed in my gardening clothes and cowgirl hat and headed over to get started. As I weeded, I thought back on the past month.

After the awkward dinner, I steered clear of joining the Serugs for future dinners. It was too uncomfortable. Abe still came over for an hour on Sunday afternoons to play cards with me, but aside from that, I hadn't seen him much at all. When I cleaned and cooked, he was at work. I started to believe he only befriended me during that week because of the "transaction." It worked, of course, and the feeling of being used crept over me any time I saw him in passing.

Tears prickled at my eyes at how easy Abe manipulated me. I wiped at them with the back of my gloved hand, smearing dirt on my cheek. How could such a nice family turn into such a conniving couple? Why would they take advantage of me like that? My nose burned red, and my eyes filled with tears. They blurred the line between the weeds and the flowers.

A light breeze blew, and I smelled the scent of fresh mulch coming from somewhere. I took a deep breath and looked down the street, but I didn't see anyone laying it. It occurred to me I needed new mulch as the irrigation hoses started to show. I stood and wiped my eyes with the backs of my arms to clear the tears from my vision.

I grabbed the keys to the Range Rover and headed to the hardware store in town. As I got to the main road, fresh mulch lay around the flower beds at the first house on the street. I couldn't believe I smelled it from that far away.

I bought ten bags of mulch, and the store associate loaded it into the back of the SUV. When I got to the house, I pulled the wheelbarrow out of the garage and wheeled it to the back of the SUV. I leaned over the pile of bags to reach the one in the back. Ow! I jerked back, holding onto my sore breasts. Why were my breasts so sore?

I ripped the bag open and poured the mulch into the wheelbarrow so I could haul it to the flowerbeds. The smell of the mulch filled my lungs. I ran to the grass and dry-heaved. The smell of mulch never bothered me before. I pulled my shirt over my nose and mouth, tempering the smell, and managed to make it through all ten bags of mulching.

By four o'clock, I was sweaty, smelly, and dirty, but the landscaping looked beautiful. I went back to the RV to wash up before making dinner.

* * *

I managed to avoid Patrona Isa most of the week, seeing her only when I made dinner. On Thursday, she came into the kitchen with a calendar in her hand as I prepared dinner. "According to the calendar, today should start your fertile window. So, starting tonight, you can stay with Abe again for the next week."

I froze. I suspected I might already be pregnant. The signs didn't hide: the morning sickness, the tender breasts, the aversion to smells that never bothered me before. Should I tell her what I suspected, or keep quiet and steal one more week with Abe before everything changed? She manipulated me. Maybe it was my turn to manipulate her. Being in Abe's arms felt good, when I managed to suppress my memories and enjoy the moments.

Nothing ever compared to how I felt with Abe. Safe. Cared for. Loved. He couldn't love me, not with Patrona Isa in his life, but I now carried his child. Could I make him love me?

She sensed my hesitation. "Look, you know I already renewed your work visa, but I can still terminate you at any time."

My eyes widened, and my eyebrows nearly hit the ceiling. Wow! She still used my job to manipulate me. She saw how little resistance I put up last month and used that power over me to her advantage. Would it ever stop?

A switch inside me flipped. If she forced me to be with her husband, I would take full advantage of it while I still could.

"Uh, sure," I said. "I'll do it."

She seemed satisfied, not sensing the defiance in my voice.

I spent every night that week and a half with Abe, staying the entire night this time instead of going home after he finished. On the last night of my time with him, I lay next to Abe with my head on his shoulder, tracing my fingers over his bare chest.

"I like this time with you," I whispered into his ear.

He turned his head toward me and looked down into my eyes as I peered back up at him. "You're a special woman, Hillary."

"I think I will miss being here tomorrow night."

"I've gotten used to you being here. It'll be a change for me too."

I couldn't tell if he meant what he said. I sighed, breathing in his earthy scent, not wanting to forget it.

***

Over the next month, it seemed every scent nauseated me. The smell of the lemon Lysol made me sick. Getting out of bed with an empty stomach made me sick. The smell of barbecue in the air made me sick. Waiting too long to eat lunch made me sick. The smell of coffee in the grocery store made me sick. The smell of the horses made me sick. I didn't even know I could smell the horses from my RV, but now I could. I couldn't hold any food down, and I worried that the baby wasn't getting the nutrients he or she needed.

Patrona Isa noticed my multiple trips to the bathroom while I cleaned the guest room one day. "Are you not feeling well, Hillary?" she asked after I walked out of the bathroom.

"I'm fine," I said, wiping my mouth with the back of my hand.

"Wait. Do you have morning sickness?" she asked, jumping up and down and clapping her hands like a little schoolgirl.

"Qué suerte, huh? I feel terrible, and you're smiling like it's a party," I said.

"Are you really pregnant?" she asked, her hands covering her giant smile, her eyes wide with excitement.

"It could be true," I said. The smell of Lysol wafted from the bathroom, and another wave of nausea hit me. I dashed back to the bathroom to empty the remaining contents of my stomach into the toilet.

"Hillary, we have to take a test to find out for sure. Wait here." She dashed out the door and returned with a long, thin box. Pressing it into my hands, she said, "Take it. Read and follow the instructions on the box and take the test. Go, go." She pushed me toward the guest bathroom.

I sighed. "Okay, Señora," I said and closed the door on her, leaving me alone in the bathroom.

This was it. I would never be able to deny the pregnancy after this test. If I was indeed pregnant. I wouldn't be able to weasel my way into Abe's bed again once she knew for sure I carried his baby. How would he react? Would he love me for helping him start his tribe? Would he love me because of the baby? It was what he wanted after all. It was what they both wanted.

I turned the box over in my hands, looking at the line drawing of the pregnant woman on the front. I slid my finger under the flap at the end of the box to open it and pulled out the instructions and a long, thin stick. This little stick could tell me if I was pregnant? It seemed impossible.

I read the instructions and smiled. Patrona Isa would have to wait...again. I put the stick back in the box and returned to the bedroom.

"It says morning is best time to do the test," I told her.

"Oh, come on," she said. "That's probably for when you first get pregnant. You have morning sickness so strong, I'm sure the test will work now."

"Look," I said, pulling the instructions out and showing them to her. "It says to take in morning."

She let out a big sigh. "Fine. But you better not forget. Put it right on the toilet before bed so you'll see it first thing in the morning." She let out a grunt. "I really wanted to be there to see the test results." Her eyes lit back up as if a light bulb turned on in her head. "Ooh, can I come over in the morning?"

"I guess," I said. I didn't want her at my home but didn't know how to refuse her either.

Patrona Isa made her plans to be at my RV first thing in the morning to observe my test and left me to finish my work on my own.

Relief washed over me. I didn't want her watching over my shoulder. I wasn't looking forward to her hovering at my home in the morning.

***

The next morning, Patrona Isa knocked at my door, pulling me from a dream. I rolled over and stretched, rubbing my eyes. Time to get this over with.

I swung my legs over the edge of the bed and stood. As soon as I stood, the nausea attacked me. I yelled "Come in," as I rushed to the toilet and flung it open, causing the box with the pregnancy test to fly across the room. Last night's dinner came out into the toilet.

Patrona Isa rushed into the little bathroom behind me and retrieved the test from the shower floor. She held it to her chest and waited for me to stop heaving.

"Ugh," I said holding onto the toilet seat for balance, my arms shaking as I tried to push myself back up. I wiped my mouth with the back of my hand. "How much time it's going to last?"

"Usually just the first trimester," Patrona Isa said.

"Trimester?"

"Yeah, the first three months."

"*Three months*?" I exclaimed. "I have to deal with this during three months?" I looked at her weakly, hating her for putting me through this. There had to be another way.

"Yeah, but we don't even know that you're pregnant yet. It's time to take the test," she said, a little too happy. She thrust it toward me.

I sighed. "Okay. Here it goes."

Patrona Isa backed out of the bathroom while I took the test, replaced the cap, and laid it on the counter. Once I finished relieving myself and washing my hands, I opened the door so she could come in and watch for the results. It didn't take long before the plus sign showed in the window of the test stick.

I was pregnant.

CHAPTER TWENTY

P atrona Isa did a happy dance of some sort right in the cramped RV living room. I couldn't help but smile. While she manipulated me into carrying her baby, it was hard to be mad at her when she radiated such joy.

The thought of a piece of Amo Abe being inside my body for the next seven or eight months kept the smile on my face. Could I make him love me now that I carried his child? But did I even want that? I still didn't know. Men couldn't be trusted.

"I'm going to tell Abe before he leaves for work," Patrona Isa said, grabbing onto my arm and bouncing with excitement.

I nodded. She turned and left the RV.

As I brushed my teeth, a thought hit me. Amo Abe and Patrona Isa trusted their Jehovah god with unwavering faith. Yet he hadn't blessed her with a child. Instead, during my very first week with Amo Abe, I ended up pregnant against all odds. The cartel used and abused me. They broke me. They injected my body with so many chemicals into my body, I doubted pregnancy would ever come. Yet now, I carried Amo Abe's baby.

Maybe their Jehovah god favored me over Patrona Isa.

When I walked into the Serug house to start my daily duties, Patrona Isa waited for me in the kitchen. "I got you an appointment with the ob-gyn in Alice. Surprisingly, they had an opening today. We leave at ten."

I nodded. "I be ready. Now I go to clean the baseboards."

She gave me little more than a glance, looking down at her phone, so I headed to the closet to pull out the cleaning supplies.

I finished the baseboards and the windows in the common areas before we left for the doctor. I climbed into the passenger side of Patrona Isa's Lexus SUV. The new car smell filled my nose as I settled into the soft leather seat. The whirring of the engine broke the silence as the car roared to life.

As we drove over the bumpy gravel road toward the highway, Patrona Isa spoke up. "I hope it's a boy. It only works to start our tribe if it's a boy."

"Will we know already?" I asked, now nervous about what would happen if it was a girl.

"No. They won't know for at least another month," she said, checking for traffic before pulling onto the paved highway.

"What happens if it's a girl?"

"We try again, I guess," she said. "Maybe you can keep the baby if it's a girl. Like I said, girls can't carry on the family line, so we would just try again for a boy."

It seemed Patrona Isa valued girls even less than Jefe Hernández did. At least el jefe could use us for profit. I started to hope the baby was a girl so I could keep a piece of Amo Abe with me forever. At least he cared about everyone, regardless of gender.

"If this is the first month, that means…" She counted the months in her head, mouthing them. "You should have the baby in early January." She sang the last sentence like a song.

More like a December baby. I deceived her into letting me be with Amo Abe after I already suspected that I was pregnant.

Patrona Isa pulled into the parking lot of a one-story concrete block building with square pillars guarding the entrance. We walked inside the clinic. The waiting room was wide, with chairs on either side of a narrow queue line to the reception desk. It smelled like fresh flowers, and I could see a colorful bunch sitting to the left on the reception counter. The tan chairs didn't appear comfortable. Small side tables filled with magazines sat between every two or three chairs.

I followed as Patrona Isa checked me in and took the intake paperwork back to the waiting room seats. The paperwork looked daunting, and I didn't know what half of the questions meant. I never filled out paperwork like this before, and the pen trembled in my hand as I filled out each box.

Date of Last Period. Answering this question could get me into hot water. If I put the true date, not counting my minor spotting last month, Patrona Isa would figure out I lied to her. What would she think? Was she happy enough that I was pregnant to overlook my indiscretion? I trembled at the possible consequences as I wrote down my lie.

After filling out what I could, I handed the clipboard to Patrona Isa.

"I don't have medical insurance, so I don't know what to fill out for those questions," I said.

"It's our baby, so we'll take care of the medical costs," she said. "We'll tell them we're paying out of pocket and cover your expenses."

Patrona Isa turned in the paperwork and spoke with the receptionist as I remained sitting, waiting. The receptionist took her credit card and handed her a receipt before she returned to the chairs.

"Hillary Morales?" a nurse dressed in purple scrubs called sometime later from a door to the right of the reception desk.

I stood, and Patrona Isa stood with me. Together we headed toward the nurse.

"Are you together?"

Patrona Isa blushed. "Well, not exactly. We aren't a couple, but she's carrying my baby."

The nurse's eyebrows raised. She turned to me. "You're okay with her joining us for the exam?"

I nodded. The nurse seemed satisfied and led us back to a room with a scale. As soon as we entered the back area, the bitter smell of cleaner hit me, causing my stomach to turn.

"Is there a bathroom?" I asked, one hand over my mouth and the other clutching my middle.

"Down the hall on the right." The nurse pointed down the hall. "Here, take this and give me a urine sample while you're in there." She handed me a cup with a lid.

I took it and dashed down the hall, making it just in time to empty my stomach of my breakfast. I wiped my mouth with a paper towel and splashed water on my face. This was getting old.

After putting the urine sample in the little silver window, I returned to the nurse and Patrona Isa, hoping the smell wouldn't overtake me again. After taking my vitals and reviewing the paperwork with me, she led us down the hall to an exam room.

"Put on this gown, open to the front. The doctor will be in shortly," the nurse said, handing me a folded-up paper gown.

I felt the heat drain from my face when I saw the monitor on one side of the room. My mind went to the TV in the bedroom of Jefe Hernández' mansion, and my lungs clamped shut. The air grew so thick, I couldn't breathe.

The nurse turned to leave, but I grabbed her arm, dropping the paper gown to the ground.

"Wait," I gasped. "Why do I have to take my clothes off?"

My heart slammed against my ribs so hard it felt like they might break. Every sound seemed loud and sharp at once—the hum of the lights overhead, footsteps echoing in the hallway outside the room, someone talking nearby. But all I could hear was the sounds from then. The memories I fought to forget. The doctors in long white coats. The other naked children lined up with me. The guns pointed at our heads. The shuffling of feet as we walked toward the medical exam. The poking with the needles. The prodding hands.

I've only had two medical exams while at Jefe Hernández' house. My brain screamed danger, even though I wasn't there. I was safe now, but my body didn't believe it. I grasped for the side of the exam table to balance myself. My eyes fixed on a spot on the wall where the memory seemed to be playing as if on a screen before me.

"Hillary?"

Patrona Isa said my name, but she seemed so far away. A fuzzy darkness wanted to imprison me, and I fought against it.

I felt a hand on my shoulder, and I jerked away from it. Stumbling, I almost fell, but arms caught me and stood me upright.

"What's happening to her?"

"I'm not sure. Let's get the doctor."

Their voices seemed far away. Gentle arms guided me to sit in a chair. The memories chided me. Blinking in quick succession, I shook my head back and forth, trying to clear them. The room came back into focus. My breaths came in sharp, shallow bursts, making my head spin. I leaned over and put my head between my legs. Breathe in through your nose and out through your mouth, I told myself.

When I lifted my head, three people stood in front of me, staring. Patrona Isa had a concerned, even scared, look on her face. The doctor watched me with a piercing gaze, and the nurse stood by like she wasn't sure what to do.

"Hillary?" The doctor's voice sounded soft, warm. "Can you hear me?"

I nodded.

"Take your time. You're safe here," the doctor said. She gestured for Patrona Isa to sit in the chair next to me as she pulled up a rolling stool. "I'm Doctor Garcia. I saw that something really hard just came up for you. I want you to know that what you've been through matters, and it makes sense that your body reacted like that."

Tears prickled in my eyes, and I swatted at them, embarrassed about my panic attack.

"If and when you're ready, we can talk about next steps," the doctor said. "But right now, the most important thing is that you feel safe and in control."

I breathed in a deep breath. In control? When was I ever in control? My whole life was out of my control. I exhaled, my eyes tracing the lines between the tiles on the floor.

"Have you ever had a pelvic exam before?" she asked.

I shook my head. I could feel my eyes widen, my eyebrows rising toward the ceiling. "What is that?"

"The pelvic exams help to check that your body is healthy. It's something we do to help care for your uterus, ovaries, and vagina. I will look outside your body first. Then I use a small tool, called a speculum, to look inside." She gestured to her private area. "I will be very gentle. After that, I will use my hands to feel from the inside and outside. It is quick, and we'll go slow. Pelvic exams can feel scary, especially when you've had something painful happen in the past. I want you to feel safe. We can use a smaller tool, take a break, or wait. This is your body, your choice."

When has my body ever been my choice? Not since the night of my kidnapping has my body belonged to me. Even after settling in Texas, safety never felt real. My body didn't belong to me. It served as a pawn in Patrona Isa's game. This baby wouldn't be mine. They forced it upon me as a payment for my job, my livelihood, my survival.

But I couldn't say all that to a doctor with Patrona Isa here. And I couldn't afford the doctor otherwise.

"You're going to put something inside me?" I asked. I tried to control my breathing so I wouldn't go back into the panic attack. I couldn't count how many times I'd been forced to put things inside me down there, either by my own hands or by the hands of others. I focused on the doctor's face so the memories would stay away. I forced myself to stay in the present.

"We'll go very slowly. I'll explain every step before anything happens. You can stop the exam at any moment. Just say 'stop' or raise your hand. You don't even need a reason," the doctor said. She smiled at me with soft eyes. "You're the one in charge of your body. My job is just to help."

I nodded.

"Let's start with your medical history, Hillary. That might be easier than the physical exam for you."

I nodded again. The doctor asked about my medical and surgical history, current medications, and any allergies. I gave quick answers, as there wasn't much to report. She asked about family history of birth defects, twins, genetic conditions. I didn't know many of these answers, so I said, "None that I know of," which seemed enough for her.

"How old were you when your periods started?"

"Thirteen, I think." I remembered the day I started bleeding, when my job changed from porn star to prostitute. I shuddered. You are not there now. Stay strong.

"What's your cycle usually like? Do you have them regularly? Are they painful? How long do they last?"

"They come every month. I get cramps, but not so bad. At the beginning they are heavy, but then they get lighter," I said. Once my job changed to cook and care for el jefe's wife, the cartel stopped giving me the shots. It took three years for my periods to be normal again, but they did eventually come back.

"So pretty normal then. Okay. Is this your first pregnancy?"

I nodded.

The doctor looked down at the paperwork I filled out. "Your last menstrual period was the beginning of last month?"

I glanced at Patrona Isa and nodded.

"Have you had any spotting, bleeding, or cramping since then?"

"Um, last month I had spotting," I said, again glancing at Patrona Isa.

"Before or after your period?"

"Um." I paused again. "I don't know if what I had last month was my period or only spotting. It was light. But I didn't pay attention in that moment."

"I see. Well, the ultrasound should help determine when the baby was conceived."

I could feel Patrona Isa's eyes boring into me. She leaned in, hanging on every word.

"Do you have any history of STDs?"

"What is STD?"

"Like HIV, hepatitis B or C, herpes, gonorrhea, chlamydia?"

"I don't know." I could have gotten any of those diseases while with the cartel; I had been with so many men. But I never even thought about that, hadn't been tested for it, and never felt sick.

"We can test for those in the blood test," the doctor said. "Have you been vaccinated against rubella, hepatitis B, COVID-19, flu?"

I shook my head.

"We can do that also." The doctor made a note in the file. She asked about smoking, drinking, and drugs. She asked about my work environment and heavy lifting. "Have you experienced depression, anxiety, or trauma in the past?"

I looked down at the floor again. The questions had been easy up to this point, but now she had trapped me. Of course, trauma shaped my past, otherwise, the panic attack wouldn't have happened. How could I get through this exam? I'd never shared any of my past with anyone, and I didn't want to do it in front of Patrona Isa.

I glanced up at the doctor, who studied me and waited. I glanced at Patrona Isa and back at the doctor.

The doctor looked back and forth from me to Patrona Isa. We played tag with our eyes. Who was "it"?

"Ma'am, do you mind if I talk to Hillary alone?" the doctor asked Patrona Isa.

"Yes, I mind," Patrona Isa snapped. "I'm paying for this visit."

The doctor paused. "I can't properly service the patient if I don't understand her medical history. I sense she's holding something back because you're here."

Patrona Isa scowled. "Whatever she has to say, she can say it in front of me."

The doctor stood and moved the rolling stool to the side of the room. "Then I'm afraid this exam is over."

Patrona Isa jumped from her chair. "Where do you think you're going? You can't just leave like that! I paid for this exam."

"Ma'am," the doctor said, "if you'd like the exam to continue, you'll allow me to speak with the patient alone."

"My husband is one of the most prominent and well-respected men in Jim Wells County!" Patrona Isa shouted. "We're paying for all services for this patient. We should be a part of the process from the beginning to the end."

The doctor stood her ground. "Yes, ma'am. I'm sure Hillary is grateful for your contribution to her pregnancy. But I cannot continue with the exam if she doesn't feel comfortable answering my questions. It is clear that your presence is causing her discomfort."

"Hillary." Patrona Isa turned her anger toward me. "Tell her you're comfortable."

I bowed my head further down and stared at the floor in silence.

"Tell her!" Patrona Isa demanded.

I didn't respond. A minute passed, maybe two.

"Ugh! Fine!" Patrona Isa said, huffing and snatching her purse from the chair. "We'll talk about this later," she said to me through gritted teeth.

I tensed up as she stormed past me and out the door.

The doctor sighed. "Is she always like this?"

I tightened my lips into a line and looked at the doctor, not saying a word.

The doctor pulled the rolling stool back over to sit in front of me, but she left space between us. She looked at the clipboard of paperwork, allowing the tenseness of the moment with Patrona Isa to pass.

Looking back up at me with compassion, she said, "It's clear you have had some trauma in your life. Whether your friend has been a part of that or not, you don't have to tell me. I'm not a psychiatrist or a psychologist, but I do recommend that you look into getting one or both of them."

I sighed. "I don't have the money to do that."

"There are programs that can help with that."

"I am not U.S. citizen. I am here on work visa."

The doctor nodded. "Do you feel safe at home?"

"Sometimes."

"Do you live with...your friend?"

"Sort of. I live on her property, but in an RV. She lives in the house."

The doctor nodded and looked back at the paperwork. "Have you ever experienced abuse? Physical, emotional, or sexual?"

I let the question float in the air, unsure of how to answer. What was "abuse" anyway? I managed to stay away from all but one physical beating at Jefe Hernández' mansion by obeying. Ruby, Crystal, and Patrona Isa all manipulated me into doing things outside of my comfort zone, things I wouldn't choose to do. Was that emotional abuse or sexual abuse or both? Or maybe life always worked that way. I had nothing else to compare it to. "Normal life," if that was what you called it, ended at age eight when Papá died.

"Have you been physically abused, Hillary?" the doctor prodded.

I paused and looked down at my hands. "Not by the Serugs."

"Have you been emotionally abused?"

"What is emotional abuse?"

"Emotional abuse is when someone uses words, threats, or control to make you feel afraid, ashamed, or like you don't matter," the doctor explained. "Maybe someone is constantly criticizing you, yelling at you, controlling what you do or who you see, or blaming you for things that aren't your fault."

"Like threatening to take away your work visa or fire you if you don't do what they want you to do?" *Ugh! I blurted that out without thinking.*

"Well, I suppose if you're not doing what you're supposed to do for work, then that would be legitimate." She tapped her pen against the clipboard, eyes narrowing behind her glasses. "But if they threaten you for other reasons when you're performing your work adequately, then that could be emotional abuse."

It did sound like what Patrona Isa did to me could be emotional abuse, but I still wasn't sure. I also didn't want her to get in trouble. If she got in trouble, would I still have a job?

"I don't know," I said.

The doctor nodded and made a note on the paper. "What about sexual abuse?"

My eyes dropped to the floor, and I clamped my mouth shut. My hands shook, and my skin prickled with cold sweat. I wrung my sweaty hands in my lap and waited in silence.

After a few minutes passed, the doctor said, "That's okay. You don't have to answer that right now. I ask because it can affect how we care for you, but I want you to feel safe and in control."

She let the silence stretch, her eyes on me, hands folded on top of the paperwork. Only the ticking clock filled the room. "Your comfort matters to me. We can go at your pace, and you never have to talk about anything you're not ready to share. If there's ever something you want to talk about, I'm here, and I'll listen without judgment."

I closed my eyes and took a deep breath to calm my nerves.

"Are you ready to try the pelvic exam, or do you need more time?" she asked. I didn't say anything. "Do you want to do the blood test first to give you some time to calm down?"

I nodded. She showed so much patience with me. I appreciated her compassion more than I could express.

"Okay. Follow me down the hall, and we'll get your blood test done. Then you can come back for the pelvic exam and ultrasound."

I stood and followed her out the exam room door. I didn't see Patrona Isa anywhere. I breathed a sigh of relief as I followed the doctor down the hall and around the corner to a small alcove with some chairs. She handed a paper to the tech.

"I'll see you in a little bit, Hillary. You're in good hands with Linda here," the doctor said, smiling at me.

"Hello, Hillary," Linda said. She consulted the paper and smiled. "Congratulations on your pregnancy."

"Thank you." I half-smiled back at her. I didn't know how I felt about the forced pregnancy, and the conversation with the doctor about my past rolled around in my head.

Linda made me feel comfortable in the chair and got to work taking several vials of blood. By the time she finished, I felt exhausted, as if my energy left my body with my blood. She gave me a bottle of orange juice to drink before I stood to go back to the exam room. The orange juice sparked my hunger. I had thrown up my breakfast, and lunchtime approached.

The nurse from the morning came back to walk me to the exam room and hand me the paper gown. "Do you feel okay enough to put this on?"I nodded and took the paper gown from her.

"The doctor will be back shortly. Dress in the gown, open to the front, and sit on the exam table," the nurse instructed before leaving me alone in the room.

I did as she said and waited on the paper sheet on the exam table for the doctor to return.

After several minutes, Dr. Garcia returned. The pelvic exam passed without another incident, nothing like this morning's panic attack. The doctor explained each step before moving forward, her voice calm. I found myself trusting her after all she did to help me feel safe this morning.

Lying on the table, I thought about the dream with Amo Abe and the little boy, the dream where Patrona Isa never appeared. Could that someday become a reality? I daydreamed about it as I tried to ignore the prodding of the doctor's hands and speculum. I forced the memories away when the doctor inserted the speculum, thinking only of the dream of being with Amo Abe and the boy, our boy.

When the pelvic exam finished, the doctor said, "Your friend will likely want to see the ultrasound. Do you want to let her back in?"

"That's fine. I hope she isn't too mad at me," I said.

"It's hard to stay mad when you're looking at an image of a baby," the doctor said, smiling. "I'll go get the ultrasound technician while the nurse gets your friend. I'll be back after the ultrasound is complete."

The doctor left, and another lady came into the room. "Hello. I'm Mandy, your ultrasound technician."

"Hi. Nice to meet you," I said.

I waited while the nurse brought Patrona Isa back into the room. When Patrona Isa saw the transvaginal ultrasound equipment, she said, "I had one of these done when they were diagnosing my endometriosis."

"Yes, it's often used for that as well," Mandy said. She prepared the probe, and I tensed when she inserted it.

Think of the dream, I said to myself. But the memory resisted coming back with Patrona Isa there. I turned my head away from her to the ultrasound monitor as it flickered to life.

"There it is," the technician said, pointing to a little spot on the screen.

"My little peanut!" Patrona Isa said, squealing with pleasure.

Mandy moved the probe around inside me, and the picture shifted. She clicked some buttons, capturing the images. "I'd say you're easily eight weeks along. Maybe nine."

"That would put the due date at..." Patrona Isa counted. "Sometime in December."

"The doctor will have to tell you for sure," the technician said, capturing more images. "There's the baby's head."

I smiled. Someone had started growing inside me. Someone I wouldn't get to keep.

My smile dissipated.

"See that flicker of light?" Mandy asked. I nodded. "That's the heartbeat. It's measuring a hundred forty beats per minute. That's a good rate." Mandy pulled the probe out. "I've got what I need for the doctor. Everything looks normal. Go ahead and change, and I'll send her in to see you."

Mandy left with the nurse. Patrona Isa moved to the other side of the room, facing away from me and examining a poster that showed pictures of baby growth by week. I changed back into my clothes.

A few minutes later, the doctor knocked on the door and came in, carrying some papers in her hand. "It's good to see everything looks normal with the baby. Based on the ultrasound, your baby is measuring nine weeks, so your due date is December twelfth."

"Wow, so early," Patrona Isa said, looking at me with a scowl on her face.

I shrunk back into the chair and looked at the floor. Why did I think I could get away with that extra week with Amo Abe?

"Here are a few photos of your baby." The doctor handed photos of the ultrasound to me and to Patrona Isa. "And here is some literature that will help you in the first trimester. I'll need to see you back in about four weeks. You can schedule on the way out. Also, you'll want to make sure you start taking prenatal vitamins and eat the right foods. I've got some information about foods to avoid and foods to eat. Lots of protein." She handed me a stack of papers.

The doctor held out her hand. "It was great meeting you, Hillary. Take care of yourself, and I'll see you soon."

I shook her hand.

She then nodded at Patrona Isa. "I'm sure I'll be seeing you as well."

Patrona Isa nodded but didn't shake the doctor's hand.

When we got to the car, Patrona Isa attacked me. "Did you know you were pregnant after the first week with Abe?"

"I...uh...wasn't sure," I stammered. "I thought the spotting was my period."

"Hmph." Her face twisted into a scowl. "What did you have to say to the doctor that you couldn't say in front of me?"

"It's nothing you'd want to know."

"About me?"

"No, nothing like that. She ask about me, not you."

"What's so secret that you can't tell me? I'm the only friend you have," she said. She pouted.

"There's many things from before I met you that you don't know," I said.

"And you don't feel comfortable telling me?" She put on an inno-cent, angel-face look.

"I'm not comfortable to say it. It's part of my past I don't want to remember."

"I see."

She didn't speak to me the rest of the car ride home, and I welcomed the silence. After the doctor kicked her out of the exam room, I had braced myself for a far greater storm. Maybe it still waited around the corner.

CHAPTER TWENTY-ONE

I was working on preparing dinner when Amo Abe came home from work. He rushed through the kitchen door and took me into his arms.

"I heard about the baby," he said, stroking my hair.

I melted into his embrace. How good it felt for a man to show love to me and not lust. His earthy scent mixed with the smell of the cooking chicken, and I smiled. I might not be his, but I now carried the baby he yearned for.

I reached up and pecked him on the cheek. "Our baby." He smiled down at me and nodded.

Patrona Isa entered the room, and we broke our embrace quicker than oil in water. I went back to monitoring the food, and Amo Abe busied himself in the junk drawer, looking for something.

"Did you see the picture of the baby?" Patrona Isa asked Amo Abe.

"No, please show me," he said pulling a pen out of the junk drawer.

"Come into the dining room, and we can sit down and look at them," Patrona Isa said.

They left me to tend to the meal alone.

Once I finished preparing dinner, I brought the platter into the dining room.

"Please stay for dinner, Hillary," Amo Abe said, motioning to the chair on his left.

I nodded and sat beside him.

Amo Abe thanked Jehovah for the food and for the baby and handed the dinner spoon to me to serve myself first. "Here, Hillary. It's more important than ever for you to eat well to help the baby," Amo Abe said, smiling at me. I might have imagined the extra sparkle in his eye.

I smiled at him and glanced at Patrona Isa. Her lips pressed into a thin line, and she drummed her fingers on the table. Amo Abe usually gave her the serving spoon first.

"Tell me about the doctor's appointment," he said to me.

"Well..." Patrona Isa started to answer, but he cut her off.

"Let Hillary tell it. The appointment was for her after all," he said.

I smiled, enjoying the extra attention. Maybe I could make him love me with his baby growing inside me. "It was interesting."

"In what way?"

"I had a panic attack."

"Oh, no. What happened?" Amo Abe asked, concern written all over his face.

"I felt uncomfortable when they told me to change into the paper gown, and then I couldn't talk about my past..." I glanced sideways at Patrona Isa. "But really, it's nothing."

"It was a big enough deal to send me out of the room," Patrona Isa grumbled.

"Oh, Hillary, I know how uncomfortable you are talking about your past," Amo Abe said with compassion. "I'm sorry that happened to you."

"What do you know about her past?" Patrona Isa asked.

"Not much. She was too uncomfortable to talk about it," he shot back to her before turning to me. "But you got through the rest of the appointment okay?"

"Yes, thank you, Señor," I said, smiling at him.

I dug into the food, devouring every bite. My hunger had increased since I got pregnant, especially since I couldn't keep many meals down with the morning sickness.

After dinner, I cleared the dishes from the table and went to the kitchen to clean them. Amo Abe followed me.

"Would you like some help?" he asked.

Surprised, I tilted my head and looked at him with a smile on my face. "Thank you, Señor. I can manage on my own."

"I like being near my baby," he said, winking at me.

I felt the heat rush to my cheeks, unsure if he was speaking about me or the baby I carried...or maybe both.

Chapter Twenty-Two

Over the next few months, Amo Abe continued to show preference to me, annoying Patrona Isa at every turn. She took it out on me by giving me more work to do. Things she used to do on her own, she now assigned to me. I didn't find myself rushing to the bathroom to pee or throw up, so I used the time to do the extra work. The second trimester treated me well.

The date of my twenty-week appointment rushed toward me. After Patrona Isa embarrassed herself at the first appointment, she sent me alone to the next two. I drove the Range Rover, and the doctor sent the bills to the Serugs. But for the twenty-week where the ultrasound would show the gender, Patrona Isa wanted to be there.

We drove in her car in silence. She hadn't been friendly to me since that first appointment. This one went much smoother.

Mandy worked the ultrasound machine again. She slathered my belly with gel and ran the probe over it, bringing the baby into view on the screen. It was so much bigger! A steady sound came out of the machine.

"That's your baby's heartbeat," Mandy explained.

I glanced at Patrona Isa, whose eyes lit up at the sound.

"The heartbeat is a hundred forty beats per minute, which is normal," Mandy said. She moved the probe around and took pictures of the baby from different angles. "It looks like the baby is measuring right around twenty weeks."

Once the ultrasound finished and I cleaned the gel off, Patrona Isa and I waited for Dr. Garcia to join us.

"Do you want to know the gender of the baby?" the doctor asked when she walked into the room.

"Yes," Patrona Isa and I said at the same time.

"Congratulations. It's a boy." She pulled out one of the ultrasound pictures to show us. "See right there? It's clearly a boy."

Patrona Isa teared up as she took the photo from the doctor. "It's a boy," she whispered.

Tears welled up in my eyes too for the baby that would never be mine. I rubbed my swollen belly, and the baby kicked. The sensation still felt new. He started kicking the week before.

The first time I felt the pressure from the kick, the three of us were sat together eating dinner. Amo Abe was telling us a story about one of his employees that handled a difficult situation with a client.

"The client was yelling at Henry about how our software wasn't connecting to his—"

"Oh," I said, interrupting Amo Abe mid-sentence.

I felt a cramp, a pressure, pushing up against my side. It didn't hurt, but I hadn't felt it before. I reached down to my belly, pushing against the cramp. I felt a tiny foot pushing back toward my hand.

"What is it?" Amo Abe jumped out of his chair and rushed to kneel at my side.

Patrona Isa narrowed her eyes into a scowl.

"I think the baby kicked now," I said. I placed his hand on my belly where I felt the pressure, but it wasn't there anymore.

"I don't feel anything." As soon as he started talking, the baby kicked again. "Oh! I feel it!"

"I believe it likes when you talk," I said with a smile. "The doctor said it hears from outside now. As soon as you speak, it kicked again."

Since that night, Amo Abe would come home from work and find me. He held his hand on my belly and talked to the baby, trying to make the baby kick for him. It was a game now, and I loved every minute. Feeling Amo Abe's hand on my belly, his warmth, his tenderness when he spoke to the baby...I never wanted it to end.

But like clockwork, Patrona Isa would come into the room with another task in hand to break us apart.

I took the other copy of the ultrasound photo from the doctor and gazed at my baby. The baby looked so much bigger than the last picture, yet still so tiny. I thought about the boy in my dream. Would he look the same? Would I be disappointed if he didn't? I relied on that dream often to suppress the memories of my past. It was almost burned into my head. Did it even matter since the baby wouldn't be mine?

That night when Amo Abe came home, he entered the kitchen.

"I heard the great news. It's a boy," he said to me, placing his hand on my belly, waiting for the kick. As if on cue, the baby kicked back at his voice.

"Yes. The baby is yours and Patrona Isa's." I looked out the window, tears prickling at my eyes.

"You'll move into the baby's bedroom while he's nursing," Amo Abe said. "You need to be close to him overnight. He'll need you."

"Patrona Isa can give him formula milk from the bottle," I pointed out. "I don't need to move into the house."

"No," Amo Abe said. "I want the very best for him, and nursing is the very best. You'll move into the house for at least that long."

At least that long...I would have to give the baby to Patrona Isa as soon as the nursing was over.

Amo Abe lifted my shirt over my swollen belly and spoke in a low voice to the baby inside, rubbing his hand over my skin. A shiver ran down my back at his touch. The baby kicked in response to his voice, and Amo Abe cooed even more to him.

Patrona Isa walked into the kitchen, holding two bags from the store. When she saw Amo Abe kneeling in front of my belly, touching it, cooing to it, she gave me a dirty look. "We've got a lot for you to do to prepare for the baby's arrival. Now that we know the baby's mine, you'll have to get the nursery ready." She thrust the bags into my hand. "Here. The guest bedroom on the left will be the nursery. Take these and put them in there."

I looked her in the eye and said, "Maybe your husband wants time with his baby. You can take the bags, no?" I thought better of my boldness and snarky attitude in front of Amo Abe and tried to soften my words a little. "I'll wait. When he's done, I'll bring the bags."

Amo Abe stood and looked between the two of us. "I can resume this after dinner. Don't let me stop you from your tasks."

Patrona Isa gave me another dirty look as I turned around and carried her bags to the guest room. I set them down on the bed and leaned up against it. What could she do to me now? She couldn't fire me or get rid of me. I had her baby inside me. She still couldn't get pregnant, and the future of her tribe curled up in my womb.

For the first time in my life, I felt some sort of control.

I took the ultrasound picture out of my pocket and unfolded it. "My little baby..." I said to myself. No, Amo Abe's baby, I corrected myself. "You'll be sleeping in this room soon." I rubbed my belly. "I get to sleep here too...for a little while."

I heard the oven ding and stuffed the picture back in my pocket. Rushing back to the kitchen, I turned off the oven timer and pulled out the chicken and rice casserole. The smell of thyme and oregano filled the kitchen.

I brought the steaming platter of food to the table and sat at Amo Abe's side without being asked.

"Please join us for dinner," Patrona Isa said, rolling her eyes when she saw that I wasn't waiting for the invitation.

I offered her a sarcastic smile. "Thank you."

Amo Abe gave the serving spoon to me first again. "Eat up. You're eating for two." He smiled at me, and his smile reached his eyes.

I smiled back at him as I took the serving spoon and helped myself to a generous portion.

Patrona Isa scowled at me as I handed her the serving spoon. I enjoyed the attention from Amo Abe. I refused to let her make me feel bad any longer. She put me in this situation after all. I didn't want to have a baby with her husband.

"Hillary, please stay after dinner to watch a movie with us," Amo Abe said as he scooped his portion onto his plate.

"I would love to. Thank you."

Patrona Isa's scowl deepened, but Amo Abe didn't notice. In fact, he seemed oblivious to her presence. He talked to me as if she had disappeared.

After dinner, I started to clear the plates as I always did, but I stopped. I decided to test my newfound control.

"My feet are so swollen. I think I'll go put them up, if you don't mind," I said, nodding toward the living room.

"What about the dishes?" Patrona Isa asked.

"Look how swollen her feet are, honey. Why don't you do the dishes tonight and let her rest?" Amo Abe said. He started to escort me to the living room.

I looked over my shoulder. Patrona Isa's mouth dropped to the floor. I winked at her and allowed myself to be led away by Amo Abe.

He settled me onto the couch, and I put my swollen feet up on the ottoman. He sat next to me and whispered to my belly, rubbing it. The baby kicked toward his voice, and he pushed back at the little foot.

Patrona Isa walked into the room and plopped down into the chair next to the couch. She crossed her arms and wore the same sour look on her face as she had at dinner.

Amo Abe pressed the play button, and Tekehentahkhwa, also known as "Beans," came on the screen in her opening interview with the school admissions officer. I leaned back into the couch to watch the movie, my belly a mountain above me. Amo Abe rested his hand on the mountain, rubbing it in circles. Patrona Isa huffed and turned toward the television. I smiled, feeling content with life, at least for the moment.

In the middle of the movie, I excused myself and went to the hallway bathroom. When I finished, I heard Patrona Isa's angry voice on my way back to the living room.

"Can't you see what she's doing, Abe?" she asked. "She's playing you. You just made me do her work!"

I ducked back into the hallway and listened.

"Did you hear her earlier when I asked her to put the new baby stuff into the nursery? She defied me!" Patrona Isa said.

"Calm down, Princess. She's carrying our baby," Amo Abe reasoned.

"It's all your fault that I'm suffering this abuse. I put my servant in bed with you, and the minute she knows she's pregnant with our baby, she treats me like I'm nothing!" Patrona Isa yelled. "May Jehovah decide which of us is right."

"No, *you* decide," Amo Abe said. "She's *your* servant. Do to her whatever you think is best."

"Fine," Patrona Isa said. "But I don't want to see you touch her anymore. It makes me sick."

I rounded the corner in time to see Amo Abe raise his hands in surrender to Patrona Isa.

"What did I miss?" I tilted my head, eyebrows raised.

They both froze and looked at each other.

"What did I miss in the movie? I haven't seen it before." I tried to act as if I hadn't heard their conversation, but I could already feel my control slipping away. The feeling in the room changed.

"Oh, um, Beans' family was just attacked by a mob," Amo Abe said.

I sat next to him, and he scooted over, away from me. He didn't touch me again the rest of the night.

When the movie finished, Amo Abe stood, smiled at me, and said, "Thank you for staying. I hope you have a good night. I'm going to bed."

He left the room without saying a word to Patrona Isa.

I stood. "I'll see you tomorrow," I said and escaped through the back kitchen door.

***

When I arrived to work the following day, Patrona Isa was waiting for me in the kitchen with several lists in her hands.

"We've got a lot to do to get ready for the baby. We've got to get the nursery ready. You'll need to move the furniture out of the room, paint the walls, put the crib together and the rest of the furniture I ordered. You'll need to pick up the paint from the hardware store and the furniture that I ordered from the furniture store."

She slapped one list on the counter. "Here's the list for the nursery. Then once you're done with that, we're going to have a special pow-wow for all of Abe's co-workers and their families to celebrate. You'll do all the shopping, cooking, and serving at the powwow. That's going to be on Friday, so it will all need to be done by then."

She slapped another list on the counter. "Here's the list for the powwow. I'm buying some more plants so the front of the house looks perfect. You can plant those once I get back from the store. And I've decided to buy some cows for that back pasture that isn't being used. I'm going to the market to look at them, but once they are here, you'll have to milk them each morning and evening.

"You got all that?" Patrona Isa asked when she had finished.

I felt my eyes widen with every new task she gave me. I stared at her with my eyebrows raised. "Uh, yes. I think."

"And don't forget your normal duties. Those still need to be done on time." She got right in my face, eyes narrowed, teeth clenched. "And if you don't stop flirting with my husband, you'll be gone as soon as that baby is out."

She turned and stormed out of the kitchen.

Chapter Twenty-Three

I wiped the sweat from my forehead with the back of my hand. It was September, and the South Texas sun beat down on me as I knelt in the front yard planting the new plants Patrona Isa brought home. The smell of mulch mixed with the musky smell of the lantana flowers filled the air, which hung thick and heavy around me. A pair of northern mockingbirds sang from the tree in the front of the yard. The air conditioner hummed from the side of the house.

I already finished my regular chores for the day, cleaning the bedrooms and bathrooms. I powered through them so I could get to her new list of things to do. To prepare for the new baby furniture, I also broke down the bed from the guest bedroom and moved it to the garage for storage. My watch now read three o'clock, the hottest time of the day, and Patrona Isa insisted the plants be planted as soon as possible.

"You're not done yet?" Patrona Isa said as she poked her head out the front door. I could feel the cool breeze of the air conditioning coming from the open door. "What's taking you so long?"

"You want it done quick? So help, then."

"Ha!" she said and went back inside without another word.

I sighed. Planting these would take all afternoon, and I still needed to go to the hardware store to pick up the paint and supplies for the nursery. My growing belly made it awkward to kneel over. I spread my knees out wide to leave room for it.

When four o'clock rolled around, Patrona Isa poked her head out the door again. "You better get to the hardware store before it closes."

"Okay. I stop what I'm doing here and go now," I said, wiping more sweat from my forehead.

"Don't forget about dinner too," she reminded me. "Abe should be home by six."

I sighed. "Yes, Señora."

"You can finish the planting after you make dinner."

I pulled off my gardening gloves and rocked back onto my feet to stand up, brushing dirt from my knees. Stomping the dirt out of the tread of my boots, I walked to the front door to grab my purse and keys before heading to the car.

I drove to the hardware store, thinking about my day. *How long will Patrona Isa keep this up?* She pushed me hard. *Cows? Really? Like we need that.*

How long can I take this? Day one hadn't even ended, and I felt exhausted, dehydrated, overheated. Thirst burned my throat, and hunger gnawed at me. *What damage did this do to the baby?* Amo Abe said he wanted "the very best for him." Did he know Patrona Isa gave me all this extra work? He said, "Do whatever you think is best," to her. This couldn't be best for his baby.

I stumbled into the hardware store and made my way to the front desk. "I'm here to pick up supplies for Isabelle Serug."

"Yes, we've got them all in the back," the man behind the counter told me. He left through a swinging door and came back a minute later pushing a cart. "Do you need help putting them in the car?" he asked, looking at my belly.

"That would be great, thank you."

I followed him out the door and pointed out my car. He rolled the cart there and loaded the supplies into the back.

"Thank you, and have a great evening," he said, waving as he rolled the cart back toward the store.

I climbed back into the Range Rover and headed home. When I got there and unloaded the painting supplies, dinnertime had rolled around already. The lantana plants mocked me from their plastic pots as I walked past them into the house. Patrona Isa was sitting on the couch, a book in hand, smiling to herself as I passed by to go to the kitchen.

Fried fish and wild rice was the quickest thing I could think to make, so I pulled out the ingredients and got started. My stomach growled at the smells, and I tasted a generous spoonful when the rice finished. My hunger brought back the memories of when I was nine, but I didn't have time for memories right now. I still needed to plant more lantana before I left for the day.

Amo Abe came home right as the food finished, but he didn't come into the kitchen today to find me. Instead, he sat at his spot at the dinner table and read the newspaper. I brought the platter of food to the table. Patrona Isa took her seat without so much as a glance in my direction.

"Will you be joining us tonight, Hillary?" Amo Abe said.

"Hillary has more work to get done before she's done for the day," Patrona Isa responded for me, not looking at me or Amo Abe as she spoke.

"Yes, I do," I said, looking down at the floor and backing out of the dining room. I felt relieved to get out of that room anyway. No way could I handle an awkward meal with them after how Patrona Isa was treating me.

I hung up my apron and headed back outside to plant the rest of the lantana. The evening sun still beat down, maybe even hotter than before. Two hours of daylight remained, and I still needed to get twenty-five pots in the ground.

At eight-thirty as the light of dusk disappeared, I covered the last plant with mulch. Twelve and a half hours of work today without any breaks, and Patrona Isa didn't seem to care at all. What did she want from me? Was she trying to keep me away from Amo Abe? If so, fine. I'd stay far away if this was the alternative.

I went around the house to the RV instead of going through it. I didn't want to see or talk to Patrona Isa. All I wanted to do was drink a gallon of water and fall into a deep sleep.

***

The next day started no better. Patrona Isa added the painting of the nursery and putting together the crib to my normal chores. It turned into another long day with no breaks. My feet swelled up by the time I got back to the RV that night. As I made my dinner at nine o'clock, I sat on the couch with my feet up while the food baked.

The smells of gallo pinto filled the RV, the sautéed onion and garlic, the toasty smell of the rice. I went two days with hardly any food. My stomach growled, reminding me how lucky I felt to be here in South Texas. I thought back to my days digging through trash heaps and wondered how my mamá survived after they took me. How did she find food without me? Maybe she strapped Jose to her body with a cloth, bringing him with her to dig through the trash piles for food.

"I miss you, Mamá," I said, a single tear slipping down my cheek. I sniffled and closed my eyes, remembering the cozy home we used to have. It didn't offer much, but I still called it home. A home with my own family. A home where I felt safe and loved. I almost forgot what love felt like.

The tears fell freely now. Maybe the pregnancy hormones intensified the emotions, or maybe the truth sank in. I would never be more than a pawn in someone else's game. Patrona Isa was using me now, forcing me to work long days, even though I carried her baby. A couple days ago I felt like I had the upper hand, but that slipped away fast.

Once, Patrona Isa felt like my only friend. Now she stood against me as my enemy. Amo Abe had acted like a friend too...when he wanted something from me. But now he tossed me away like leftovers, letting Patrona Isa decide what to do with me. I was alone.

What good did this life even offer? Maybe dying would feel like mercy.

Maybe the trash heaps offered more than this place ever could. I survived for a year doing that as a child. Maybe I could do the same here.

The timer dinged. I wiped my tears away with a tissue and lifted the warm pot of gallo pinto from the stove. After spooning some onto my plate, I sat at the small dining table. The sun had already disappeared by the time I took my first bite of the day. The familiar blend of rice and beans, cooked with onions and garlic, grounded me. I added a spoonful of crema and a slice of fried cheese on the side. When I pulled my fork away, the cheese stretched with it. The salt and spice danced on my tongue, and the hot cheese stung the roof of my mouth.

It wouldn't be easy to leave this behind. It didn't offer luxury, but it gave me all I needed. A life on the street would be much more difficult, especially with a baby.

How much more of Patrona Isa's hard labor could I take? How much more of her hatred could I take? She despised me for being able to conceive.

"It wasn't my idea!" I yelled into the emptiness. "I didn't ask for this!"

I sighed and looked down at my food. I took only three bites before losing my appetite. My stomach twisted into knots. I took a few gulps from my water glass, trying to loosen it up.

"What do I do, Mamá?" I asked to myself. "What would you have done if you were me?"

What a different life I would have if Papá hadn't died.

***

Knock, knock, knock. I rolled over and groaned. My alarm hadn't gone off yet, and the knock interrupted my dreamless sleep.

Knock, knock, knock.

"Who is it?" I called, covering my face with my pillow.

"Wake up, sleepyhead!" Patrona Isa's voice came through the RV door. "It's time to get to work."

"Today's Wednesday. It's my free day," I called back from the bed.

"There's too much to get done. No day off for you today."

"What? You joke, right?" I said groaning.

"Nope. I expect to see you in no more than thirty minutes at the house," Patrona Isa called back through the door. I heard her footsteps go down the stairs and away from the RV.

I rolled over. Could she do that? The clock read 7:35 a.m. Maybe she planned on giving me a different day off this week. The powwow was Friday, so maybe I'd get the entire weekend off instead. Ugh, could I survive another three days with twelve hours of manual labor and no breaks?

I swung my legs around to the edge of the bed and dragged myself to my feet. I should have left yesterday, walked away and never turned back.

After getting ready, I walked across the backyard to the house and through the back door. Patrona Isa waited in the kitchen.

"You're late," she said, looking at her watch.

"I don't even know why I'm here. I wasn't supposed to work," I said through gritted teeth.

"How dare you talk to me like that. I'm your boss. I make the working hours, and I say you're working today. And tomorrow. And Friday. And Saturday."

"Is this how it will be now? Only one free day each week?"

Patrona Isa stood at the counter with lists spread across it, pencil in hand. "Who said anything about a 'free day'? When the baby comes, you won't get a day off, so we might as well start now."

I felt my mouth drop open, and I stared at her. "Watching a baby is different than planting flowers under the sun and painting with no air."

"I suppose it is, but the house won't clean itself. The groceries won't get purchased on their own. The food won't get prepared by itself.

You've got a lot to do before Friday, and there will be plenty more after that as we prepare for the baby to come."

"Ugh." I threw my hands up in disgust and glared at her. "I already do enough. I'm not doing more."

The slap across my face was unexpected and stung, my head jerking to the side from the impact. I heard a ringing in my ear. I raised my hand to my hot cheek. I was stunned and looked at her with my mouth and eyes both wide.

"That's what you get for being rude." Her lips curled into a crooked little smile. "Here's a list of things that need to be purchased at the store in preparation for the powwow. Some at the grocery store. Some at the department store." She handed me a list. "Once that's done, I'll let you know what's next."

I snatched the list from her and stomped out of the kitchen toward the front door. Grabbing the Range Rover keys, I headed out the front door to the car.

My back ached from the planting and mulching on Monday, and now my cheek stung from her slap. Climbing into the car had grown harder with my belly in the way. When I got to the end of the neighborhood street, I paused. Turning right would take me toward the store. Turning left would take me...well...away from here. What would Patrona Isa say if I drove away and never came back?

I turned left.

I hadn't been this way before, but I bumped over the gravel road until it came to a paved road. I took a left onto the road and kept going until I found a gas station. The gas tank neared empty, so I filled it up using Patrona Isa's credit card. I could go a long way on a tank of gas. How far could I get?

I bought a large bottle of water and some snacks from the gas station store before getting back in the car. I turned the radio up and headed south. The air conditioning blasted, blowing my hair around my face. The ranch land and oil rigs flew by.

I was free! A huge smile stretched across my face. I thought it might break. In time Patrona Isa would come looking for me, for her car, for her credit card. But right now, I felt like I could take on the world.

I drove without a clue where to go. I just kept driving. I took a left at the next major intersection and drove through Kingsville. Once I got through the city, I took another left. My foot must have been heavy on the gas as I bounced to the music, letting myself enjoy the moment.

Blue and red lights flashed in my rearview mirror.

"Ugh!" I shouted. Fear shot through me. Was I speeding? What if Patrona Isa reported the car stolen? What if she tracked me with the credit card transaction? What if they found my forged citizenship documents?

I couldn't let them catch me. I hit the gas and shot forward. I drove through a remote part of the state, far from traffic. Nothing surrounded me but flat, dry land. My best chance at disappearing came from the dust clouds rising off the gravel farm roads.

A dusty farm road crossed ahead between Kingsville and Bishop, and I skidded left off the highway onto it. Swerving around a tractor, I zoomed down the road, dust kicking up behind me. The cop trailed close behind, but the dust blocked my view and kept me from seeing how close they were. Turning another corner, I bumped over a narrow road, past a farmhouse.

I could see a river or a stream in front of me, but I couldn't tell how deep it was. Could the Range Rover go through it? I pressed harder on the gas pedal, but at the last minute, I hesitated. Turning the wheel, I slammed on the brakes, in time to stop before going into the river. The car swerved to the right, putting it between me and the cop car.

Slamming the car in park, I dashed out the door and started running along the bank of the spring. I could see a clump of trees ahead of me. Maybe I could reach them and hide. I huffed harder, not stopping to look back to see if the cop was closing in. I could hear the sounds of footsteps and heavy breathing behind me. He...or she...was close.

I flung myself into the trees, the branches grabbing onto my hair, pulling it. The branches weren't very giving and tore into the flesh of my arm. I ran through the trees until I reached the stream. Seeing a bush on the bank, I curled myself into a ball behind it and awaited my fate. Blood dripped down my arm onto my shorts.

The police officer found me by the spring of water in the wilderness, the San Fernando Creek. "Hillary, servant of Isabelle, where have you come from, and where are you going?"

I flinched against the wrath I expected from a man forced to chase me, but what I saw surprised me. The sunlight blazed behind him, casting a glowing halo around his figure. Kindness and peace softened his face. He didn't hold a gun or a stick. Instead, he extended his hand to help me up.

I took his hand, and warmth spread through me, starting at his touch and flowing through my whole body. The scratches from the branches disappeared, healing in an instant, as if they never existed. He pulled me to my feet, and peace settled over me like nothing I'd ever felt before.

When I caught my breath and noticed him waiting for an answer, I replied, "I'm running away from Patrona Isa."

The man said to me, "You must go back to her and submit to her mistreatment."

My eyes widened. I couldn't go back. Patrona Isa worked me to death, and she didn't even care. Tears prickled my eyes as I shook my head. I dropped back down to my hands and knees in the dust by the spring, eyes closed, feeling defeated.

The man said to me, "The baby you carry will be one of many in your family line. Jehovah will give your son many children. Your descendants will be too many to count."

Jehovah. Patrona Isa's god sent this man as a messenger. What did Jehovah want from me? Why must I even believe in a god that would leave Patrona Isa barren and cause her to have such strife with me? We were supposed to be friends!

The words the man spoke echoed in my head. "Your descendants will be too many to count." That worked out good for Patrona Isa and Amo Abe. They got the baby they wanted. This child fulfilled the exact promise they claimed Jehovah gave them, the one Patrona Isa couldn't fulfill herself.

I thought back to the conversation they shared after her last fertility treatment failed. Jehovah never told them to involve me. That idea came straight from Patrona Isa. She and Amo Abe clung to Jehovah's promise, but when His timing didn't match their expectations, they took matters into their own hands. The strife between Patrona Isa and me didn't come from Jehovah. It came from her lack of faith.

And now Jehovah expected me to return and submit to her? That felt so unfair. I hadn't done anything to deserve this. I was a pawn in their game.

I looked into the face of the man sent to bring me a message from Jehovah. Once again, he helped me to my feet, peace and warmth radiating from his hand.

"The Lord has heard your cry," the man said to me. "You have conceived and will have a son. You will name him Ignacio, for he will be a fiery man, like a wild donkey. His hand will be against everyone, and everyone's hand will be against him. He will live at odds with all his brothers."

Like a wild donkey, strong, a survivor. Like me.

He will live at odds with his brothers, like I'm living at odds with Patrona Isa right now.

In this place, have I actually seen the One who sees me?

We walked back to the Range Rover together. Before he left, I said, "Thank you." I paused to look up into the blue, cloudless sky and said to the man, "Jehovah is the God Who Sees."

He smiled and nodded at me and walked toward his car.

I climbed into the Range Rover and gulped down some water from my water bottle. At the spring, the water flowed over the rocks and down past the bush in the distance where I hid.

This spring is a well of the living One who sees me.

I had no idea how to get back home, so I plugged the address into the navigation tool in the car. By the time the directions populated the screen, the cop car was nowhere in sight.

CHAPTER TWENTY-FOUR

Patrona Isa worked me hard over the next few months. She always found another chore for me to do. But I did everything without complaining or arguing after the encounter at the spring.

Jehovah stood with me. I'd endured so much in my life already, and somehow, I would get through even this. I was a survivor, like my son would be.

Patrona Isa did allow me one day off every couple of weeks, and Sunday, December seventeenth, five days after my scheduled due date, marked that rare break. My belly swelled so much, I struggled to sleep. I tossed in the bed, trying to find a comfortable position, a pillow wedged between my knees. I got up every hour to pee, the baby pressing hard against my bladder. My stomach cramped with contractions most of the night, but they seemed mild.

I turned onto my left side and felt a pop inside my belly. A sudden urge to pee overwhelmed me, and I dashed to the bathroom, fluid dripping down my leg.

As I sat on the toilet with fluid streaming out of me, a cramp gripped me. The contraction hit harder than the previous ones, and I moaned through it. The baby was coming.

Alone in the RV, my heart started racing. This marked the moment I never planned and never wanted, but I now had to face the pain of birthing my son...no, Amo Abe and Patrona Isa's child.

Fluid kept pouring, and I froze, unsure what to do. I didn't want to get up off the toilet and tell Patrona Isa it was time, not while dripping like this. I grabbed a pad and did my best to catch the fluid as I pulled up my panties. I couldn't sit here all day.

Another cramp hit me, knocking me off my feet and back onto the toilet seat. I bent over my swollen belly and moaned in pain. I needed to get to them. As soon as the cramp subsided and I caught my breath, I pulled up my pants and waddled through the RV to the door. I managed to get down the steps and across the lawn before another cramp hit me. I crumpled to the ground on all fours in the moonlight and groaned through the pain. *How was I going to get through this?*

When the cramp passed, I dashed to the back door and pulled it open.

"Patrona...Isa," I panted as I called through the house, trying to catch my breath. My voice sounded so quiet though I tried to yell out to her. I waddled through the house to the master bedroom and pounded on the door. "Patrona Isa!"

Another cramp gripped me, and my knees gave way, dropping me to the floor. I held my belly as I whimpered.

Patrona Isa flung the door open and looked down at me as she pulled the belt of her robe around her to tie it. "Is it time? The baby's coming?"

I didn't answer as the pain silenced me.

She turned and dashed back into the room. "Abe, wake up!" I heard her say from behind the door. "The baby is coming!"

I caught my breath when the cramp passed and used the doorframe to pull myself to a standing position.

Patrona Isa came out of the room, dressed in a green V-neck short-sleeved blouse and short black jean shorts, her hair pulled into a messy ponytail. She looked gorgeous as always. Amo Abe followed her, also dressed.

The maternity nightshirt and loose maternity shorts felt frumpy compared to them. But another cramp hit me, and I almost fell to the ground. Amo Abe caught me and held me up as I panted through the pain.

"The contractions are coming fast! We better hurry if we're going to make it to the hospital in time," Patrona Isa said, pulling at Amo Abe's arm.

I stumbled along with him holding me upright. I couldn't see where we went, as my eyes were squeezed shut. He guided me through the house, out the door, and into the backseat of his Bronco. I curled up into a ball on the seat, allowing the pain to pass as they climbed into the front seats.

"Seatbelt, Hillary," Amo Abe said as he started the car.

I moaned but sat back up and managed to get the seatbelt clicked around my enormous belly.

Once he backed out of the driveway, he wasted no time bumping down the gravel streets to reach the highway.

"Ahhh!" I groaned as another cramp hit me. I curled up toward my tummy against the will of the seatbelt.

"Hang in there. We're less than ten minutes away," Amo Abe said as he sped around the curve and onto the highway, gravel flying as the tires left the dirt road.

I gasped for breath and sat up straight again as the contraction passed. The car entered town, but Amo Abe didn't slow down. He sped through the streets until he pulled into the hospital parking lot.

Another contraction squeezed at my stomach as we parked.

"I'll go check us in," Patrona Isa said, jumping out of the passenger seat and racing into the building. She left Amo Abe to help me out of the car and across the parking lot as another cramp hit me. I collapsed into his arms, curling around my belly and panting through the pain.

"You've got this," Amo Abe said.

But he did this to me. I turned to him and growled, "This is *your* fault."

He shrunk back, still holding me up so I wouldn't fall as the pain overwhelmed me.

When we got to the entrance, Patrona Isa rolled the wheelchair to me. I plopped down in the chair, sweat running down my forehead into my eyes. I wiped it away and tried to take calming, slow breaths. The rest wouldn't last long before the pain was back. I could feel a pressure pushing at me when I sat, as if the baby might burst out.

The wheelchair moved through the halls, but I felt far away from myself. The rooms, nurses' stations, equipment all went by in a blur as the chair rolled through. It stopped inside a hospital room as another contraction hit me.

"The baby...is...coming!" I yelled at no one in particular through gasps. "He's...coming...out!"

"It's okay, ma'am. Let's get you in the bed," the nurse said with unnerving composure.

I almost fell out of the chair, squatting on the ground, breathing through the pain. He had to be coming out. I felt a pressure in places I shouldn't feel pressure. I stayed in the squatting position until the cramp passed. The nurse helped me to my feet, out of my clothes, and into the hospital gown. If I wasn't rushed between contractions, I might have found the decency to feel embarrassed about undressing in front of them. But I didn't care.

When I lay down, she checked me to see how far along I was. "Wow! You're already fully dilated and ninety percent effaced. The baby will be coming very soon. I'll go get the doctor." She put her hand on my knee. "Hang in there. It's almost over."

She put a sheet over my legs and left the room. I laid my head back on the elevated bed, feet in stirrups, and closed my eyes, enjoying the temporary rest.

It ended way too soon, with another contraction. My whole body tensed up, pushing toward the baby. I screamed and doubled over toward my feet.

"I see the head! Look at all that dark hair," Patrona Isa cried, peeking under the sheet.

"Where's the doctor?" Amo Abe said, pacing back and forth. He went to the door to look out as the nurse returned with the doctor and another nurse.

"Is she pushing already?" the doctor asked, rushing to me.

She sounded far away. The voices around me became muted, slow. My body folded over itself, pushing as hard as it could to rid myself of the one who had grown inside me for the past nine months. Sweat poured over my face, dripping onto the sheet draped over my legs. Pain, as if someone were tearing me apart, radiated from my private areas and up my back. Black spots formed in my vision, and soon my world went dark.

Ignacio was born on December seventeenth at four o'clock in the morning.

When I regained consciousness, I lay in a different room than the one where I gave birth. Patrona Isa cooed to the baby in a chair beside me.

"You're awake," Amo Abe said, moving a tendril of hair behind my ear. He stood next to the bed, leaning over me. His soft hand stroked my cheek.

"What happened?"

"You passed out just as the baby was born," he said. "Your blood pressure dropped. They had to give you more fluids, but they didn't seem too worried."

"How long have I been out?"

"About twenty minutes. They cleaned the baby, got his measurements, and did all the things they normally do. You haven't missed much," Amo Abe said as he adjusted the blanket around me. "I told them we're naming him Ignacio Morales Serug."

"I do not want him to have her name," Patrona Isa said through gritted teeth.

"She carried it for us. She deserves to have at least the middle name."

"Can I see the baby?" I closed my eyes, still weak.

"He's mine," Patrona Isa snapped.

"Honey, let her see the baby. She's going to be nursing him until he's weaned," Amo Abe said, taking the baby from Patrona Isa's arms.

She didn't object, but the look on her face said that she didn't agree.

Amo Abe placed the baby into my arms. He looked so tiny, so breakable. But a love unlike any I felt for any man in my life oozed out of every pore in my body as his baby smell reached my nose.

This baby came from me. He grew inside me and entered the world through me. He carried my genes. His mouth, eyes, and facial shape mirrored Amo Abe's, but his nose, ears, and perfect brown skin came from me.

He nuzzled into my chest, and I lost it. Tears fell from my eyes, but I wiped them away before they hit baby Ignacio's red, blotchy face.

"He's so perfect," I whispered. I put my finger into his tiny fist, and he closed around it. He nuzzled closer to my breast.

The nurse came in. "You're awake," she said and smiled. "I see you've met your son."

"*My* son," Patrona Isa snapped.

The nurse ignored her. "It looks like he's trying to feed. Do you want to try nursing?"

Uncertainty filled my mind. The nurse unsnapped the shoulders of the hospital gown and exposed my left breast. I glanced over at Amo Abe, and he turned away toward the door.

"I'm going to get a snack from the vending machine," he said over his shoulder as he walked out of the room.

Baby Ignacio turned his head to my breast as if he knew what to do. His little mouth suckled at my nipple. He felt like sandpaper against it, and I sucked in a breath. He pinched and tugged at it, trying to get milk out. I expected the pain to end after birth, but a whole new pain took its place.

"Ouch!" I cried, jerking away.

"He's not latching properly," the nurse said. "I can get the lactation consultant to come by and help teach both of you."

My heart sank. It's a good thing Patrona Isa claimed this baby as her own, because I already felt like I had failed as a mother. Tears filled my eyes.

"It's okay. Most mothers and babies don't get it on the first try," the nurse reassured me.

I sniffled and looked down at baby Ignacio. He moved his head back and forth over my breast and let out a little cry.

"Let's try again."

She helped position Ignacio over me and touched his mouth to my nipple, so he opened wide. He clasped his mouth over my breast and started sucking. I could feel a gentle pulling as he sucked.

"There you go!" the nurse said.

The precious baby sucking at me, his eyes closed, looked so content. How could I give him up?

PART THREE

SOBREVIVIENTE

CHAPTER TWENTY-FIVE

Amo Abraham burst through the front door, shouting, "Quick! Take twenty-four pounds of flour and make bread."

I poked my head out from the hallway. Patrona Sara watched television in the living room and jumped up at his sudden command.

A month ago, Jehovah changed the names of both Amo Abe and Patrona Isa, and I was still struggling to get used to it. I didn't know a god could change someone's name, but Jehovah was different. I never knew what to expect. Amo Abe now went by Abraham, and Patrona Isa now went by Sara.

"What's going on?" Patrona Sara asked.

"We have guests!" Amo Abraham said, his huge smile stretching across his face, his eyes wide with excitement. "I'm going out to grill the meat we just got from that calf from the herd. We're going to serve them dinner."

It was fall break, and Ignacio had just started his last year of middle school. Over the past thirteen years, Canaan Ranch had expanded into a cattle ranch, and Ignacio cared for the herd and built and strung fences when he wasn't in school.

"Twenty-four pounds of flour makes a lot of bread!" I said, joining the conversation.

"Yes, this needs to be a feast fit for a king," Amo Abraham said. He turned and dashed back out of the house.

Patrona Sara and I looked at each other.

"A king or a city?" she asked as she headed for the kitchen.

I shrugged and smiled, amused at Amo Abraham's request. "Should he be running like this so soon after surgery?" I asked as I followed her.

Both Amo Abraham and Ignacio were circumcised just two days before at the request of Jehovah.

"Absolutely not! The doctor said both he and Ignacio should be resting for at least a week. But I can't control that man. He does what he wants to do," she said, giving me an exasperated look.

I pulled out the five-pound bag of flour from the pantry. "We're a little short," I said, chuckling.

Patrona Sara looked at our stash. "I can go get more if you want to start with those."

"Sure," I said, shrugging again.

If she wanted to do exactly as Amo Abraham said, I would comply, regardless of how ridiculous the request seemed.

"I have enough baking powder, but we'll need more eggs too?" I called after her as she left the room.

By the time Patrona Sara got back from the store with the other twenty pounds of flour and the eggs, the dough was ready for the first five loaves.

"I'm going to check on Abraham and the meat," she said. "You can handle the bread."

I nodded, since that wasn't my specialty. I preferred cooking in the kitchen rather than on the grill.

She left me alone in the kitchen again. I started working on the other loaves, pondering how ridiculous it seemed to make so much bread for one meal. How many guests would join us? Where did these mysterious guests come from?

Two o'clock rolled around. Only six loaves would fit into the oven at once. If Amo Abraham wanted twenty-five loaves of bread, it would take more than four hours to make. I popped the first five into the oven while I mixed up the next six and waited for them to rise.

The back door opened as the smell of freshly baked bread filled the kitchen. Ignacio walked in, knocking dirt off his boots. The smell of roasting meat wafted into the room from outside. Patrona Sara must have been cooking the meat over the firepit.

"Hello, Miss Hillary," Ignacio said.

Patrona Sara unofficially adopted him once I finished weaning him at two years old. Though no paperwork was filed, she took full responsibility for him and pushed me away. She never told him I was his mother. He knew me only as the household servant, the nanny. My heart ached every time I heard him call me "Miss Hillary." I was his mamá, and he didn't even know it.

"Hi, Ignacio," I answered, busying myself with the mixing of the next batch of bread. "Who's making the meat? It smells delicious."

"Oh, Eddy is grilling it. Mom and Dad gave it to him to cook it," he said.

"He's very good with the grill, so I'm sure it will taste as good as it smells."

"Have you seen our guests?" he asked.

I glanced up at him. His face shone with a mixture of astonishment and excitement. "No, they haven't come inside the house yet, and I've been in the kitchen all afternoon making the bread for dinner."

"They're quite...interesting." He paused, fiddling with the hem of his shirt. He launched into a story. "Okay, so I'm walking in the field, minding my business, and I see them in the distance. I swear they glitched reality," he said, eyes wide. "Like, the vibes? Not human."

"Wow, that is very interesting," I said, raising my eyebrows and trying to decipher what he said. Kids spoke so strangely these days.

"When Dad came to get me, I saw them closer up. They look normal—T-shirts, sneakers, whatever—but something was off in the most extra way. Like they were glowing without glowing? They made eye contact, and I felt read. Pure 'I see you' energy. Gave me goosebumps and inner peace at the same time," he said, closing his eyes and tilting his head back, face toward the ceiling. His dark locks of hair were tied back in a ponytail that flowed down his back.

"Like a movie or dream? Not like real life?" I felt grateful that he was talking to me for more than a two-minute conversation.

"And when they talked, it hit different. Not loud, but somehow it echoed in my bones. Not even kidding." He raised his eyebrows, his chestnut eyes wide.

I smiled at him and studied his face. He grew up so quickly. I could still remember the days when he woke me up in the middle of the night crying his hungry cry. I stayed in the nursery with him, sleeping on a daybed, for two years as I nursed him.

Once he weaned, though, Patrona Isa banished me to the RV, and I saw Ignacio only at dinnertime. She had claimed him as hers from the start, after all. That plan had been in place all along. But I felt the missing piece of me most when I saw him.

"How many of them are there?" I asked. My curiosity rose as we baked so many loaves of bread.

"Three of 'em, but one's def giving main character energy. Like, total boss vibes compared to the other two."

"Only three?" I asked in disbelief. Why were we making so many loaves of bread for three guests?

He nodded.

"Well, okay then. I'm looking forward to meeting them and having this experience too, Ignacio," I murmured, soaking him in with my eyes.

"Anyway, I better get to the restroom. I really need to pee," he said and disappeared from the kitchen.

I sighed. A mother's love never left you, even if your child did.

I turned back to my dough-making. The oven dinged, and I took the loaves out and added six more. Eleven loaves done. Halfway through. I took the first five off the cooling rack and out of the loaf pans so I could use the pans for the last loaves.

What could we serve with this bread and meat? I rummaged around in the refrigerator. Several blocks of cheese that I made earlier in the week from the cows' milk sat on the shelf. Bread, cheese, meat. Not the best meal. Not a meal fit for a king, in my opinion, but it would have to do.

I sliced the cheese into thin slices and arranged them on a platter with a loaf of sliced bread in the middle. One loaf should be good enough to get started, and I could bring out another when it ran out. I pulled out another platter and lined it with aluminum foil, giving Eddy a place to put the grilled meat. The oven needed forty more minutes to finish this round of bread. The last six loaves sat in the pans, ready to bake once the oven was freed up.

Ignacio walked back into the kitchen. "It low-key smells amazing in here."

"Thanks, mijo," I said. "Is everybody eating in the dining room?"

"Nah, they're outside on the patio. It's mad nice out today." He reached the door and waved bye as he left.

I grabbed the foil-lined platter and headed out the back door toward the patio on the side of the house. The pleasant South Texas winter greeted me. At four o'clock in the afternoon, the temperature held at a cool, clear seventy degrees. The low sun cast long shadows from the trees over the patio.

Three strangers gathered around the firepit next to Amo Abraham, Patrona Isa, and Ignacio, the flames from the fire illuminating their faces. Heat radiated from the grill to the side of the patio, and Eddy stood next to it flipping meat over with tongs. The smell of grilled veal filled the air.

"I might need a bigger plate," Eddy said when he saw the platter I brought him. He motioned to the plate full of uncooked meat beside him and raised the lid of the grill to extract the finished pieces.

"I have the bread and some cheese ready, Amo Abe. You want me to bring it out now, since some meat is cooked?" I asked.

"Yes, Hillary, that would be wonderful. Please bring out some fresh milk as well to drink."

I rushed back inside to get the food, milk, plates, cups, and silverware. Patrona Sara followed me inside to help bring everything out. Soon the feast lined the table behind the firepit. I left to go back inside, and Patrona Sara followed me, stopping me at the back door.

"What do you think of our guests?" she whispered.

"They seem nice. Different," I said.

"Yes, different, for sure."

"Where is Sara, your wife?" I heard one of the guests ask.

Patrona Sara shrunk back toward the door at the mention of her name, pushing me back out of their view with her.

"She must be inside the house with the servant," Amo Abraham answered.

"I will surely return to you when the season comes 'round again, and your wife Sara will have a son," one of the guests said.

Patrona Sara grabbed onto me and pulled me inside the back door into the kitchen. She laughed as she closed the door behind her and leaned up against the door.

"Did you hear that?" Patrona Sara said through chuckles. "I was just diagnosed last week with early menopause, and that joker just said I'm going to have a child."

I backed away from her and shrugged. "I don't know. He seemed serious."

"Will I really have the pleasure of having a child of my own now that I am old, especially when my husband is recently circumcised?" she asked, plopping down onto the kitchen chair.

"Does the circumcision make it so he can't have a baby?"

"I'm not really sure how it works."

"I hope not, because Ignacio was circumcised too. I don't think Jehovah would tell you to circumcise him if he couldn't help you make your tribe like He wants for you."

"I don't know," Patrona Isa said, grabbing her apron after she rose from the kitchen chair. Her eyes darted to the doorway, always measuring appearances. "Let's get another platter of food to bring out to them so it looks like we've been doing something."

The oven dinged as she helped me slice another loaf of bread. I pulled out the finished loaves and added the last loaves of dough to the oven. After we sliced the bread and cheese, she carried it out to the table.

When Patrona Sara came into view with the platter in hand, the visitors looked over at her.

Addressing Amo Abe, one of them said, "Why did Sara laugh and say, 'Will I really have a child when I am old?'"

Patrona Sara froze in place. The color drained from her face. Her eyes met mine, and I shrunk into the background.

"Is anything impossible for Jehovah?" the visitor said. "I will return to you when the season comes 'round again, and Sara will have a son."

Patrona Sara shook her head back and forth, her face still pale. "I did not laugh."

I could see the platter of food trembling in her hands. She tried to set it down, and it clattered on the table as she steadied it.

"No! You did laugh," the visitor insisted.

His words carried across the patio, louder than the crickets singing in the grass. The air felt heavy and still, as if the wind had stopped to listen.

Sara kept her eyes on the platter, refusing to look up, while the scent of roasted meat lingered around us.

Chapter Twenty-Six

F our months later, I carried a platter with fried fish and wild rice into the dining room at dinnertime. Amo Abraham sat in his normal seat at the head of the table, Ignacio at his left and Patrona Sara at his right. I never ate with them now. Their family seemed complete, and I wasn't included. My dream of me, Amo Abraham, and my son eating dinner together never came true.

As I set the platter of food down, Patrona Sara's favorite meal, on the table, she covered her mouth with her hand and sprinted from the table down the hallway. I raised my eyebrows at Amo Abraham, and he shrugged, his forehead creasing as his eyes darted after her, lips parted like he wanted to ask why.

A couple minutes later, she peeked her head into the dining room from the hallway. "Hillary, can you please take the food away?"

"Is everything okay, honey?" Amo Abraham asked. "What's wrong?"

"Something about the smell..." She trailed off. "I can't take it."

"Honey, it's your favorite meal. I don't understand," Amo Abraham said.

"Nor do I, but I can't do it," she said, pinching her nose between her pointer and thumb.

"Do you want me to make something else?" I asked. I picked up the platter and carried it out of the dining room, looking over my shoulder for her response.

"No, it's late. Let's just go out to eat tonight. I need to get away from the smell," she said, crinkling her nose.

Amo Abraham and Ignacio rose from the table and joined her as she grabbed her purse and walked out the front door.

How bizarre. Patrona Sara never had any problems with this meal in the past. It reminded her of her childhood on the reservation. She asked for it at least once a week.

Well, I wasn't going to let it go to waste. I prepared myself a plate of wild rice with a fish fillet on top and put the leftovers away in the refrigerator. Alone, I sat at the kitchen table to eat.

***

The next day, I pulled into the driveway after doing the grocery shopping. Amo Abraham had left for work and Ignacio for school. I never knew what to expect from Patrona Sara while at work. She still played tennis, volunteered, and did other things outside of the house. Sometimes she stayed at home, and sometimes she didn't.

I pulled the groceries out of the back of the Range Rover, four bags in one hand and three in the other and lugged them up the front steps to the door. Setting them down on the porch, I checked the door to see if I needed my key. The door gave way, so I pushed it open and picked the grocery bags back up. As I carried them through the house toward the kitchen, I passed by a sleeping Patrona Sara on the living room couch.

Strange. In my twenty-four years of working for Patrona Sara, I never saw her sleeping outside of normal sleeping hours. Shrugging it off, I took the groceries into the kitchen to put them away and then got started deep cleaning the kitchen.

When the time came to clean the living room, I tiptoed around Patrona Sara as she slept on the couch. She stirred, stretching her arms over her head and yawning.

"You missed tennis, Señora," I said.

She shot up into a sitting position, looking at her watch. "Oh, no! What time is it?"

"It's already after noon."

"I slept the whole morning away," she groaned. "I don't know what's wrong with me. I'm just so tired, all the time."

"Maybe you're getting sick?"

"I hope not!"

"Isn't it flu season still?" I asked.

"Not really. It's February. Flu season should be behind us by now."

"I don't know then." I pulled the vacuum cleaner out of the hall closet. "Is it okay for me to vacuum?"

"Yes, of course. I'm getting up. I shouldn't have slept for so long." She yawned again.

"Ignacio has his roughstock clinic after school today. Do I need to take him, or are you going to do it?" I asked.

"I can take him today. That way you can have dinner ready when we get home." She stood. "I gotta pee." She headed to the restroom, mumbling under her breath about not being able to understand why she felt so tired.

After finishing the living room, I went out back to weed the raised vegetable beds that Patrona Sara made me put in when I was pregnant. The ranch sustained itself, and the vegetables we grew came in handy and made for some delicious meals. So did the cows, which I milked first thing in the morning and right before I left for the day. Raw milk and fresh cheese counted as definite benefits. And the bulls gave Ignacio plenty to practice on for his rodeos.

The breeze felt good, bringing in the smell of freshly cut grass and the herbal scent of new mesquite leaves. The air grew heavy, though, as I pulled the last weed from the bed. The afternoon thunder clouds stood like mountains on the horizon, threatening to splatter their big drops onto the parched land. Maybe Ignacio's clinic would be cancelled, or maybe they would finish before the first raindrops hit the earth. He should be at the arena by now.

Gathering my gardening tools, I headed back inside to make dinner. An hour later, I finished cooking, but no one had come home yet. Someone should have arrived by now.

Every bad possibility ran through my head. Did Ignacio get thrown too hard from a bucking bronco? Did he get trampled? Did he get charged by a bull? My heart raced at the thought. Why did we let him do such a dangerous sport?

I forced myself to slow down. He no longer belonged to me. For two blissful years, I had mothered him, nursed him, loved him. Now, he wasn't my responsibility, yet I still cared. The bond remained, though he didn't know I was his mother. To him, I was nothing more than the nanny. The household servant.

I paced back and forth in the living room, glancing out the window each time I got close to the front door. Where were they? My watch read 6:37 p.m. Most days they ate dinner no later than six o'clock. But it wasn't too late. Maybe they hit traffic. Maybe they got held up. Did Amo Abraham go to watch after he got off work? Did the roughstock instructors hold them back for some reason? Someone should have been here by now.

I slumped onto the couch, biting the skin around my fingernails. *It's fine. Everything is going to be fine.* But I couldn't dismiss the uneasy feeling that something was wrong.

My cell phone was in the RV, but I couldn't wait much longer before the cows needed milking. I set the food on a heating pad to keep it warm and put my boots on to head out to the pasture. The rain had come and gone, and the smell of wet soil and wildflowers filled the evening air. Some of the cows lined up near the barn, but I still needed to round up the others. I trudged through the muddy field.

"Cooome on, girls! Come on in!" I called to the cows, but my voice sounded softer than usual.

They started coming in but slowed down. Maybe they could sense my distraction.

I leaned on a fence post, looking out toward the road for any sign of either Amo Abraham's or Patrona Sara's car, but still didn't see them.

I whistled at the cows.

Did Patrona Sara say she would be late? Did I forget about some reason she might be late? No. I remembered her saying she would take Ignacio so I could get dinner ready. There should be no reason they weren't back by now. I sighed.

Once I gathered all the cows and got them in line, I prepared the first one for the milking machine. The machine hummed as the milk pulsed through. I left every few minutes and looked out the barn door to see if anyone arrived home, but no one did.

By the time I returned from milking the cows, the clock read eight o'clock. Still, no one was home. I walked to my RV to get my cell phone and dialed Amo Abraham's number.

"Hello?"

"Amo Abraham, where are you?"

"I'm at the hospital with Sara and Ignacio."

"What happened?" My heart started racing.

"Everything is fine. They were in a car accident on the way home from roughstock practice, but they okay. The doctors wanted to check them out anyway."

"Phew."

"The car is pretty messed up, so I'm bringing them home."

"I was so worried that something happened to Ignacio during the roughstock clinic. I could barely function milking the cows this evening."

"The accident happened afterwards on their way home."

"I feel a little better now. Thanks for letting me know," I said. "And you're sure everyone is okay?"

"Yes. We'll be home as soon as we can. You know how slow hospitals are."

***

After a sleepless night, I walked in through the back door to see Ignacio eating cereal at the kitchen table.

"Mijo," I said, dashing over to give him a hug. "I was so worried when I heard about the car accident."

"Yeah, it was low-key scary, but we're good," he said, half returning my hug with one hand.

"I'm so happy you're okay," I said.

"Have you heard about Mom?" he asked.

"No, what happened? Is she not okay?"

"Bruh, she's preggo," he said.

"What's 'preggo?'" I asked.

"She's literally pregnant."

"What?" I asked. I backed up and put my hands over my open mouth.

Pregnant? Like the visitor from four months ago said would happen. After all these years, all the failed fertility treatments, the waiting. After forcing me to have her child for her, the child sitting right there in front of me, she was pregnant. Could this be?

"Looks like I'm leveling up to big brother status," he said, spoon hovering above the milk, his grin tugging at the corners of his mouth. "I'm hoping I'm not stuck on baby duty." Then he studied me. "But like...that's kinda your job, right?"

I stood, still speechless at this new information. I nodded but couldn't respond. Ignacio went back to his cereal.

I floated into the living room to see if I could find Patrona Sara and confirm what Ignacio had told me. She wasn't around.

Ignacio came into the living room, grabbed his backpack, and headed out the front door to go to the bus. "Catch ya later," he said over his shoulder before the door slammed shut.

My head swirled with thoughts. What had the visitors said? I racked my brain to remember. Something like, "I will surely return to you when the season comes 'round again, and Sara will have a son." Señora Sara just turned forty, young for menopause, but old to have a baby.

Could she be carrying a child? Would Patrona Sara have a son of her own?

Patrona Sara emerged from the hallway, glowing. "Hillary, did you hear the news?"

"Yes, ma'am. Ignacio told me." I sank back onto the sofa, the stiff fabric scratching the backs of my legs, while her smile seemed to brighten the whole room. "How did it happen?"

"They thought I had cracked a rib in the accident and were going to give me an X-ray. They asked if I was pregnant, to which I laughed and told them, 'I doubt it,' but they wouldn't proceed without confirmation. They did a urine pregnancy test, and it was positive," she said, beaming from ear to ear.

"That's so wonderful. You've been trying for so long," I said, trying to be happy for her.

"Yeah, finally, when I turn forty. It's going to be a geriatric pregnancy. I feel so old saying that," she said, laughing. Then grasped her side, drawing her breath in. "Ouch. I did actually crack a rib. I'm going to get some ice." She strolled past me and into the kitchen.

Anger boiled up inside me. She was pregnant. She hadn't needed to force me into bed with Amo Abraham after all. The pain. The trauma. The past I left behind coming back to haunt me. It was all for nothing. My son knew me as nothing more than the nanny. Patrona Sara enjoyed all of Ignacio growing up, and now she got to do that again with this new baby.

I drew in a deep breath and released it. It didn't matter. The past was the past, and I could do nothing to change it.

CHAPTER TWENTY-SEVEN

Patrona Sara busied herself with preparations for the baby. I became the taxi for Ignacio's rodeo and archery practices, which meant I prepped dinner ahead of time so it would be easy to heat up once we got home.

But it also allowed me to spend more time with Ignacio. He acted like a typical teenage boy who didn't talk much to adults and kept his nose in his cell phone. I tried, often unsuccessfully, to carry on conversations.

"How was school today?" I asked one day as I drove him home from school after archery practice.

"Fine."

"Anything exciting happen?"

"No."

"Did you have any tests or quizzes?"

"Yeah."

"How did they go?"

"Fine."

"How are your grades?"

"Fine."

"Are you interested in any girls at school?"

This question made him pause and look up from his phone, a blank look on his tan face. He shrugged, then went back to his phone.

I kept peppering him with questions and getting one-word answers the entire way home. I would try again tomorrow. He had no interest in engaging with me, despite my obvious attempts.

Once I got home, I prioritized dinner and milking the cows. I left Ignacio in the living room and went to the kitchen to heat up dinner. Casseroles and slow-cooker meals dominated our menu since I spent the usual dinner-prep hours taking Ignacio places. Sometimes Patrona Sara would cook, but most of the time she read *What to Expect When You're Expecting* or picked out paint colors and accessories for the baby's nursery.

After milking the cows, I went back into the house and found Patrona Sara sitting in the nursery floor organizing baby clothes, her legs crossed around her swollen belly.

"Do you get anything more than one-word answers from Ignacio?" I asked.

She looked up from the pile of clothes and shook her head. "He's a teenage boy. I don't get much more from him than the bare minimum."

"It's so frustrating. This year is my first time engaging with him since before kindergarten, and his face is in that phone all the time," I said, throwing my hands in the air.

"We probably shouldn't have given the phone to him, but 'everyone else had one,'" she said, mimicking his voice.

"It's good to know I'm not the only one he acts like that to."

Patrona Sara let out a burst of laughter. "You're definitely not."

***

I tried again the next day after I picked Ignacio up from school to take him to his bareback bronc-riding lesson.

"What's been the best part of your week so far?" I asked.

"I'm goated at archery. Nailed some bullseyes yesterday," he said, not looking up from his phone.

Nine words marked progress, and I cherished my minor win. "Goated?"

"Yeah, greatest of all time. I nailed it."

"Do you have any competitions coming up?" I asked. "I'd love to see you compete."

"We start competing in a few weeks."

"Well, maybe I'll get a chance to see you. I hope so."

He shrugged, still staring at his phone, thumbs flying over the keypad.

"How are things going with your friends?" I tried next.

"Good."

Back to square one. "Who's your best friend these days?"

"Oliver."

Strike two. I needed to think of a question that would require more than one word. "What do you and Oliver do for fun?"

"He does bareback with me. And sometimes we play video games."

We pulled into the small gravel parking lot of the practice arena behind one of the ranches outside of town. A few rusty pick-up trucks lined the fence around the arena, their tailgates facing the fence. Lawn chairs sat between them with several nervous women leaning forward to see the action. A country song blasted from a speaker in one of the trucks. A musty smell of sweat mixed with horse manure hung in the air along with the dust kicked up by the hooves of the horses.

"You got your chaps and glove?" I asked.

He nodded toward his backpack and headed toward the arena entrance. He reached another boy that looked about his age and did some sort of special handshake.

I opened the back of the Range Rover and sat on the tailgate to watch. Teens of all ages mulled around inside the arena, waiting for practice to begin. Some looked like seniors, strong as the broncos. Others looked smaller and baby-faced, like Ignacio, who hadn't yet hit his growth spurt.

The head coach limped into the arena and called them all together. He led them to the fifty-five-gallon plastic barrel mounted on springs for their groundwork where each boy got a few turns with the drills.

After adjusting Ignacio's handhold on the rigging, one of the pick-up riders pulled the barrel back and let it go.

"Don't lean back too soon," the coach corrected Ignacio. "Toes turned out, spurs above the shoulder."

I wasn't sure where the "shoulder" sat on the barrel, but Ignacio seemed to understand, and he corrected himself.

The coach made the older boys demonstrate how to bail, and the younger ones copied their technique until the coach appeared satisfied. Soon the time came for chute work. The older, more experienced boys went first, taking turns on the two bucking broncos. The younger boys watched, pacing and swinging their arms as if they tried shaking off their nerves. When the third boy made it the full eight seconds, everyone cheered and hollered.

Ignacio made it four seconds before he bailed, and they were the longest four seconds of my life. I wasn't sure how rodeo moms did it.

I shook and sweat as I watched, turning away most of the time, teeth clenched and peeking through my arm. As soon as he hit the ground, I flinched.

Maybe he should stick with archery. It seemed a lot safer than this.

"He made it halfway!" a mom sitting in a lawn chair near my car yelled in my direction. She threw me a thumbs up.

My face formed into a half-smile, and I sent her an unenthusiastic thumbs up back. I didn't fit the rodeo life. I vowed to beg Patrona Sara to drive him next time, though I doubted she would. She now owned a new car but hesitated to take it to the arena. I didn't blame her.

At the end of practice, a sweaty, dusty Ignacio climbed into the car, tossing his backpack in the back seat. A puff of dust floated into the air as it landed. I coughed.

"Careful, nene. You'll get the car all dirty," I said.

"Ha. Hard to prevent that in this sport," he said, stretching his arms above his head and moving his upper body back and forth.

"Looks like you might have some bruises, or at least some sore muscles after that practice," I said, eyes wide. "This is the first time I've seen it. It looks pretty scary up there."

"Yeah, a little," he said, scratching the back of his head, dirt falling to the seat around him. "But the adrenaline rush is outta this world."

I shook my head as I started the car and bumped over the gravel driveway onto the road. "I guess it's going to take some getting used to, watching you up there like that. You ever have any friends get seriously hurt bailing?"

"Nah. I mean, we all get banged up a little, but nothing serious."

"One of the other moms was pretty impressed that you lasted four seconds. I guess that's good for someone your age?"

"That's actually solid for my age, not gonna lie. Oliver only lasted three."

"Good job then, mijo. I'm proud of you," I said, smiling. I managed to draw a full conversation out of him.

"Thanks, Miss Hillary."

***

When I finished dinner, I brought it out to the dining table. Amo Abraham and Patrona Sara sat at their places at the table. Ignacio was missing.

"I think he's in his room doing homework," Patrona Sara said. "Can you go tell him dinner's ready?"

"Yes," I said, nodding.

I headed down the hall to his bedroom. His door stood closed, but I opened it without knocking. He faced the computer, his back to me. The screen displayed a scene clearly unrelated to his homework.

I gasped. My hand flew to my open mouth. I backed out of the room into the hallway, still staring at the screen. My whole body started trembling.

The scene looked all too familiar to me. The four-poster mahogany wood bed. The cream Egyptian cotton comforter with the gold embroidery. The girl, not much younger than Ignacio, naked, staring into the camera. I could see the fear peeking out from behind her blank expression. She didn't want to be there. She was being groomed, forced. For the duration of her adolescent life, she would be nothing more than a sex slave.

A wave of nausea hit me, and I grabbed my stomach with my other hand. Memories from a quarter of a century ago came flooding back. The life I tried to bury deep inside came rushing at me like a raging river.

How did Ignacio find the videos? Did he watch videos of me? Or did they show new girls? I shivered. How many girls had they exploited? Were still being exploited even today?

Anger rose inside me. I could feel the heat on my cheeks. My trembling from the memories became rage. I balled my fists up, looking for something to throw at the computer screen.

Ignacio hadn't heard me open the door. He hadn't heard me gasp. He was too engrossed in the video to hear his surroundings. He didn't notice me picking up the half-drunk water bottle from the top of the bookshelf and throw it at the computer screen.

It whizzed past his ear, and he jumped backwards. The chair tilted back and dumped him on his back onto the floor.

He looked horrified—his eyes wide, face flushed red, jaw hanging open as if he didn't know what to say. Maybe for getting caught watching something he shouldn't have been watching. Maybe because I scared him when I chucked the water bottle at the screen. Maybe a combination of both.

"What are you doing?" I growled through clenched teeth.

Ignacio scrambled to his feet and stepped in front of the computer screen to hide it. "I...I..." he stammered, backing up so his butt grazed the desk. The button and zipper of his pants hung undone, and he yanked the zipper closed.

"Please don't tell Mom or Dad," Ignacio begged. He reached behind him and shut the laptop without taking his eyes off me.

"Why? Why would you do that?" I asked, pain in my voice.

I hurt for the girls whose lives would forever be changed by that terrible cartel. They looked so young. So innocent. So clueless about what was happening to them, how the life had changed them, desensitizing them to what they were doing.

"I don't know," Ignacio stammered. "Oliver showed it to me. I guess his father watches it too."

"Oliver is not a good friend then," I snarled.

He was taken aback by my reaction. "Why is it such a big deal?"

My eyes narrowed, and my temper flared. "Do you have no consideration for the feelings of others? For the lives of others?" I spat at him. "I know what that girl is feeling behind that fake smile."

I wanted to say more. I wanted to tell him that I had been that girl. That I fought my way out. I wanted to tell him how it changed my life forever. How it still left me broken because of it. How could I make him understand?

I took a deep breath and sighed. "Let's talk later, nene. Come see me in the RV tonight. Dinner is ready."

He nodded. He searched my expression, seeming to find something that surprised him. His cheeks still wore the pink of embarrassment as he left his room and headed to the dining room.

I left the house and headed to the field to round up the cows for the evening milking. So many thoughts ran through my head as I herded them in line and sat to hook up the first cow. A tear escaped the corner of my eye, and I didn't bother wiping it away.

I hated feeling like a victim—weak, helpless, vulnerable. I wanted to feel strong, like a survivor. But seeing that little girl on the same bed I used nearly twenty-five years ago brought back so much pain. I felt transported back to that moment, back to that house.

How could my son have fallen into the temptation of looking at videos like that? Why were so many men tempted to watch that material?

If it weren't for them, the cartel wouldn't have anyone to sell their porn to. If it wasn't a money-maker, they would have no reason to kidnap girls and force them into that type of lifestyle.

I felt defeated. I tried to lock the memories away for ten years. Then Patrona Sara forced me to be with Amo Abraham, and I relived my past all over again. Now, thirteen years later, I must face it another time. Could I ever get away from it and live my life like a normal person?

I finished milking the cows and headed back home, wondering if Ignacio would come see me. I dreaded having a conversation with him. This should be a talk his dad or mom had with him. But as his biological mother, whether he knew it or not, I felt some responsibility to help him, particularly with this topic.

To my surprise, Ignacio was waiting on the steps of my RV when I returned from the barn. I took off my boots at the entrance, and he did the same. I motioned to the couch for him to sit. He took a seat, farthest away from the entrance, and looked down at his hands. For once, his phone wasn't in them.

"Thank you for coming, Ignacio," I said. He still looked embarrassed. "You were brave to come here, after what I saw earlier."

He nodded and looked into my eyes as I sat beside him.

I sighed, trying to collect my thoughts and say the right thing. "I probably shouldn't have this conversation with you. It should be your dad or mom—"

He cut me off, jerking his head in a hard no. "No! They can't know about this."

I sighed again. "You're growing up now, and I know it is normal to feel curious about sex and about bodies. That's okay. But there is something I need you to understand about porn."

He looked down at his hands again, wringing them in his lap. His cheeks pinked at the word "porn."

"Porn is not real. It doesn't show real love or real relationships. It is made to get our attention and make money. And the people who make the money are very bad people."

He looked up at me with slight interest.

"The way it shows sex is fake," I said. "And it's very disrespectful, especially to women. Most of those girls in porn...they don't want to be there. Some of them are pushed to do it, forced to do it. It is not something they do because it makes them happy. Many feel like they have no choice."

Ignacio tilted his head, as if he was thinking about what I said. He was listening.

I continued, "Maybe Oliver or his dad say something different. But I know your mom and dad want you to grow up to be someone good. Someone who respects others, especially women. Real love means trust, respect, and care. Porn does not teach that."

What did I know about real love? Was I capable of teaching this boy, my son, about love when I didn't know the first thing about it?

I sighed again. I was sighing a lot today. "I know this world is very difficult and full of a lot of temptations. If you ever want to talk about anything, and you don't feel you can talk to your mom or dad, you can always talk to me. You will not get in trouble. We can talk about anything, okay?"

Ignacio nodded. He looked down at his hands, and then he looked up into my eyes. "Thanks, Miss Hillary. Look...I'm sorry about earlier.

You won't tell Dad or Mom, will you?" He gave me the most pathetic look I had ever seen on him.

"No, mijo. This is between you and me. Just please, don't do it again," I pleaded.

He stood, and I stood with him. He gave me a quick hug. I wanted so much to hold on longer, to impress in him how much he hurt me through those actions.

But it wasn't my place to do so. This conversation should have been between him and Amo Abe. I would not say a word, as long as I didn't see it again.

CHAPTER TWENTY-EIGHT

I gnacio entered high school. In two months, he would turn fourteen. He already hit his first growth spurt and stood as tall as me. He started to look more like a man.

Patrona Sara went into labor overnight in early October, but I didn't find out until later that day. When I walked into the house after milking the cows, silence greeted me. Ignacio had already left for school, and I assumed Amo Abraham left for work. Patrona Sara was nowhere to be found. I busied myself with cleaning the bathrooms and bedrooms like I did every Monday.

I picked Ignacio up from the high school after archery practice.

"Is there a baby yet?" Ignacio asked as he climbed into the Range Rover.

"Huh? I haven't seen your mom all day."

"Yeah, they went to the hospital this morning. Before I went to school."

"No wonder I hadn't seen her," I said. "She's usually around at least part of the day. No one told me."

"I'll text Dad." His thumbs flew over the keypad of his phone. After a few minutes, he said, "She still hasn't had it yet."

"It might be just you and me tonight then," I said.

When we got back to the house, we still hadn't heard from them. I decided to make gallo pinto with carne asada, a Nicaraguan classic. If the night belonged to the two of us, I could imagine being back home with him as my son.

When I finished dinner, I peeked my head into Ignacio's room and let out a thankful sigh. No porn filled his computer screen today. Maybe he listened to me.

"Time for dinner, mijo," I said.

As we ate, I couldn't help but remember the good times back home. Papá never made enough money for carne asada, but gallo pinto served as an almost daily meal. Before he got sick, he would bring home beans and rice from the market after work. I would help Mamá soak the red beans in the well water I brought from the village. She soaked them overnight and rinsed them and some long-grain white rice in more water the next day. In the afternoon, she cooked the rice in one pot and the beans in another pot over the hot coals in the backyard firepit. The smoky taste from the open fire made it unforgettable.

This gallo pinto didn't have the smoky taste of a backyard firepit, but it still tasted good.

"This was what I ate nearly every day when I was a little girl," I told Ignacio as he scooped food onto his plate.

"Where are you from again?" he asked.

"Nicaragua. I lived there until I was nine," I said, hoping he wouldn't ask too many probing questions about after that time.

"What is it like there?"

I smiled and stared into the distance as I remembered the good times with Papá and Mamá. "Well, we lived in a very small house."

I looked around the dining room. "It wasn't much bigger than this room...maybe a little bigger."

His eyes grew wide as if he couldn't imagine living in such a cramped space.

"The village was small too. All the houses were in a circle around our well. We didn't have running water, like a sink or shower or toilet. Once I was old enough to carry it, I had to go to the well each morning and fetch water for the day."

"How did you use the restroom?" he asked, still amazed at the simple life I lived.

"There were holes in the ground in the backyards, kind of near the tree line."

He crinkled his nose and gave me a disgusted look.

"Things were different there. That's for sure," I said.

"Did you like living there?" he said, displeasure still dripping from his words.

"It was a simple life, yes, but it was a good life. I loved my papá and mamá very much. They took good care of me when they could."

"What did you do, like, for fun?" he asked.

I enjoyed the interest he was taking in what he thought was a terrible life. I never thought of it that way.

"We played fútbol, or soccer as we call it here in Texas. We swam in the river. We climbed trees."

"The trees near where you pooped?" he asked and laughed.

His joking stung, but I could see how a teenager would think it funny.

"Further in the forest, not right at the tree line," I assured him.

His phone rang, interrupting our conversation. He answered it. "Hello? Oh, great! I'll tell Miss Hillary... See you soon... Love you."

He set the phone down and turned to me. His wide smile reached his eyes, like Amo Abraham's did when genuine happiness lit his face. "They had the baby. It's a boy. They said we can come visit in the hospital."

"Okay. Perfect timing," I said as I finished the last bite of my food. I stood to clear the dishes, but Ignacio held his hand up.

"I've got this. You go milk the cows so we can leave as soon as you're finished," he said.

His awareness of my chores and willingness to help out surprised me. He must be eager to see his baby brother.

I smiled and nodded at him. "Thank you, Ignacio. That's very responsible of you."

I left him to clean up the leftovers and dishes and went to herd up the cows. Most of them already stood near the barn, ready to be milked. I gathered the couple stragglers and hurried through to get the milking finished. Even on a quick day, it could take an hour to get them all milked.

When I returned, the leftovers were put away and the dishes were rinsed and put next to the sink. It wasn't the way I would have done it, unfinished, but it was good enough for now. I found Ignacio sitting in the living room, eyes in his phone, thumbs flying over the little keypad.

"You ready to go?" I asked.

He nodded and jumped up from the couch with a smile.

We walked out the front door and climbed into the Range Rover.

"Are you excited about being a big brother?" I asked.

"I'm not even sure how I feel," he admitted. "I mean, ever since Mom got pregnant, she's barely talked to me. It's been all about the baby."

I nodded in sympathy. He wasn't wrong.

"I mean, like, you've been more of a mom to me than Mom has," he observed, fiddling with the strap of his seatbelt and not looking my way. "She didn't come to my archery competition because she was at a doctor's appointment. She didn't come to my rodeo because she was too busy putting the nursery together. She never picks me up anymore from anything. You do all that."

"Your mother loves you, Ignacio. You know that, right?" I tried to cover for Patrona Sara, but Ignacio was right. Ever since she became pregnant with her own child, the child she had raised as her own for eleven years seemed to take second place. As if he didn't matter anymore.

It didn't make any sense to me. She wanted to start a tribe. That was what both she and Amo Abraham had been saying since the beginning. That was what their god told them to do. It was why she forced me to give her a child. But a tribe took a lot more than one son to make. Two sons would make the tribe bigger faster. Why did she seem to be rejecting Ignacio in favor of the new baby?

Ignacio seemed excited about the baby coming at dinner, but now it seemed like he resented it. "Yeah, I guess."

"What about your dad? He's still been taking you on hunting and fishing trips on the weekends, right?"

"Yeah, actually more of them, so that's been nice. I guess there are ups and downs to having a baby around. I just hope I don't have to change any diapers."

I laughed. "Well, that's what I'm here for. I changed almost all of your diapers when you were a baby."

"Mom didn't do that?"

"No, I slept in the room with you and took care of you in the middle of the night," I said. "It was part of my job at the time."

My mind wandered back to those early years before he weaned. Waking up to his cry. Picking him up from the crib and inhaling his baby powder smell. Holding him to my breast to feed him, his tiny hand curling around my finger. Seeing his smile when he felt full. Feeling his tiny body against my shoulder when I burped him. And then changing him before swaddling him and putting him back down to sleep. It seemed like a lifetime ago, but the memories still remained.

"Are you going to do that for this baby?" Ignacio asked.

"I don't know what your mother wants me to do for this one. That's up to her."

He huffed.

We drove the rest of the way in silence. When we arrived at the hospital, I parked, and we walked in. The sterile hospital smell hit me as we walked through the door. The last time I came here, I gave birth to Ignacio, and the memories flooded back. Ignacio was now as tall as me and nearly a man. How did the years rush by? I felt grateful to still be a part of his life...even if he didn't know who I really was.

We made our way to the maternity ward. As we were finding the Serugs' room with the help of Ignacio's text messages with Amo Abraham, a man walked by, his face shining like the son.

"Wait, was that one of the visitors we had last year?" Ignacio asked, peering over his shoulder at the man disappearing into the elevator.

"Yes! I think it was," I said, eyes wide.

As we reached Patrona Sara's room, I remembered what the visitor had said, that he would return in a year and Patrona Sara would have a son. He had kept his promise.

The hospital room was small, but private. Patrona Sara sat up in the hospital bed cradling the new baby. Amo Abraham sat beside her in a chair, his eyes fixed on his new boy. He looked up when we arrived and smiled.

"Ignacio, meet your baby brother, Isaac," Amo Abraham said with pride in his voice. He drew the baby out of Patrona Sara's arms and brought it over to the couch where Ignacio had sat. He placed the baby into Ignacio's waiting arms.

"Hi, baby Isaac," Ignacio cooed. Then he looked up at Amo Abraham. "Why is he so red?"

Patrona Sara's eyes narrowed, and a scowl came over her face.

Amo Abraham didn't notice. "Most babies are red-faced and blotchy when they're first born. It will go away with time."

Ignacio took the explanation. He put his finger inside the baby's hand, and Isaac grasped onto it. Ignacio looked up and smiled. "I think he likes me."

He looked back down at his baby brother and wiggled Isaac's arm around, a tiny hand still grasping Ignacio's finger.

"He's so small," Ignacio said with awe. "I could break him in half with my bare hands."

"Don't you even say that," Patrona Sara growled at him.

"I didn't mean it like that. I just meant that he's so small." He stopped when he saw his mother's angry face. His eyes widened. "I would never," he insisted, looking right into her eyes.

Her face softened, and she nodded.

"Your mother's a little emotional right now, Ignacio," Amo Abraham said. Patrona Sara glared at him. "That's normal during pregnancy and while a new mother is nursing. Let's not say anything to upset her, okay?"

Ignacio nodded and turned his attention back to Isaac. "His nose is so tiny," he said, touching his finger to the tip of the baby's nose.

"Don't touch his face!" Patrona Sara yelled.

Ignacio jumped at her stern tone and jerked his hand backward. "Um, maybe I shouldn't touch him at all," he said, standing up and handing Isaac back to Amo Abraham.

"Maybe you shouldn't," Patrona Sara said.

"I'm ready to go now, Miss Hillary," Ignacio said.

I nodded and led the way out the door. Amo Abraham followed.

"Buddy," Amo Abraham said to Ignacio. "Sorry about your mother. I can't explain it all, but I can explain her last statement. When babies are first born, their immune system is very weak. She didn't want you to give your brother any germs from your hands through his nose or mouth. Does that make sense?"

"Sure, Dad, whatever."

"Sorry, son. She's a little on edge. Maybe I can take you hunting this weekend. Get us both out of the house for a bit. What do you say?"

Ignacio's face lit up. He smiled at his dad. "Bow hunting?"

"Absolutely."

"Okay."

"I love you, buddy."

"Love you, Dad."

"We should be back home no later than tomorrow evening," Amo Abraham said to me.

I nodded.

Once we moved out of earshot and nearly out of the hospital, Ignacio said, "Wow! Mom has gone crazy with this new baby."

"She definitely has the new mother hormones," I muttered. My jaw tightened, fists clenched as we pushed through the sliding doors.

How could she forget the son she already had?

CHAPTER TWENTY-NINE

Patrona Sara didn't want any help from me for the new baby, so I kept doing my regular work. She spent all her time with Isaac and all but ignored Ignacio.

"Jehovah has made me laugh," Patrona Sara as she bounced baby Isaac on her knee. He giggled with glee. "Everyone who hears my story will laugh with me. Who would have said to Abraham that Sara would nurse children? Yet after all the fertility treatments failed, I have given birth to a son for him."

I gasped, wondering if Ignacio would know what she meant by this. Patrona Sara didn't seem to care.

"I can pretty much do whatever I want now. Mom doesn't pay any attention to me," Ignacio said in the car on the way home from his bareback bronc lesson one day.

"But you're getting a lot of time with your dad," I said, trying to look on the bright side.

Amo Abraham took Ignacio camping, hiking, fishing, hunting, or to a rodeo every weekend.

"True. At least someone still loves me."

Ouch. Did Patrona Sara know what her actions did to Ignacio? Did she even care?

"I'm sure your mother still loves you too, Ignacio," I said. If nothing else, his real mother loved him. If only he knew.

Ignacio did what he could to impress his mother. He kept his grades up. He won his next archery contest. He even changed a few diapers. But Patrona Sara paid no attention to the son she had mothered for the past fourteen years.

I could feel the tension in the house growing. Ignacio resented Isaac. His feelings might have even bordered on hatred. When he was old enough for solid food, Isaac sat in a high chair at Patrona Sara's right hand at dinners. She made all his baby food and fed him while everyone else ate the food I made.

One night, while I made dinner in the kitchen, Ignacio stared at his phone in the living room, and Isaac toddled around. Patrona Sara had left the room for something, leaving the boys by themselves. I heard Isaac crying and peeked my head into the room. He had fallen on the floor, as toddlers often did.

"You better be quiet, or the monsters are going to come eat you," Ignacio hissed at him as Patrona Sara walked back in the room.

Isaac cried even louder, now scared of the monsters.

"Ignacio!" Patrona Sara scolded. "Why would you try to scare the baby?"

When she picked Isaac up and coddled him, Ignacio rolled his eyes and continued playing on his phone.

Another day at dinner, Isaac was in a playful mood. Patrona Sara fed him carrots and blueberries. The rest of the family ate roast venison from the deer Amo Abraham and Ignacio brought home from their last hunting trip. Isaac flapped his hands around as Patrona Sara fed him. He smacked too hard, causing the spoon with the blueberries to fly across the table and hit Ignacio right in the chest.

Ignacio jumped up from his chair, looking down at the blueberry stain on his favorite shirt. "You stupid baby! No one actually wants you around, you little brat!"

When I heard the scraping of the chair legs on the floor, I ran into the room.

"Ignacio!" Patrona Sara reprimanded. She looked at Amo Abe. "Do something. He can't talk to Isaac like that."

Amo Abraham sighed. "Ignacio, that was not kind."

"He just ruined my favorite shirt!" Ignacio countered.

"We can get it out, can't we?" Amo Abraham said. He looked at Patrona Sara.

" Yes, let me see what I can do." I motioned for him to take off his shirt. He did and handed it to me. I could see the irritation on his face. I took the shirt into the kitchen to run cold water through it and work the stain out.

By Isaac's second birthday, he no longer nursed. Patrona Sara and Amo Abraham planned a huge celebration, inviting everyone they knew. All of Amo Abe's co-workers, the families the Serugs met from town, and Patrona Sara's mommy group all planned to come. Even Patrona Sara's family from Minnesota also planned to be in town for the celebration. We expected at least a hundred guests, for a two-year-old's birthday party.

Ignacio never had a party that big for any of his birthdays. He would soon turn sixteen, and they didn't plan to have a party for him. Sixteen should feel like a much bigger deal than two. The Serugs hadn't thrown an extravagant celebration when Ignacio weaned. The whole party felt like overkill, but what did I know?

Patrona Sara handled the theme, decorations, and party favors. She gave me recipes from Pinterest and told me what to make. I played my part by keeping the house spotless and preparing the food exactly as she wanted it.

We repurposed the powwow arena to a party area for the weekend. Tents circled the area with tables and chairs beneath them. A large section remained open for dancing, and a live band set up alongside it. The drummers who played at the powwow would also be present to entertain.

A special tent covered the food tables. Cupcakes were stacked high on cupcake stands. A red, green, and blue fruit platter sat next to a giant vegetable plate in the shape of a number two. Cheesy queso and bean dip filled a fancy bowl with a matching bowl of chips for dipping. Venison jerky and cornbread covered other fancy platters next to a bowl of wild rice. A charcuterie board offered cheeses and meats, with a platter beside it with deli roll-ups in the shape of flowers.

And that only covered the appetizers. Amo Abraham manned the grill for the main course. He lined up his beside several others borrowed from his co-workers near the entrance to the food tent. The smell of venison filled the air.

The mild October weather greeted the guests as the party started. Wrapped gift boxes were piled up on a table near the entrance in a mound taller than the guest of honor. I sat at a table near the grills, ready to help if Amo Abraham needed me.

"Does he really need all these gifts?" Ignacio asked, rolling his eyes. He sat near the edge of the tent, a table away with Levi, one of Amo Abraham's co-workers' children who was nearly thirty years old now. He glared at Isaac with jealousy. "Did I get a party like this when I turned two?""Not that I can remember," Levi responded. "I've never seen anything like this."

The drummers circled the grandfather drum and started playing. People got up and danced. Isaac ran to the center of the dance floor and tried mimicking the dancers.

"Look at him, always the center of attention," Ignacio grumbled.

"Well, it *is* his party," Levi reasoned.

"But he's so annoying! So clumsy," Ignacio said as Isaac fell over for the third time.

"He's two," Levi said. "You can't expect him to have perfect coordination."

"I can't stand that baby. I hope they send him away or something," Ignacio spat.

As he spoke, Patrona Sara walked past the table and heard him.

"What did you just say?" she asked.

Ignacio stood from his chair and looked right at his mother. "I said, 'I can't stand that baby, and I hope you send him away or something,'" he said through clenched teeth.

"Maybe I'll send *you* away, and then you won't have to worry about him," she said back to him, jaw tight. She gave him an evil look and stomped away.

I couldn't believe what I heard. Did she really say that to him? She wouldn't do something like that! I watched her as she strutted to the dance floor and picked Isaac up, nuzzling him in her neck. He wiggled, and she put him down. He went on dancing, shaking his butt and trying to move like the other dancers who loved every minute of his cute movements.

Seeing Isaac remained in good hands, she walked toward Amo Abraham, who grilled the meat. He looked up at her approach and smiled. But when he saw the look on her face, his face fell.

"Get rid of that servant woman and her son. Send them away," she demanded when she reached him.

"What are you talking about, honey?" Amo Abraham said.

She huffed and paced next to him, looking at the ground. "He was mocking Isaac. He's been doing this constantly. Being mean, teasing him, scaring him. I can't stand it any longer."

"Sara, calm down. We can't just send them away. He's my son."

"The son of that woman will not be an heir along with *my* son, Isaac."

"They're both my sons, Sara. You're overreacting. Let's talk through this later."

"You don't even care about me, do you?"

"Don't turn this around to be about you. This is my son you're talking about," Amo Abraham snapped. "It's the middle of the party. Let's talk about this later."

"Fine." She turned on her heels and stormed off.

Amo Abraham closed his eyes and tilted his head toward the sky. He took a deep breath and let it out in a long sigh. He gave a slow shake of his head and went back to cooking.

I faded into the background, trying not to be seen. She meant it. She planned to send Ignacio away. But she wouldn't send him away alone. She intended to send me away too.

How would that even work? Ignacio didn't know who his real birth mother was. Surely Amo Abraham would set her straight. Surely, he wouldn't let her send us away.

***

The next morning, I came to the house to finish cleaning up after the party. It was Saturday, and Amo Abraham, Patrona Sara, Ignacio, and Isaac were sitting in the living room. Isaac played with his toys on the floor. Ignacio sat in the chair tapping on his phone, and Amo Abraham and Patrona Sara relaxed on the couch.

"Hillary, please come in," Amo Abraham said. "We all need to talk."

He waved at the empty chair. I sat.

"Ignacio, put the phone down. There's something I need to tell you," Amo Abraham said. "Something we've kept from you."

Ignacio looked at his father with raised eyebrows.

I stiffened, knowing what was coming. My palms began to sweat, and I wrung them in my lap. I could feel the heat in my face.

"Mom..." Amo Abraham looked at Patrona Sara then back at Ignacio. "Isn't your biological mother."

Ignacio's eyebrows came together in confusion. His eyes clouded. He tilted his head and looked at Amo Abraham, waiting for more.

"Mom wasn't able to have children, so Miss Hillary helped us and had you with me. Miss Hillary is your biological mother."

I swallowed the lump in my throat and peeked up at Ignacio to see his reaction.

His mouth dropped open, and he met my eyes. "Miss Hillary is my mother?" "This can't be real." He put his face in his hands, propping his elbows on his knees.

"Yes. I'm sorry, son," Amo Abraham said. "It wasn't right for us to keep this so long from you."

Patrona Sara hadn't said a word yet, but she kept a smug look on her face.

"Yesterday, Mom...er...Sara...was pretty upset about what you said about sending Isaac away," Amo Abraham said. "She came to me demanding that I send you away."

"I was pissed. He gets all the attention. You used to love me," he said, waving his finger at Patrona Sara. "You used to care about me. Then this thing comes around"—he pointed at Isaac—"and you've barely so much as looked in my direction. How do you think that makes me feel?" Tears filled his eyes and spilled down his cheeks.

"Well, it won't matter after today anyway," Patrona Sara said.

Amo Abraham put his hand out to quiet her. "Let me handle this, please. Don't make it harder than it already is." He turned his attention back to Ignacio. "I know, son. It hasn't been easy for you. I've tried to pay as much attention to you as I can to make up for it."

Ignacio wiped at the tears and sniffled.

Amo Abraham's eyes teared up now too. "I love you, very much. You're my son. I'm your biological father. Nothing will ever change that."

His voice caught in his throat. Tears flowed down his cheeks, and he took a deep breath.

"Jehovah came to me in a dream last night and told me to let you go. To do as Sara requested," Amo Abraham said. Then he lost it. He sobbed into his hands. He stood and pulled Ignacio up into a hug. "I'm so sorry, son."

They cried together.

"You can't do this, Dad," Ignacio sobbed. "You can't just send me away like this."

I froze. I couldn't breathe. My heart pounded so loud, I couldn't think straight.

"Take your hiking pack. It has your tent,"Amo Abraham choked out. "And take your bow and arrows. Sara will fill my pack with the leftovers from last night. Hillary can take that one, and you'll have food."

Patrona Sara jumped up, a little too eager to help get us on our way. She disappeared into the kitchen.

I remained frozen in the chair, mouth open, eyes wide. I couldn't believe this was happening. I served the Serugs with unwavering loyalty for twenty-six years. After running away, I came back only to face more work and fewer days off. I never complained or argued. I gave Patrona Sara everything she wanted. And now they planned to throw us out after all that?

What about poor Ignacio? He had to feel so confused. His father claimed to love him yet was sending him away. With no plan in place. *Take your pack? Is that all he can do? What about school? What about all his rodeo training? What about his future? Can a dad send away his fifteen-year-old son without a plan?*

I waited for the cruel joke to be over, but it never did.

"Dad, please!" Ignacio's voice cracked as he lurched forward from the couch. " You can't kick me out. What will I do? How will I survive?"

"Fill the hydration bladder too," Amo Abraham called to Patrona Sara over his shoulder, as if he were packing for a weekend trip instead of banishing his son. He turned to Ignacio. "I've taught you all about camping, fishing, and hunting. You can live off the land, like our ancestors did. You've got your tent. Miss Hillary will be with you to help."

I couldn't move. Maybe if I sat here forever, we wouldn't have to leave. I stared up at Amo Abraham in disbelief.

"You're really kicking us out," I managed to whisper.

He nodded, a sad look on his face, and hugged Ignacio. Amo Abraham broke the hug and looked at him. "You're going to be a great tribe some day. He promised me that. You will survive. Thrive even."

I swallowed hard and closed my eyes. I let them fall to my hands, propped up by my elbows on my knees. Thoughts swirled around in my head. What would we do? Where would we go?

Patrona Sara came back into the room, lugging the full pack. "There's plenty of food here, and the water is full," she said, setting it next to me.

It leaned against my leg, and I shrugged away from it as if it burned me. I felt dead inside, like my whole world had crashed down to nothingness.

Ignacio clung to Amo Abraham's arm, crying, not wanting to let go. "Don't do this, Dad. I was only joking." He looked down at Isaac, content playing with his truck on the floor. "He's not that bad."

Patrona Sara sneered at him. Ignacio's hatred for Isaac fueled her hatred for him. It would be hard to mend that relationship.

Amo Abraham saw that Ignacio wasn't going to get his pack ready. He walked toward Ignacio's room, Ignacio trailing behind. "You're almost sixteen now. That's nearly old enough to be on your own anyway. You can get a job, help your mother."

"My mother? I barely know her. She's just the nanny," he whined as they disappeared into his room.

My heart ached within my chest. He was right. To him, I was "just the nanny." He never knew me as anyone more until today. I loved him all these years from afar, not allowed to get any closer until Patrona Sara got pregnant. Could he see me as his mother?

They came out of his room and back into the living room, Ignacio with his cowboy hat on his head and hiking boots on his feet. Amo Abraham carried Ignacio's hiking pack and handed it to Patrona Sara. "Fill the water in here too."

She took it with difficulty and left to fill the hydration bladder.

"You're making a mistake, Dad," Ignacio sobbed.

"I have to follow Jehovah's orders, son. I know you'll be okay. He promised me that," Amo Abraham said as Patrona Sara returned, dragging the full pack.

She tried handing it to Ignacio, but he refused to take it. Amo Abraham took it and guided Ignacio to the front door.

Patrona Sara walked over to me. "He's always been your son. Now you can be his mother." Her tone sounded steady, without malice or disgust. She waved toward the door where Ignacio and Amo Abraham stood. "He's yours to take care of now."

I held back my tears. If I responded, the tears would pour out. Anger burned inside me. I stood, my legs shaking. I pursed my lips, holding back the words I wanted to hurl at them about how unfair and cruel they acted. After all these years, I had imagined leaving on good terms. Instead, the odds were stacked against us, and they didn't even care.

I picked up the pack and walked to the door.

Amo Abe turned to me. "I'm sorry, Hillary. You've been a good servant. A good friend. I know you'll be a good mother to your son."

"I need to get my papers. What about his birth certificate?" It came out as a whisper.

Patrona Sara jumped into action getting Ignacio's paperwork.

My hands shook as I took the folder with the birth certificate and Social Security card from her. I fumbled with the zipper and tucked them away in Ignacio's pack.

Amo Abraham opened the door for us, and we stepped out into the sunlight. He helped me into my pack as Ignacio swung his onto his back and secured his bow to the side.

I glanced at the Range Rover as I walked past to go to the RV and get my fake Mexican documents, the only paperwork I had. They hadn't offered us any means of transportation. No place to live aside from the tents in our packs. I couldn't get a job without a work visa. Ignacio was my only hope for survival. Would he accept me as his mother, or would he be mad that I hadn't told him the truth all these years?

The steps to the RV seemed like a mountain too tall to climb. I set the pack down before scaling them. I didn't have many possessions. The Serugs gave me everything I needed.

I lifted the bench of the dining table to retrieve my paperwork from the hidden compartment, grabbing the small wad of cash I saved from my earnings. It would be enough to stay in an extended-stay hotel for a few months, long enough for us to figure out what to do next.

I changed into more comfortable shoes and grabbed a couple changes of clothes, my cell phone, and my wide-brimmed hat. If we walked, I needed shoes that would hold up.

I descended the stairs and stuffed my papers, clothes, and money into my pack next to the food Patrona Sara packed that wouldn't spoil, enough for a few days, if we rationed properly.

Swinging the pack onto my back, I looked at Ignacio. "Where should we go?"

CHAPTER THIRTY

SOUTH TEXAS RANCH LANDS

We headed left out of the neighborhood, following the same route I'd driven in a frenzy before Ignacio's birth. The gravel road lay empty, dust swirling over the barren land. No sidewalks lined the road, but few cars passed.

I turned to Ignacio as we walked, not sure where to start, but wanting to say so much. "I'm so sorry you had to find out this way. I love you so much and wanted to tell you, but I couldn't."

"Why not?" Ignacio's voice cracked, his hands deep in his pockets as his steps quickened against the gravel. He glanced at me, eyes shining with fresh tears. "Were you ashamed of me?"

"No! Not at all." I sighed. I owed him an explanation, and now we had all the time in the world. "It wasn't my choice."

"What did Dad say? You helped them by having me for Mom?"

"It's complicated," I said. I kicked a large rock off our path. I started the story with reluctance. "Jehovah told your parents...er...your dad and Patrona Sara that they were supposed to start a new tribe. Your mom...er...Patrona Sara had tried to have children for a long time. She spent many days in Houston at a fertility clinic trying to make it work. Eight years she tried for a baby but could never get pregnant.

"I was working for them this whole time. They brought me from Mexico to be their nanny, but I worked for them for ten years, and no baby ever came. Patrona Sara got impatient."

How much should I tell him? He'd known her as his mother for nearly sixteen years. I couldn't tell him that she forced me to have sex with his father. She'd done a lot of rotten things, but she still raised him for fourteen years. He was still figuring out his feelings for me, and I didn't want his mind to be tainted by how he was conceived.

"She asked me to have a child with your dad. For her," I said, weighing each word. "The child I would have was never supposed to be mine. I got pregnant easily, after the first month with your dad. When you were born, I stayed with you the first two years. When you stopped nursing, Patrona Sara took you as her own.

"I never wanted to let you go, mijo, but they made me. Patrona Sara was going to fire me if I ever said anything, and then I would never have seen you again. I made sure I was still near you, to watch you grow up. But at that point, she was your mom. I was 'just the nanny.'"

"All this time, I could have known you. All this time, I thought *she* was my mom," he spat out.

I sighed. "I know, mijo. It's a terrible, awful situation. If I had known it would come to this, I never would have let them take you in the first place. I feel like I missed out on fourteen years of your life. I love you. I've always loved you. And your father loves you too."

"He said he loved me. But he kicked me out," he said, anger building in his voice. "All those weekends together. All those years. All for nothing." His bottom lip quivered.

"He does love you, Ignacio. I know he does."

"Then why would he let her kick me out?" he demanded.

"I wish I knew."

We walked along in silence. The warm October sun beat down, and I welcomed the shade from my wide-brimmed hat. A car passed, kicking up dust. I coughed and sipped from the hydration bladder to rid my throat of the dirt.

"At least those weekends of hunting, fishing, and camping will help you now," I said, breaking the silence. "I don't know the first thing about any of that."

"I guess Dad did prepare me for living on my own in the wilderness."

"I can cook over an open fire...some. We used to do that when I was a little girl," I said. "But we'll find a place to stay. We just have to figure out where."

He nodded. "I can't believe Dad took my phone," he muttered. "He cut me off from everyone."

"Sorry, mijo. This whole thing is unfair to you," I said. "Life is unfair. It sure has been for me. A ti y a mí...la misma mala suerte nos tocó."

"Huh?"

"We have the same bad luck."

Eventually the dirt road ended onto a narrow, paved road. We continued straight past forests of oaks and mesquite trees and fields of cattle. The sun shone high overhead, baking the pavement. A warm breeze blew around the smell of the sunbaked gravel mixed with the sweet aroma of the mesquite trees. Mockingbirds sung their tunes at us as we trudged along.

I realized that I never found joy in nature. Since the kidnapping, I stayed inside the house most of the time. Even when I milked the cows or tended to the gardens at the Serugs' house, I didn't appreciate the sounds and smells. Now I was forced into it. Could I learn to like it?

My legs ached. We had walked for three hours now. How long could I walk in one day? My job kept me active, but I never exercised. Ignacio was fitter from all his rodeo training, while I stood thirty years older than him. I doubted I could keep up. Would he leave me behind? Even now that he knew I was his biological mother, would that change anything for him?

"Can we take a break?" I asked.

"Sure."

We moved off the road to the edge of the forest under the shade of the trees. I sat, leaning up against a tree trunk, stretching my legs out in front of me. I glanced at Ignacio. He sat against a neighboring tree, shoulders hunched, eyes staring off into the distance. Fifteen, tall, strong, with the same stubborn set to his jaw that I saw in myself every morning in the mirror. But now he seemed breakable. Like a branch under too much weight.

"Mijo...how are you feeling about all this?" I asked. My voice faltered, and I cleared my throat to try again. "About me?"

Ignacio didn't answer right away. He didn't even look up. I waited, my heart pounding. His jaw tightened, and he blinked fast, as if keeping something from spilling out.

"I don't know," he said after what felt like hours. "Everything feels fake. Like I'm in someone else's life. Like I missed something obvious. Everyone was in on the joke except me."

I nodded and looked down at my hands. "I didn't want you to find out like that. I...I wanted to tell you so many times. But I wasn't allowed. Your father—" I stopped myself. I wouldn't point fingers.

He looked straight into my eyes like a grown man carrying age, wounds, and a restless search for meaning.

"Were you ever going to tell me?" he asked. "Or were you just gonna keep cleaning around me for the rest of my life?"

The words hit hard, but I took them. I deserved them. I had asked myself the same question a thousand times.

"I don't know," I murmured. "I was scared. And I didn't want to hurt you. Or confuse you. You had a life, a name, a family. I thought if I stayed close, I would at least get to see you grow up. That was enough."

Ignacio let out a dry laugh, hollow as a drum, with no hint of joy. "Enough for who?"

I didn't answer right away. His hands were clenched in his lap, knuckles white.

"Enough for me," I said. "It was enough for me to watch you grow up. To be near you. Even if I had to pretend to be nothing more than the housekeeper."

His head dropped to his hands, covering his face. I reached for him, aching to hold him like when he was two and scraped his knee on the porch step. But I didn't move.

"Why didn't you fight for me?" he said, his voice cracking.

"I did," I whispered. "But maybe not in the way you wanted. I stayed. I loved you in every quiet way I could. I gave you what I was allowed to give. When Isaac came along, and I was allowed to be more involved in your life, it was the best thing for me."

He looked up at me, his eyes red, as if he wanted to cry, but no tears formed. "I don't know what to call you."

"You don't have to call me anything," I said. "Just...don't shut me out. Don't leave me alone. Please."

He didn't answer right away. But after a moment, he moved to sit next to me. Tears...happy tears...stung my eyes. I didn't move. I sat beside him in the quiet, letting the truth sink in.

After a few minutes of silence, I sighed. "We better get moving. I'm not sure where we want to stop for the night."

He got up first and held his hand out to help me up.

I smiled at him and took his hand. "Thank you."

Maybe we still had a chance. Maybe he wouldn't hate me forever for not telling him I was his mother. Maybe we could build a family together after all this.

***

We camped in a field under the stars. Ignacio taught me how to build the tent. We gathered sticks, and he taught me how to build a campfire. He shot a rabbit with his bow for us to eat along with some of the food Patrona Sara packed. I felt grateful for the many weekends he went away with Amo Abraham, learning to live off the land. I never would have survived on my own.

The next day we continued south. I didn't know our destination, and neither of us had a plan. We followed a narrow, gravel ranch road, avoiding the larger highways. The sun beat down, and the air hung heavy.

"Have you seen a river lately?" Ignacio asked.

"No, why?"

He swatted a mosquito off his arm. "I'm running out of water. And I haven't seen any rivers or lakes lately."

I pulled my wet hair up off my neck and tucked it under the hat. "We haven't passed much of anything, other than cows."

"If we can find a river, I have a filter we can use to refill the water."

I pulled my cell phone out of my pocket and opened the map app. The loading circle spun and spun. No service. I sighed and turned it off so it wouldn't waste battery searching for service. Why didn't I think to download the map before we left?

"I'll be on the lookout," I said, glancing toward the horizon.

We trudged on as the sun got higher and hotter. Sweat poured down my back under the pack, and my shirt clung to my body. The brush rustled with cicadas, and the air smelled of mesquite and dust. My boots kicked up puffs of dust that stuck to my sweat-slick skin.

I sucked out the last of the water from the hydration bladder in my pack. "I'm out of water."

"Yeah, I've been out for a few hours now," Ignacio said. He had slowed over the past mile.

"You doing okay?"

Ignacio's face was flushed a blotchy red, and his lips had turned pale. His shoulders sagged beneath his pack.

"Let's take a break. You don't look so good," I said.

He wiped his forehead with a shaky hand. "I'm fine." But his legs moved like a newborn calf's.

I dropped my pack and stepped toward him, reaching for his arm. His body felt too hot, too limp. "You're not fine."

He swayed and dropped to one knee.

"Okay, come on. Over here." I scanned the horizon and spotted the only patch of real shade for miles.

A scraggly mesquite tree, young and low to the ground, clung to life in the parched land. I half carried, half dragged him under it, yanked off his pack, and eased him to the dust.

"Just sit. Don't talk. Just breathe."

His breath came fast and shallow. I yanked off his shirt, hoping the faint breeze might cool his skin. I fanned him with the fabric, desperate to stir more air. My hands shook as I searched for a way to bring his temperature down.

"Ignacio, I need you to talk to me," I said. "Just stay with me, okay?"

He gave a slight nod. Then, after a minute, he said, "It's not just the heat."

I waited.

His mouth opened again, trembling. "I can't believe Dad would send us away like this. What was he thinking?" Tears sparkled in the corner of his eye.

My throat tightened. "I'm really sorry, mijo."

He looked at me, his eyes red, a tear streaking his cheek. "Mijo...that means a lot more now than it meant before I knew who you really are."

I felt his pain. If I knew this would be the outcome, I would have told him long ago.

"How do you just reject your own kid?" Ignacio asked. "How do you shut the door like that and never open it again?"

"I don't know," I whispered. I wished I could offer wiser words that could fill the void in his chest.

Ignacio curled his body, hugging his knees and resting his head on them. His shoulders shook as he tried to hide his tears from me. He was so young but already tainted by grief and pride.

"He didn't even care," he cried. "He didn't even watch us leave."

I gathered him into my arms, and he didn't resist. He let me hold him, like I did when he was two.

"He just shut the door and shut us out of his life. Like we're nothing."

"I know," I murmured. "I know, mijo. I saw it too."

His skin burned against mine, his voice still fading. But in that moment, he needed my arms more than he needed shade.

"I thought he loved me," Ignacio said.

I had no answer for that. I didn't know anymore. I held him closer, tears soaking into my shirt, the damp seeping through to my skin. My chest ached as if it might cave in, each breath shuddering under the weight pressing from inside. I rocked him, the motion steady, trying to hold my tears in.

"I'm sorry," I breathed into his hair. "I should've kept you safe. I should've..."

"You did," he whispered. "You didn't leave me. He did."

I didn't deserve his love, his forgiveness. All I could offer was a promise I didn't even know I could keep. "I'm not going to let you die out here, mijo. I swear, I won't."

I laid him down in the shade with care and walked away to give him space. Not far, a few yards maybe. Enough for him to fall apart without feeling watched.

I didn't want him to see me cry too. We had no water, no father coming to look for him, only us and the relentless heat. I didn't know what to do. I sat in the dust, close enough that I could hear him breathe, fast and shallow, but still going. The shadow of the tree couldn't reach me. The heat pressed against my skin. I deserved it.

I pulled my knees up to my chest and wrapped my arms around them. I didn't look at him. I couldn't. His suffering burned into me, a suffering I had dragged him into. My breath came in shallow bursts, threads of control slipping through my fingers. I clenched my jaw. I couldn't let my fear or my anger show, not while my son still breathed.

We weren't supposed to be here. Not like this. The two of us, kicked out like trash. I hadn't done enough to prepare us for this. No map. No plan. Not enough water.

My fingers curled into the dry dirt beside me. Crumbling clods broke apart in my hand like everything else I touched.

Ignacio trusted me. I saw it in the way he hadn't complained when the last of the water disappeared. Now he sat under a tree, curled up like a child, his body dying from heat and heartbreak.

And I couldn't do anything about it.

I pressed my forehead to my knees and squeezed my eyes shut. My skin felt sticky with sweat and dirt. I could still hear his breathing, but it felt thinner now, further away. The sound that made a mother's blood go cold.

I should have begged harder. Should have fought more. Should have stayed, screamed, clawed at the door until Amo Abe let us back in. But I sat there, frozen in the chair, while he got the packs ready, trying to hold it all together.

I opened my eyes to the sunlit dirt. Dry, cracked. Like me. I dug my fingers into it again, desperate to ground myself, to feel anything real. I was failing at mothering all over again. I couldn't protect my son. I couldn't protect myself. The tears welled up inside me, and I couldn't control them any longer.

"What's the matter, Helena?"

At the sound of my real name, I jerked my head up. It wasn't the voice of Ignacio. Who else was out here with us, and how did they know my name? I scanned the barren land around me but saw no one. Was I hearing things?

"Don't be afraid, for Jehovah has heard the boy's voice right where he's crying."

The voice came from above, as if the sun itself spoke to me. I squinted toward the sky and saw a figure, terrible and beautiful all at once. An angel. Not soft and sweet, like a child's painting, but a being of power, clothed in light so pure it felt like it might shatter my eyes. Its clothes shimmered like liquid gold. Its face blazed brighter than the sun. Wings stretched high behind it, alive with light.

I shielded my eyes with my hand. My heart pounded in my chest, so hard I felt it would run away.

"Get up!" the creature said. "Help the boy up and hold him by the hand. I will make him into a great tribe."

I looked from the creature to Ignacio, so weak and feeble. And then I saw it. A well of water waited on the other side of the tree!

I jumped up and grabbed my pack, fumbling with it to figure out how to fill the hydration bladder. The water from the well felt cool and pure. I hurried to fill the bladder and dashed back to Ignacio.

"Small sips. Not too fast," I said as I placed the straw into his mouth.

He took a few gulps, then leaned back against the tree, breathing like he'd finished a sprint. His eyelids drooped, and sweat ran down his temples.

A hawk called in the distance, and a breeze stirred the dry ground.

He took a few more gulps.

"We're going to be okay," I said.

Chapter Thirty-One

We stayed by that well for several days. The old mesquite tree and the tufts of dry grass around us gave us enough kindling for a campfire to cook and keep warm in the cool winter nights.

On the third day, Ignacio spotted her. She stood out on the horizon, probably a mile away, all alone. She reared on her hind legs, neighed, and galloped away as if fear drove her.

"Did you see that?" he asked.

I nodded. "I wonder if it belongs to anyone."

"There's no one else around. No one for miles...as far as the eye can see."

We hadn't seen anyone since we started camping here by the angel's well. We camped far enough away from any streets, far enough away from any herds of cows.

The next morning, I peeked my head out of my tent and saw the horse again. This time she drank out of our well, twenty yards away from our tents. I froze, not wanting to scare her off. She was a coffee-colored mare with burrs in her mane, her tail matted in disarray, like a wind-blown bush. She looked like a horse that probably escaped from a ranch years ago. Not tame and not branded.

She lapped the water, oblivious to the two humans nearby. Ignacio stirred and unzipped his tent. The horse heard the noise and took off as he emerged. He caught a glimpse of her retreating.

"Wow. It was close to us this time," Ignacio said, his eyes wide.

"She found our water source."

"Maybe she'll be back then." His voice was full of hope. He'd grown up around horses, trained with them, and competed at junior rodeos with them. We hadn't been gone long, but to a kid, a week felt like a hundred years. I felt certain he already missed them.

When the horse returned, Ignacio leapt into action, spending every day for two weeks trying to catch her. Ignacio sat motionless beside the tree while the horse drank from the well. At first, the horse wouldn't let him close. She ran away when she saw him. But he had something in him that made animals pause. He didn't rush or grab. He just waited.

Eventually, she stayed when she saw him. His mouth moved, but I couldn't hear what he said from a distance. He drew on his training from Diego and Daniel and from his roughneck coaches. There were no arenas surrounding him now, no chutes, no crowd. There was only wide-open country, his voice, and his stubbornness.

He tossed her a piece of apple. At the sudden motion, she backed up, ready to run away. But she paused and looked at the apple in the dust. Then she looked at him. She took a step toward it, toward him. She bent down and sniffed the apple and sucked it into her mouth. She looked at him again, as if thanking him, before she turned and trotted away.

The next day, the horse came back to the well. This time, Ignacio took an apple and a piece of old rope from the bottom of his pack. He didn't go to her but crouched nearby. He held out his hand with the apple and let the horse decide.

I peeked out from behind my tent as she stepped forward toward him. He held his hand out high, flat, with the apple balancing on top. She took it from him.

I bit my lip, tears stinging behind my eyes as he spoke in a low, steady voice to calm her. He slipped the rope around her neck, and though she shivered, she didn't bolt. With one hand, he patted the side of her neck and spoke to her in his soft voice.

After a moment, he climbed onto her back. There was no saddle or reins, only his calloused hands and strong grip I'd seen him use to stay on broncs twice her size.

Ignacio leaned forward and whispered something I couldn't hear before tapping her side with his heel. The mare took a step, then another. Her pace stayed slow and uncertain, but she kept moving, willing enough to show she'd decided Ignacio wasn't her enemy.

I covered my gasp with my hands. He was riding her. After two and a half long weeks of waiting, of building trust with her, he was riding her. This skinny, broken-hearted kid, abandoned by his father and left with nothing, now rode a wild horse in the wilderness. Not because anyone handed it to him, but because he'd earned it. One slow breath, one quiet day, one step at a time.

He caught my eye and smiled. I smiled back, though my hands still trembled. We still didn't know our destination, but now we wouldn't be walking. We would be riding. We could make it to the next river without running out of water again.

***

Whisper became our companion over the next week. We stayed by the well while Ignacio tamed her. She carried traces of long-ago training, dulled by the years without use, but she learned it again with ease. When Ignacio wasn't hunting, he spent most of his day with her.

"We need to move on from here. The food Patrona Sara packed is gone, and I'm tired of eating just meat," I said one morning. I shouldn't complain. If it weren't for Ignacio's archery skills, we would have starved already.

"I don't want to leave until we're sure Whisper won't buck you off," he said. "Let's try having you ride her."

I hesitated. Ignacio handled horses with a skill I could never match. I had ridden the Serugs' horses plenty of times, but always with a saddle. Sweat slicked my palms at the thought of climbing onto this wild horse with only a rope. Still, we had walked for miles, and riding would spare my raw, blistered feet.

"Won't she sense my fear?" I asked, backing away. "My inexperience?"

"Yes, which is why you need to get comfortable with her too. She's very good with me, but she's still a wild horse." He cupped his hands beside her. "Here, use my hands to help you get up."

I climbed on as he held the rope, my shirt heavy with sweat. As soon as I settled in, Whisper snorted beneath me, hooves pawing at the dirt. Her back felt slick from Ignacio's morning ride. Her sides quivered with distrust; her ears flicked back toward me.

Whisper screamed through her teeth and exploded. Her front hooves came up in defiance. The world tilted. I slid down her slick back, grabbing for anything I could, but there was nothing to hold onto.

"Hold on with your legs!" Ignacio shouted up to me. "Lean forward!"

I tightened my legs around her body, but she didn't yield. I hung on for a second, but then gravity won. I slid further down her back and slammed into the dirt behind her. A huge dust cloud engulfed me, filling my mouth and eyes. I coughed, rolled, and spat into the dry ground.

Ignacio tugged Whisper away from me so she wouldn't kick me in the face with her hind legs.

"That was not nice, girl," he scolded her.

I didn't get up right away. I sat there, blinking down at the ground, still coughing. A thousand things ached. My backside felt sore, bruised.

A shadow came toward me. I looked up to see Ignacio, his face pale, brows pinched.

"You okay?" he asked.

I forced a breath out and pushed myself up to my knees. "I'm fine."

"You sure?" He held out his hand to help me up.

"Maybe I can guide, and you can ride," I suggested.

"I'd like to get her to the point where both of us could ride her together," Ignacio said. "That would make our journey much quicker."

"I just want to find a grocery store." I dusted my pants off. "And maybe a real shower."

We tried a few more times, Ignacio directing me on how to lean forward and tighten my grip around Whisper's body with my legs when she bucked.

"Be the horse, Mom."

My heart stuttered. I blinked through the dust. He'd never called me that before. I swallowed hard. The pain in my bottom dulled. I focused all my effort on leaning forward when she tried to buck again. This time, I stayed on.

Whisper sensed that I felt more comfortable, more confident. She whinnied and settled down. I sat upright on her back, smiling down at Ignacio.

"You riding with me?" I asked, reaching my hand down toward him.

He nodded, took her hand, and swung up in front of me. I draped my arms around his waist. He looked back at me. "You ready, Mom?"

There it was again. That word. I blinked hard against the sting in my eyes. "Yes, mijo."

***

The land stretched out, empty and silent. Aside from a couple of cars at the start, we hadn't seen a single person in the month we'd been walking.

The dirt road ended at a two-lane paved road, but it looked deserted. Ignacio slowed Whisper to a stop to check for traffic. Seeing none, we continued onto the dirt road across the street. Whisper veered to the left on another dirt road, and Ignacio let her lead.

"Look there!" Ignacio cried. "It's a lake...or pond...or something."

The water sparkled in the distance. I sighed. We made it.

Ignacio slid down and helped me off. Whisper walked to the water and started lapping. The lake wasn't big—I could see across it—but it welcomed us like an oasis in the dry land we traversed.

I set Ignacio to pitching the tents while I washed off. I felt so dirty, so sweaty. We both longed for baths. I tossed my boots and socks on the shore and walked into the lake, fully clothed. My clothes needed washing anyway.

The water felt cool, soothing. My feet squished into the mud at the bottom of the lake. This was the first time I had washed myself since leaving Patrona Sara's house. We could draw water from the well and wipe down with rags, but to immerse myself in water felt like a luxury.

Memories of splashing and bathing in the river near our village in Puerto Cabezas flooded my mind. A tear pricked at my eye. Those days felt so simple. We were poor then, but I didn't know. Now, I was the poor mother trying to raise her son.

I emerged from the water, dripping along the bank. The breeze felt good against my wet skin and clothes. Ignacio tied Whisper to a tree and set up the tents in the shade below it.

"Your turn, mijo," I said.

When he disappeared in the direction of the lake, I pulled out dry clothes and changed in my tent. No need to risk getting chafed from the wet fabric.

I gathered sticks for our campfire as I waited for Ignacio to return.

The sun dipped low in the sky when I heard the crunch of tires on the dry gravel road. I tensed, unsure whether to hide in the tent or step out to see who approached. Perhaps it was a rancher, maybe the one who owned the land where we camped. Would he kick us out?

A green bar striped the side of the vehicle. My stomach sank.

Border Patrol.

Ignacio was still away at the lake washing up. I didn't call for him. I eased up and raised my hands, like I'd seen people do on the news, even though I wasn't doing anything wrong. Not really. We only wanted to rest and figure out what to do next.

Two agents climbed out of the truck. The older one, white, had sun-leathered skin and mirrored sunglasses. The younger one, possibly Hispanic, carried a look of caution rather than aggression. The older one spoke first.

"You folks camping out here?"

I nodded. "Yes, sir. Just for the night."

"This private land?"

"I...I don't know. We didn't see any signs. We stayed close to the road."

The younger agent glanced toward the brush, where our tiny dome tents sagged in the breeze. I heard the crunch of Ignacio's footsteps returning from the lake.

"You have ID?" the older one asked.

I nodded and dug through my pack, handing him my Mexican passport and my work visa card, still valid, still legal.

He flipped through them, frowning. "Says you're authorized to work in Alice."

"I am," I said. "I was working there. Cleaning houses. But my boss...she let me go. I didn't have money for the bus."

"And your son?"

I turned. Ignacio stood behind me now, his clothes making mud in the dirt below him. His voice cracked when he spoke.

"I'm a citizen," he said.

The older agent raised an eyebrow. "You got proof of that?"

Ignacio reached into his pack and pulled out a crumpled folder. Inside lay his Texas-issued birth certificate. Nothing else.

The agent took it, held it up to the light. "No photo ID?"

"He's only fifteen," I said. "We weren't planning to travel like this. Everything happened fast."

The two men stepped aside to speak. I couldn't hear what they said, but I could guess.

When they came back, the younger one knelt a little, addressing Ignacio.

"You got any relatives nearby, mijo?"

Ignacio glanced at me. "Not really."

The agent looked at me. "You know it's not legal to camp here without permission. And you're not where your visa says you should be."

"I know. I wasn't trying to hide," I said, twisting the strap of my backpack between my fingers. The sun beat down, hot on the back of my neck, and my voice cracked. "We just...we needed time. I didn't know what else to do."

The older agent huffed, then handed back our documents. "We're not gonna arrest you. But we have to report this. You're out of status, geographically speaking. That might trigger a notice later. ICE may contact you."

I nodded, swallowing hard.

"As for him," he continued, jerking his thumb toward Ignacio, "he's a U.S. citizen. But if you get detained or deported, he can't go with you unless you sign paperwork saying it's voluntary. Without that, he stays."

I felt Ignacio shift beside me. His shoulder brushed mine. He didn't say a word, but I could feel the fear coming off him like heat.

The younger agent softened his voice. "You need to find shelter. A bus station. Something. We're letting you go for now, but if you're found like this again, they won't be as kind."

"Gracias," I whispered.

The older agent turned back toward the truck, but I couldn't let him leave. Not yet. Not without asking.

"Señor?" My voice shook. I swallowed and tried again. "If I get deported...can he come with me?"

Both men stopped.

The younger one turned first. He looked at me, then at Ignacio. Fifteen years old, too thin from walking, trying hard to look like a man but blinking back fear like a boy.

The older agent rubbed the back of his neck. "He's a U.S. citizen. We can't deport him."

"I know," I muttered. "But he's my son."

"If you get detained," the younger one said, slower now, "you'll be processed. You might be offered voluntary departure. If you sign the papers, you can request that he leave with you, but it's not automatic. Depends on who's handling your case."

"And if I don't sign?" I asked.

He hesitated. "Then he stays. ICE would notify child welfare or try to contact relatives. You'd have to figure something out fast."

I turned to Ignacio. He looked down at his shoes, jaw clenched. He wouldn't cry, not in front of them, but I could see it in the way his fingers balled into fists.

"He won't stay," I said. "Not without me."

The older agent shrugged. "Then if it comes to that...you'd better make sure his name's on the paperwork. And hope someone on the other end approves it."

It wasn't a yes. It wasn't a no. It was the gray I'd been living in for years. Ignacio could come with me...if I asked. If they let him. If they didn't decide otherwise. But if they took me, it might not matter what

I said. It would come down to them, men in uniforms and government systems that didn't know what it meant to be someone's mother.

They headed back to the truck, but the younger one turned back.

"Try Centro de Indulto Benéfico in Edinburg," he said. "It's about thirty miles south of here. They might be able to help."

I nodded and smiled a weak smile of thanks.

They got back in the truck and drove off, their taillights blinking red against the dirt as the road swallowed them up.

Ignacio came and stood beside me. "You wouldn't leave without me, right?"

"No," I whispered. "Never."

"We need to get to Edinburg."

"We'll leave at first light. Whisper needs rest."

Chapter Thirty-Two

Between Encino and Linn Texas

When the sun rose, we packed up camp and headed toward Edinburg. Thirty miles seemed doable in a day, as long as we could find some water along the way. We stayed off the highway on ranch roads and fields to try to avoid the Border Patrol.

Whisper's hooves beat steady against the dirt, but my heart beat louder. Thirty miles. That was all. Thirty more miles, and maybe someone would tell me we still had a chance. That I could stay with him. That I could be his mother on U.S. soil.

The sun pressed hot on my neck. I glanced at the back of his head. My boy, my son. It took thirteen years to have him as my own. His shoulders were getting broader, his jaw harder. I wondered what he was thinking about as we trudged along.

If they deported me, would Amo Abraham take him in? Patrona Sara made it clear she didn't want him there. Would they force Amo Abraham to step up and be the father he chose not to be? Otherwise, how could Ignacio stay without me? Who would he stay with? Who fights for him when he messes up or gets sick or gets scared?

They said he belongs here, and I don't. But I carried him into this world with blood and breath and every part of me. And now they want to split us apart like it's nothing. Like it's paperwork. I'm not a missing form. I'm his mother.

I almost laughed when the agents gave me the warning with their plastic smiles. One of them seemed empathetic, but he had to do his job. "We're letting you go for now." For now. What did that mean? Tomorrow? Next week? Would Border Patrol track us down at night, when we were sleeping, when we felt safe?

No, I wouldn't let that happen. I would get us somewhere. I would ask questions, find lawyers, beg if I had to. But I would not let them take me from him. If they tried, I would chain myself to him, scream in their faces, throw myself in front of the bus, I didn't care.

The wind picked up and blew dust across the dirt road. I wiped my face with my hand. Sweat or tears wet my palm. Maybe both.

They didn't see me. They saw numbers. But if they looked harder, they'd see a mother and her son trying to stay together. Two people who found each other mere weeks earlier, heading to a place that might give us a little hope.

The situation overwhelmed me as we trotted along. My chest felt tight, and my shoulders sagged.

I remembered the angel when Ignacio had heat exhaustion. What did it say? Jehovah would make him into a great tribe. I could hold onto hope for him, but what did that mean for me?

Ignacio's voice interrupted my thoughts. "Mom, there's a pond ahead."

"That's great. I bet Whisper is thirsty and needs a break."

"I wonder how far we've gone."

"We've been going steady for three hours. We're probably halfway there," I guessed.

Halfway to freedom or halfway to failure, I wasn't sure.

Whisper lapped the pond water as we sucked water from our packs. Riding didn't dehydrate us as much as walking did, but my sweaty shirt still stuck to my back. I walked around, stretching my weary legs. My butt felt sore from the bouncing motion on Whisper's back.

"Do we have any food left in the pack?" Ignacio asked.

My stomach growled in response. I knew the answer, but I opened the pack anyway to check. "No, we've eaten it all."

"I'm going to take Whisper to graze in that field over there. I'll take my bow and see if I can catch dinner." He motioned to a field off the road with tall, wiry grass swaying in the breeze. It looked like the perfect grazing pasture.

"I don't want to let you out of my sight, Ignacio. What about Border Patrol? What if they take me while you're gone?"

"Yeah, okay. Um, take the packs and hide under that bush." He pointed to a shrub a little way off the road. "You should be able to see me from there. Yell if anyone comes."

I sighed. He was right. Whisper needed food as much as we did. With all the commotion with the Border Patrol yesterday, we hadn't eaten dinner or breakfast.

"Take your birth certificate...in case you need it." I rifled through his pack and pulled out his birth certificate from the folder. "Put it in your pocket."

He folded it and did as I told him. I hoped it wouldn't get too sweaty that the writing would smudge away, but I didn't want to risk him not having it. If Border Patrol questioned him, he would lead them straight to me.

I stuffed the packs under the bush and tangled myself in the branches, hoping I couldn't be seen. I could still peek through and see where Ignacio headed. He promised not to go too far, but a piece of my heart seemed to walk away with him.

"Be safe," I whispered, but he couldn't hear.

I counted the minutes silently to myself. His hunting trips could take hours if no animals crossed his path. Whisper might scare them off, making it take even longer. We needed to get moving again if we hoped to reach Edinburg. I didn't know what time a place like Centro de Indulto Benéfico would stop taking guests for the night, or if it even did. But I didn't want to take any chances.

Thirty minutes passed. I searched the field and spotted Whisper bending down to chew on some of the seed heads dangling from the grass stalks like little flags. I didn't see Ignacio, and my heart quickened.

Thirty more minutes passed. Whisper shifted, but Ignacio still hadn't appeared. He said he would stay close. My head pounded, and I let out a huff of breath through gritted teeth. If he didn't return before I counted the next thirty minutes, I would go after him.

My feet felt numb, and I shifted my weight in my hiding place. The branches scratched my bare arms. I began to count again.

Seventeen minutes later, Ignacio rose out of the grass holding the ears of a rabbit, his bow hanging over his shoulder. He took Whisper's rope in his other hand and guided her toward my hiding place. I let out a breath of relief and emerged, glancing over my shoulder at the road.

We gathered sticks for our campfire to cook the rabbit and went as far away from the road as we could, hoping the fire wouldn't attract any attention. This was the first fire we started since the Border Patrol incident yesterday. I hesitated, but we had no other way to eat.

I tore the cooked rabbit meat off the bones with my teeth. The taste of rabbit wasn't new to me anymore. It had become the most common animal Ignacio caught, and we lived off them most of the journey. I didn't hate it, but I couldn't wait to get to a town and to a grocery store.

The food reinvigorated us, and as we stomped out the fire, I smiled.

"Ready to get going?" I asked, anxious to get closer to our destination.

"Let's do it."

We packed away the few things we used for the meal, along with his birth certificate, and climbed onto Whisper. She whinnied, and Ignacio rubbed her neck as we started south again.

An hour later, I heard tires crunching on the gravel behind us. I tensed up, peering over my shoulder.

A white truck approached us from behind. Ignacio saw it too and led Whisper off the road into the fields. He started heading west, away from the road, into the barren ranch land. He kicked Whisper into a gallop, and we sped away from the road, away from the truck, away from danger.

I glanced over my shoulder. The truck wasn't following us. Phew!

Ignacio slowed Whisper down to a trot and turned her back south.

"That was a close one," Ignacio said.

"Yeah. I don't know if that was Border Patrol, but I'm glad we didn't wait around to find out."

We headed southeast back toward the road and back on track to Edinburg.

I felt tired and sore when we spotted the first sign of a town in the distance. When the *Welcome to Edinburg* sign came into view, I choked up. We made it.

We walked down the streets of the town, looking in the shop windows. A market loomed ahead, and I gasped and pointed. "Ignacio, let's stop there."

Whisper sauntered over to the market, and we tied her to a bike rack outside.

I hesitated. "We can't bring our packs in. They'll think we're stealing."

Ignacio stroked Whisper on the neck. "I can stay out here with Whisper and the packs while you go in."

I nodded. He should be safe in this small town with the horse. I went inside the store.

Only a month had passed since I last stepped into a grocery store, but it felt like years. My mouth watered at the sight of the produce, so fresh, so colorful. I put apples and carrots into the basket. Those would last if we needed them to, and Whisper would enjoy them as well. I added beef jerky and crackers. We couldn't carry too much.

"Ma'am, do you know how to get to Centro de Indulto Benéfico?" I asked the lady at the checkout.

She looked at me and at the bills I gave her. Counting them, she put them in her drawer. As she handed me the change, she smiled. "It's two blocks to the south, then turn left and go three more blocks."

I took the bags and thanked her.

As I walked out of the store, I dug out an apple to give to Whisper. Ignacio grinned when he saw my offering. I held it up toward her nose, and she chomped it out of my hand.

"We're close," I said as we climbed on Whisper's back. I gave him the directions.

In less than five minutes, we reached the shelter. It wasn't much to look at from the outside—a squat block building with peeling paint.

But when I opened the door, hope and warmth spilled out like a river. We stood at the entrance, almost afraid to cross the threshold.

A friendly young woman who couldn't be much older than Ignacio greeted us, clipboard in hand. Her name tag said Gloria, and her smile looked warm and inviting. Gloria. Like the glory of the angel that saved us in the wilderness, this woman could save us again.

"Welcome to Centro de Indulto Benéfico. You're safe now."

I didn't move at first. I waited for Border Patrol to come bursting out or for someone to yell or the door to slam shut in our faces. But then a man took Whisper's rope, and another woman came outside and handed Ignacio a burrito wrapped in foil. I could smell the beans through the paper.

"We need help," I said before the tears started coming down in waves.

All the pent-up emotions, the hidden anxiety, the fear came out at once. I tried to be so strong for Ignacio's sake along the journey, but I couldn't be strong forever. At least we stood at a place that could help us...hopefully.

Gloria looked at me again. "We have room. You can rest here. We'll help you figure out what's next."

She led us to an intake room, handing the clipboard to an older woman and leaving to greet the next guest. The air felt cool. I heard children laughing somewhere down the hall. The smell of rice, beans, and soap filled the air. And I felt something I hadn't felt in a long time—peace.

I told the older woman our story, about Amo Abe kicking us out, about the trip south, about Ignacio's heat exhaustion and the well, about the Border Patrol. She hung on every word and nodded where appropriate.

"You've had a difficult journey," she said. "But it sounds like God has been with you, protecting you."

I nodded, wiping my tears with my hands.

She gave me a tissue. "You are safe here. We can help."

I didn't know what would happen tomorrow, but tonight we had food and a roof over our head, and that was enough.

CHAPTER THIRTY-THREE

EDINBURG, TX

The shelter smelled like boiled beans, bleach, and wet shoes. A fan rattled in the corner, barely cutting the heat. Ignacio sat on the edge of a cot, elbows on his knees, his face blank. I sat beside him and tried not to think about the past month.

We'd made it this far. That was something.

The cot creaked every time I shifted. The mattress was thin, barely more than fabric stretched over springs. Ignacio lay down without a word and pulled the blanket up to his chin. His feet stuck out the end. I watched his chest rise and fall and waited until his breathing evened out before I let myself close my eyes.

I didn't sleep much. The room stayed loud with whispers, babies crying, and the distant clang of pots in the kitchen. Someone coughed for hours. My back burned from riding Whisper for so long. My stomach felt hollow.

But we had a roof. For one night, we could rest.

The next morning, Gloria found me wiping crumbs off our blanket with the edge of my sleeve. She held the same clipboard, a fresh sheet clipped on top.

"There's a ranch outside town," she said. "South. They've got space for a housekeeper. The owners sponsor work placements and help with paperwork."

I stood up and straightened my shirt. "What kind of ranch?"

"Dude ranch. Mostly tourists. They want someone for the guest rooms. We've had several successful placements with them in the past. They said they'd take a kid, too, as long as he's in school."

I looked at Ignacio, who sat cross-legged on the cot, pulling a loose thread from his sleeve. He looked up at me but didn't say anything.

"You'll get housing," Gloria said. "Small but clean. Bus picks him up at the gate."

I didn't ask what they'd seen in my file or if they knew my passport was fake. I didn't want to give her a reason to change her mind. "Do I need to meet them first?"

Gloria shook her head. "They already said yes."

I nodded. "We'll take it."

She handed me a manila envelope. "Your placement papers. Don't lose these."

I took the envelope and folded it in half, tucking it into the front of my pack. The paper felt too clean for my hands.

"Your ride's in ten minutes," she said, and walked off to the next cot.

I sat back down beside Ignacio. He looked at me, waiting.

"We're going to a ranch," I said, my eyes bright with hope. "You'll have school. I'll have work."

He nodded once and zipped up his backpack. We didn't hug or celebrate. Everything still seemed unreal. But we stood up and walked to the door together.

***

Señora Karen stood outside the row of guest rooms at the Tri-Flowers Ranch with a clipboard tucked under her arm. Sweat darkened the collar of her work shirt. Her boots left clean imprints in the dirt as she stepped toward me. The cabins stretched along the fence line, each one with a small porch, two dusty rocking chairs, and a metal number nailed beside the door.

She pointed at Room Four. "That one's open. You'll stay there."

Ignacio and I followed her across the yard, gravel crunching under my shoes. The sun beat into the back of my neck, relentless and hot. Behind us, a horse let out a sharp snort, the sound echoing from the barn. The wind shifted, carrying with it the pungent bite of manure mixed with the dry sweetness of hay.

"You'll handle all the guest rooms," she said. "Beds, bathrooms, windows. Keep the porches swept and the coffee stocked. Clean towels are in the cabinet behind the laundry building."

She handed me a ring of keys. The metal felt hot in my palm. "Ignacio's school bus pulls up at seven each morning. It waits five minutes. Don't miss it."

Ignacio nodded, eyes wide, scanning the area.

"Take a moment to settle in, then you can start cleaning the rooms that have already been vacated." She handed me the clipboard. "This will show which rooms need to be completely turned and which ones are just a refresh."

"Thank you, Señora." I took the clipboard and walked toward the cabin.

"Let me know if you need anything." Señora Karen turned and walked toward the main lodge.

I unlocked Room Four and stepped inside. The air smelled like soap and sun-warmed wood. The cabin was small and plain. It had one had a small table, two chairs, two small beds with stiff mattresses, a television, an air conditioning unit, and a kitchenette with old tile counters. I soon found out that all the cabins were nearly the same.

Once I dropped my backpack on the bed, I looked around the room. "This will do. It's simple, but it's a roof over our head."

Ignacio sighed, shoulders slumped. "It's better than living off the land, but I miss home."

I closed the distance between us and pulled him into a hug. "I know, mijo. Me too."

The keys jingled in my hand as I picked up the clipboard to study it. Fifteen cabins needed cleaning. I headed next door to get started.

I peeled the sheets off the bed and opened the windows to let the dust out. By the time I finished cleaning the first room, sweat soaked my shirt, and my back ached. I moved on to the next one.

I worked until the light changed and the heat started to settle. The guest rooms were plain, but the city guests called it charming. I saw it simply as easy to clean.

***

Señora Karen came by once a day. She didn't hover or ask questions. She ran her finger across surfaces and checked under the sinks. One day, she pulled a hair from a pillowcase and said nothing. After that, I started checking everything twice.

Each morning, I grabbed my mop, rag, and spray bottle. I moved room to room without losing pace. I emptied trash bins, scrubbed showers, swept porch steps, and tucked the corners of every sheet. Tips started showing up under mugs and inside pillowcases. A few guests left thank-you notes with handwriting I couldn't always read.

At night, my fingers burned from bleach, and my knees ached when I stood. No one asked if I was tired, and I didn't expect them to.

Ignacio spent most evenings learning the ranch. He put the skills he had learned back home to good use. Señor Edward took a liking to him and kept him busy stringing fences and killing coyotes with his bow. From the porch, I watched him come in at night, his shoulders sagging under the weight of honest labor. His hands were cracked, his clothes heavy with dust, yet there was a light in his eyes I hadn't seen since we left home.

I worried over him still but seeing Señor Edward nod at him with quiet respect eased some of the fear I carried. Ignacio was finding his place here, even if it was through blistered palms and the sharp twang of bowstring. When he walked back to me in the evening glow, the sky painted red behind him, I thought perhaps the ranch was giving him something I no longer could: the chance to grow into himself.

And though I said nothing, I held on to that hope as tightly as I once held his small hand in mine.

***

A few weeks in, I was wiping down the sink in Room Six when Señora Karen stepped into the doorway. She didn't speak at first. Her eyes moved across the floor, the bed, the corners of the room.

"Your passport says you're from Mexico?" she asked.

I kept my focus on the faucet and decided to tell the truth. "Nicaragua, actually. Puerto Cabezas."

She leaned into the doorframe and crossed her arms. "Do you have family there?"

"My mother and my brother. Rosa and Jose Downs."

The wind shifted outside. Dust scraped against the porch boards.

"How long has it been since you've seen them?"

I let out a small laugh. "Too long. The last time I saw them, I was nine years old."

She stared for a moment longer, her jaw set. Without another word, she stepped back outside. "Would you like to find them?"

The question caught me off guard. My eyes brightened, betraying me, and I felt the corners of my mouth twitch with something between a smile and a plea. "Yes, very much."

"Then let's try."

***

By the end of the month, I could clean all eight rooms in one day without rushing. My hands stayed dry and cracked from the chemicals, but I worked fast and stayed focused. Señora Karen stopped checking behind me. I knew where every extra towel was folded, which lights flickered, and which cabinet latches stuck.

One evening, I sat on the porch of Room Seven with a bucket at my feet and a rag still damp in my hand. The sun stretched long across the pasture, turning the dirt the color of rust. Two cows moved along the fence, kicking up dust. I leaned back into the chair, listening to the creak of old wood beneath me.

I closed my eyes and pictured home. Waves crashed against the dock, steady and alive. My mother's voice carrying across the yard, and rain hammering our tin roof in the small village near Puerto Cabezas. I didn't know where she slept now or if José had lived long enough to grow into a man. But I had sheets to fold, a boy to raise, a room waiting each morning, and a boss offering more than wages. She was willing to sponsor my green card and help me search for my family. That was enough to keep me moving.

EPILOGUE

"Jose?" I asked, squinting through the airport at a man with my eyes and facial features.

The man's lit up with a smile that stretched across his face. He dropped his duffel and ran, arms outstretched, into my arms. "Helena!"

I embraced my brother for the first time in forty-three years. My bottom lip quivered, and tears tinged the corner of my eyes. "It's so good to see you, brother. I've missed you and Mamá so much, God rest her soul."

"We have so much to catch up on."

"Let's talk in the car."

He grabbed his duffel and followed me to the parking lot.

"You work here?" Jose said pointing at the Tri-Flowers Ranch logo on the side of the van.

"Yes, for seven years now. They sponsored my green card to help me get citizenship."

"So you got your citizenship?"

"Yes, thank you so much for your help," I said, smiling at him. "I couldn't do it without you helping me with my birth certificate and Ignacio sponsoring me."

I searched a long time to find Jose. It was easier to find people with technology, but Jose still lived in the village in Nicaragua, the same one I grew up in. We didn't have technology then, and they still didn't have it now. But I longed for contact with my mother and brother, to have a family of my own again. I also needed him to help get the right paperwork for my green card and citizenship application. I refused to leave Ignacio in the United States for fear they wouldn't let me return if I left, but the search was on. It took me five years to find him.

"Señora Karen is my boss and the sweetest woman," I said. "She and Señor Edward sponsor green cards for many migrants who work at the ranch. Ignacio's fiancé also works there."

We climbed into the van and began the forty-minute drive to the ranch.

"Tell me about Ignacio," Jose said as he settled into his seat.

"He's a great kid. Twenty-two now. Owns his own business, just like his dad. But he works outdoors, mostly bow hunting, killing and butchering meat. He also puts up fence posts for the ranches around here. He's very smart and strong. I'm so proud of him."

"I can't wait to meet him."

"Tell me about your family."

"Maynor just turned eighteen," he said, drumming his fingers against his leg. "He works at the dock with me. Anielka got married two years ago, right before Mamá died. She's nineteen. Pregnant with her first child."

"Wow, I've missed so much! And you're carrying on Papá's legacy, working at the docks."

"Yes. They're the biggest employer in the area," Jose said. "I don't remember Papá, but Mamá showed me the only picture she had of him."

We both paused, honoring our late parents.

"Thank you for buying my flight." He reached over and touched my hand. "I don't know how to repay you."

As soon as Ignacio popped the question, I started saving. It took a year to gather enough money for Jose's flight and passport.

"I wanted you to be here, brother," I said, smiling back at him. "I've longed for you and Mamá since the day I was taken away. This trip, you being here, is a dream come true." I glanced sideways at my brother, all grown up with kids of his own. I'd lost so many years.

I pulled into the long drive, passing under the Tri-Flowers Ranch sign with its three lilies etched in steel, grateful my brother would be here to see my son get married.

***

The sun shone through the small church window. The ceremony neared its start. I secured the collar buttons around Ignacio's narrow black tie. I gave him a kiss on the cheek.

He looked so sharp, so mature.

"Are you ready, mijo?" I asked him, smoothing down a stray hair I could barely reach.

He stood so tall now. A tear stung my eye. I blinked it away. I refused to cry.

"Yes, Mom," he said, smiling back at me. His dark eyes glowed with tears of his own. He pulled me into a hug and stood there for a long moment. "I love you."

"I love you too, mijo," I wiped at the wetness under my eye to keep my mascara from smearing. I struggled to accept that I would no longer hold the most important place in his life. "It's time."

Ignacio escorted me to my seat in the front pew and climbed the stairs to join his groomsmen on the small stage near the altar. A few dozen people filled the rows of the church, waiting with anticipation for the ceremony to begin.

The music started, and the bridesmaids traversed the short aisle to join Ignacio and the groomsmen on the stage. The song changed, and the rear doors opened, revealing Aurora dressed in a beautiful, lacy white dress with her father by her side. She'd pinned the front of her hair up, letting brown curls spill down her back under her veil. She spotted Ignacio and her smile grew, her face bright with joy.

Aurora's father passed her hand to Ignacio's, and they stood together on the stage while the priest blessed the church, the guests, the ceremony, and the couple.

I dotted at my eyes with a tissue when the ceremony finished. They were happy tears, of course. I introduced Aurora to Ignacio shortly after she started working for me at the ranch, where I was the housekeeping manager. She worked hard, carried a bubbly personality, and won me over almost instantly.

We filed out to the tents and tables set up in the church yard for the reception. The smell of tamales, beans, and rice filled the tent. Once the guests were all settled, Gloria raised her glass for a toast to the new couple.

"When Ignacio first walked into Centre de Indulto Benéfico seven years ago with his mother, I had no idea I was meeting the guy who would one day marry my future best friend. And when Aurora arrived at Centre de Indulto Benéfico two years ago, I still couldn't see the full picture. Placing both of your families at the Tri-Flower Ranch might have looked like a coincidence to us, but it was never random. God was weaving something beautiful all along.

"I feel blessed to have seen your journey through trials, healing, and now joy. Sometimes it's in our lowest moments that God plants seeds for our greatest blessings. He was there for you then, and He'll be with you now. May God always remain at the center of your marriage. And may He bless you with more love, laughter, and unshakable faith than you can count.

"To Aurora and Ignacio!"

We all raised our glasses.

***

The music played on. Guests danced. Plates emptied and filled again.

I sat still for a while, watching them. Ignacio held Aurora by the waist, swaying in a slow circle while the sky faded into lavender.

I thought back to the years that came before this one. I had been rejected by many people: the men, the cartel, and finally Amo Abe. The hardest to swallow had been the rejection from my son's father. He had kicked us out with no place to go, no hope, nothing but fear and a long road ahead of us.

The ache of doing whatever I had to for us to survive, for me to finally mother my own son, had been great. I wanted peace for him more than anything. I hadn't expected the kind of joy we were finally experiencing now.

I stood, walked out to the edge of the tent, and looked back toward the church. Its windows caught the last of the light. A breeze moved through the grass, lifting the edges of the tablecloths.

I glanced toward where my brother sat smiling at his nephew. With my family, with my job at Tri-Flowers Ranch, and with my United States citizenship, I was no longer rejected. I finally felt like I belonged.

I placed my hand over my chest and closed my eyes for a second. *Thank you.*

I didn't need to say it out loud. The one I was speaking to had seen me all along.

ASSOCIATED SCRIPTURE:

C hapter 10:

When Abram entered Egypt, the Egyptians saw that the woman was very beautiful. When Pharaoh's officials saw her, they praised her to Pharaoh. So, Abram's wife was taken into the household of Pharaoh, and he did treat Abram well on account of her. Abram received sheep and cattle, male donkeys, male servants, female servants, female donkeys, and camels.

But the Lord struck Pharaoh and his household with severe diseases because of Sarai, Abram's wife. So, Pharaoh summoned Abram and said, "What is this you have done to me? Why didn't you tell me that she was your wife? Why did you say, 'She is my sister,' so that I took her to be my wife? Now, here is your wife. Take her and go!" Pharaoh gave his men orders about Abram, and so they expelled him, along with his wife and all his possessions.

Genesis 12:14-20 NET

Rejected Notes:

Abram is Abe; Sarai is Patrona Isa/Isabelle; Pharaoh is Jefe Hernández; Hagar is Honey, Eliezer is Eddy

In Rejected, Abe and Isabelle go to Mexico to evacuate from a hurricane. The cartel's falcons see her at the border and praise her beauty to el jefe, Hernández. Jefe Hernández takes Isabelle to be his wife. Shortly after, the entire cartel is struck with a strange illness that causes rashes. Abe confesses to Hernández that Isabelle is his wife and not his sister. Hernández sends them away, with their dowery gifts, which includes Honey, Eddy, Barry, and Daniel.

***

Chapter 13:

But Sarai was barren; she had no children.

Genesis 11:30 NET

Rejected notes:

Sarai is Patrona Isa

***

Chapter 14:

But look, the word of the Lord came to him: "This man will not be your heir, but instead a son who comes from your own body will be your heir," The Lord took him outside and said, "Gaze into the sky and count the stars – if you are able to count them!" Then he said to him, "So will your descendants be."

Abram believed the Lord, and the Lord considered his response of faith as proof of genuine loyalty.

Genesis 15:4-6 NET

***

Chapter 15:

The Lord said to him, "I am the Lord who brought you out from Ur of the Chaldeans to give you this land to possess."

But Abram said, "O sovereign Lord, by what can I know that I am about to possess it?"

The Lord said to him, "Take for me a heifer, a goat, and a ram, each three years old, along with a dove and a young pigeon."

So, Abram took all these for him and then cut them in two and placed each half opposite the other, but he did not cut the birds in half. When birds of prey came down on the carcasses, Abram drove them away.

When the sun went down, Abram fell sound asleep, and a great terror overwhelmed him.

Then the Lord said to Abram, "Know for certain that your descendants will be strangers in a foreign country. They will be enslaved and oppressed for four hundred years. But I will execute judgment on the nation that they will serve. Afterwards they will come out with many possessions. But as for you, you will go to your ancestors in peace and be buried at a good old age. In the fourth generation your descendants will return here, for the sin of the Amorite's has not yet reached its limit."

When the sun had gone down and it was dark, a smoking fire pot with a flaming torch passed between the animal parts. That day, the Lord made a covenant with Abram: "To your descendants I give this land, from the river of Egypt to the great river, the Euphrates River

– the land of the Kenites, Kenizzites, Kadmonites, Hittites, Perizzites, Rephaites, Amorites, Canaanites, Girgashites, and Jebusites."

Genesis 15: 7-21 NET

Now Sarai, Abram's wife, had not given birth to any children, but had an Egyptian servant named Hagar. So Sarai said to Abram, "Since the Lord has prevented me from having children, have sexual relations with my servant. Perhaps I can have a family by her."

Genesis 16:1-2b NET

Rejected Notes:

Ur of the Chaldeans is Ur Street in the Native American tribe of the Chaldeans; the Amorites are the Klebergs; the Kenites, Kenizzites, Kadmonites, Hittites, Perizzites, Rephaites, Amorites, Canaanites, Girgashites, and Jebusites are the Klebergs, Hebbronvilleites, Falfurriasites, Edinburgites, Raymondvilleites, Aliceites, Harlingenites, McAllenites, Brownsvillites, and Encinoites (all cities in south Texas).

Patrona Isa / Princess tells Abe to have sex with Hillary so they can build a family through her.

***

Chapter 17:

Abram did what Sarai told him.

So after Abram had lived in Canaan for ten years, Sarai, Abram's wife, gave Hagar, her Egyptian servant, to her husband to be his wife.

Genesis 16:2c-3

Rejected Notes:

Hillary lived at Canaan Ranch for ten years before Patrona Isa gave her to Abram to treat her "as a wife."

***

Chapter 18:

He had sexual relations with Hagar, and she became pregnant.

Genesis 16:4a NET

***

Chapter 19:

Once Hagar realized she was pregnant, she despised Sarai.

Genesis 16:4b NET

***

Chapter 22:

Then Sarai said to Abram, "You have brought this wrong onto me! I allowed my servant to have sexual relations with you, but when she realized that she was pregnant, she despised me. May the Lord judge between you and me!"

Abram said to Sarai, "Since your servant is under your authority, do to her whatever you think best."

Genesis 16:5-6a NET

***

Chapter 23:

Then Sarai treated Hagar harshly, so she ran away from Sarai.

The Lord's angel found Hagar near a spring of water in the desert –
the spring that is along the road to Shur. He said, "Hagar, servant of
Sarai, where have you come from, and where are you going?"

She replied, "I'm running away from my mistress, Sarai."

Then the Lord's angel said to her, "Return to your mistress and
submit to her authority. I will greatly multiply your descendants," the
Lord's angel added, "so that they will be too numerous to count."
Then the Lord's angel said to her, "You are now pregnant and are
about to give birth to a son. You are to name him Ishmael, for the Lord
has heard your painful groans. He will be a wild donkey of a man. He
will be hostile to everyone, and everyone will be hostile to him. He will
live away from his brothers."

So Hagar named the Lord who spoke to her, "You are the God who
sees me," for she said, "Here I have seen the one who sees me!" That is
why the well was called Beer Lahai Roi. (It is located between Kadesh
and Bered.)

Genesis 16:6b-12 NET

Rejected Notes:

Patrona Isa gave Hillary so many chores that she didn't have time to
eat during the day. When Hillary tried to resist, she slapped her across
the face. Then Hillary took the car and fled. She ends at a river between
Kingsville and Bishop.

She meets a man, a police officer, who glowed and exuded peace and
kindness. He tells her to go back and submit to Patrona Isa.

***

Chapter 24:

So Hagar gave birth to Abram's son, whom Abram named Ishmael. (Now Abram was 86 years old when Hagar gave birth to Ishmael.)

Genesis 16:15-16 NET

Rejected Notes:

Abe was 36 when Hillary gave birth to Ignacio.

***

Chapter 25:

No longer will your name be Abram. Instead, your name will be Abraham because I will make you the father of a multitude of nations...Then God said to Abraham, "As for your wife, you must no longer call her Sarai; Sarah will be her name.

Genesis 17:5, 15 NET

This is my requirement that you and your descendants after you must keep: Every male among you must be circumcised. You must circumcise the flesh of your foreskins. This will be a reminder of the covenant between me and you....Abraham took his son Ishmael and every male in his household (whether born in his house or bought with money) and circumcised them on that very same day, just as God had told him to do. Now Abraham was 99 years old when he was circumcised; his son Ishmael was thirteen years old when he was circumcised.

Genesis 17:10-11; 23-24 NET

The Lord appeared to Abraham by the oaks of Mamre while he was sitting at the entrance to his tent during the hottest time of the day. Abraham looked up and saw three men standing across from him.

When he saw them, he ran from the entrance of the tent to meet them and bowed low to the ground.

He said, "My lord, if I have found favor in your sight, do not pass by and leave your servant. Let a little water be brought so that you may all wash your feet and rest under the tree. And let me get a bit of food so that you may refresh yourselves since you have passed by your servant's home. After that you may be on your way." "All right," they replied, "you may do as you say."

So, Abraham hurried into the tent and said to Sarah, "Quick! Take three measures of fine flour, knead it, and make bread." Then Abraham ran to the herd and chose a fine, tender calf, and gave it to a servant, who quickly prepared it. Abraham then took some curds and milk, along with the calf that had been prepared, and placed the food before them. They ate while he was standing near them under a tree.

Then they asked him, "Where is Sarah your wife?" He replied, "There, in the tent." One of them said, "I will surely return to you when the season comes round again, and your wife Sarah will have a son!" (Now Sarah was listening at the entrance to the tent, not far behind him. Abraham and Sarah were old and advancing in years; Sarah had long since passed menopause.) So, Sarah laughed to herself, thinking, "After I am worn out will I have pleasure, especially when my husband is old too?"

The Lord said to Abraham, "Why did Sarah laugh and say, 'Will I really have a child when I am old?' Is anything impossible for the Lord? I will return to you when the season comes round again, and Sarah will have a son." Then Sarah lied, saying, "I did not laugh," because she was afraid. But the Lord said, "No! You did laugh."

Genesis 18 NET

Rejected Notes:

Jehovah changes Abe's name to Abraham and Princess/Isa to Sara. Both Abraham and Ignacio are circumcised as God required.

While Sara is not as old as the Sarah of the Bible, she had already experienced early menopause, causing her to question whether she could have a child.

*****

Chapter 26:

The Lord visited Sarah just as he had said he would and did for Sarah what he had promised. So Sarah became pregnant.

Genesis 21:1-2a NET

*****

Chapter 28:

Sarah became pregnant and bore Abraham a son in his old age at the appointed time that God had told him. Abraham named his son – whom Sarah bore to him – Isaac.

Genesis 21:2-3 NET

Rejected Notes:

Isaac is called Ignacio in *Rejected*.

*****

Chapter 29:

The child grew and was weaned. Abraham prepared a great feast on the day that Isaac was weaned. But Sarah noticed the son of Hagar the

Egyptian – the son whom Hagar had borne to Abraham – mocking. So she said to Abraham, "Banish that slave woman and her son, for the son of that slave woman will not be an heir along with my son Isaac!"

Sarah's demand displeased Abraham greatly because Ishmael was his son. But God said to Abraham, "Do not be upset about the boy or your slave wife. Do all that Sarah is telling you because through Isaac your descendants will be counted. But I will also make the son of the slave wife into a great nation, for he is your descendant too."

Early in the morning Abraham took some food and a skin of water and gave them to Hagar. He put them on her shoulders, gave her the child, and sent her away.

Genesis 21:12-14b NET

Rejected Notes:

Abraham gave Hillary leftover food from the party in a hiking pack with a hydration bladder. Both Hillary and Ignacio had hiking packs with full hydration bladders when they embarked on their journey.

***

Chapter 30:

So she went wandering aimlessly through the wilderness of Beer Sheba.

When the water in the skin was gone, she shoved the child under one of the shrubs. Then she went and sat down by herself across from him at quite a distance, about a bow shot away; for she thought, "I refuse to watch the child die." So she sat across from him and wept uncontrollably.

But God heard the boy's voice. The angel of God called to Hagar from heaven and asked her, "What is the matter, Hagar? Don't be afraid, for God has heard the boy's voice right where he is crying. Get up! Help the boy up and hold him by the hand, for I will make him into a great nation." Then God enabled Hagar to see a well of water. She went over and filled the skin with water, and then gave the boy a drink.

Genesis 21:14c-19 NET

Rejected Notes:

Hillary and Ignacio wander the ranch lands of south Texas. Ignacio gets heat exhaustion, which causes him to be at risk. She sets him in the shade of the only tree around.

***

Epilogue:

God was with the boy as he grew. He lived in the wilderness and became an archer. He lived in the wilderness of Paran. His mother found a wife for him from the land of Egypt.

Genesis 21:20-21 NET

Rejected Notes:

Ignacio becomes an archer who kills the invasive coyotes on the ranch where Hillary works. Hillary finds a wife for him, Aurora, who is from Mexico.

Join the Fight for Freedom

For survivors like Helena, the pain doesn't end with escape. Freedom is only the beginning of a lifelong journey through healing. The memories and the fear don't go away, and the hope that somehow life can be rebuilt doesn't come overnight.

Every day women remain trapped in the same darkness Helena fought to survive. Others are free but still carry the invisible scars. You can help bring light into those places through organizations like El Pozo de Vida, Street Grace, Love146, The A21 Campaign, and The MeKong Club, which offer safety, counseling, and restoration for women in Mexico and beyond.

Visit lizard-books.com/advocacy to learn more and stand behind survivors. Healing takes a village, and every act of compassion helps rewrite a life.

Scan here to find out more.

Want New Release Updates?

Keep in Touch with Elizabeth

Are you interested in being the first to know when Elizabeth releases her next story?

Are you interested in a free book promo or two?

Then follow Elizabeth on social media and join the mailing list.

Website: lizard-books.com

Facebook: @lizardbooks

Instagram: @lizardbooksllc

TikTok: @marathonmom9

Substack: elizabethsimonauthor.substack.com

LinkedIn: elizabethsimoncpa

Sign up for the newsletter at www.lizard-books.com/contact-elizabeth

Scan here to stay up to date!

IF THIS STORY MOVED YOU...

LEAVE A REVIEW TODAY

Every review helps another reader find the courage to open this book.

Review on Ama-
zon

Review on
Goodreads

BEFORE THERE WAS REJECTED

THERE WAS BARREN: THE CONTEMPORARY STORY OF SARAI

B arren was the story that started it all.

When a car crash claims their parents, Isabelle Serug and her older siblings are left reeling—orphans in the snowy reaches of northern Minnesota. Taken in by two brothers from their tribe, the family clings to hope, faith, and each other to survive.

But when a divine calling urges them to leave everything behind for an unfamiliar land, Isabelle is swept into a journey that will test the limits of love, loyalty, and belief. As their new life unravels, she must face impossible choices and find the courage to rise when everything around her falls apart.

A modern reimagining of the biblical story of Sarai, Barren blends culture, contemporary drama, and timeless themes of betrayal and redemption. In the heart of every storm lies a choice: give up, or believe the promise is still worth fighting for.

Read for FREE on Kindle Un-
limited or buy on Amazon

Buy on BarnesandNoble.com

DISTRESSED: A CONTEMPORARY STORY OF ISAAC

COMING IN 2026

When sixteen-year-old Isaac accompanies his father on what's supposed to be a simple camping trip in the South Texas brush country, he expects heat, rattlesnakes, and awkward conversation. He doesn't expect a knife, ropes, or his father whispering that God demands obedience.

Shattered by betrayal, Isaac runs away, bleeding, terrified, and unsure whether he's escaping his father...or God.

His desperate flight leads him to Ignacio, the older brother his family never talked about, the one who was cast out years ago under a cloud of religious justification. Ignacio carries the same scars Isaac is just beginning to understand, and offers what Isaac needs most: safety, honesty, and the freedom to breathe without fear.

But healing isn't simple. The past does not stay buried. Isaac must confront more than trauma. He must face the truth about the faith that shaped him, the family that broke him, and the future he's terrified to claim.

Distressed is a haunting, deeply human reimagining of the story of Isaac set against the stark landscapes of modern South Texas. It's a story about survival, brotherhood, and reclaiming the pieces of yourself someone once tried to sacrifice.

ACKNOWLEDGEMENTS

Writing Rejected was a journey I could not have walked alone.

First and foremost, I give glory to God. Without Him, this story would not exist. He wrote the first version in Genesis; I have only adapted it in hopes that today's world might connect with its truth in a new way. To Him be all the glory.

To the Suncoast Long Writers Group, thank you for being my alpha readers, for listening to early drafts, and for offering your wisdom and encouragement along the way. To Kayle Buchanan, Michael Grigsby, and Lisa Dunbar, my beta readers, your thoughtful insights sharpened the story and gave me confidence in its direction. To Clara Abigail, my editor, your keen eye and steady hand helped refine this book into its best version.

I am deeply grateful to Matthew Friedman of the Mekong Club (www.themekongclub.org), whose expertise and guidance ensured that the most difficult and sensitive portions of this novel, particularly those dealing with human trafficking, were handled with accuracy and care.

To my family, thank you for being my source of strength and unconditional love through the long nights of research and writing.

And finally, to you, the readers: this story exists because of you. Thank you for turning these pages, for engaging with difficult truths, and for allowing these voices to be heard. Your willingness to enter into this narrative is the greatest honor a writer could hope for.

With gratitude,

Elizabeth Simon

ABOUT THE AUTHOR

Elizabeth Simon is a storyteller at heart. A native of Ohio now living in sunny southwest Florida, she began writing stories as a teenager, scribbling characters and plot lines between homework and youth group. Life took her down a different path into the world of accounting, corporate compliance, and risk management. But the love of storytelling never left her.

For over two decades, Elizabeth built a respected career helping organizations uphold ethics and integrity. She's been a featured writer in Compliance & Ethics Professional and Fraud Magazine and has spoken across the country on doing what's right—even when it's hard. But behind the spreadsheets and boardroom presentations, a deeper calling stirred: to tell stories that wrestle with truth, faith, identity, and redemption.

Her debut novel, Barren, is the first in a powerful series that blends Biblical themes with timeless struggles—legacy, betrayal, love, and the search for belonging. Inspired by her deep study of Genesis and authors like Francine Rivers, John Grisham, and Karen Kingsbury, Elizabeth writes with both heart and grit, weaving suspense and spiritual insight into every chapter.

When she's not writing or leading in the corporate world, you'll find her reading, reflecting, or walking near the water, dreaming up the next story that just won't let her go.